The Warrior King

A Love Story with Criminal Interruptions

Also by Wendy Murray

A Mended and Broken Heart

On Broken Legs

Facing Forward

Sacred Journeys

Day of Reckoning

The Warrior King

A Love Story with Criminal Interruptions

WENDY MURRAY

ecco qua press

Beverly, Massachusetts

This book is a work of fiction. The location, historical information about the Maya, and the archaeological data are true to events surrounding the year in which the book is set: 1993. Since that time, archaeologists have modified conclusions depicted in this narrative. Those changes are noted in the Acknowledgments. Further, the tribal names used in the story are fictional, with the exception of a few, which do not assume a significant role in the story. Otherwise, all names, characters, institutions and incidents are used fictitiously.

THE WARRIOR KING. Copyright©2010 by Wendy Murray. All rights reserved. Printed in the United States of America. For information address Ecco Qua Press, 54 Lothrop Street, Beverly, MA 01915.

•

Library of Congress Cataloging-in-Publication Data

Murray, Wendy.

The Warrior King / Wendy Murray.—1st. ed.

ISBN 978-0-615-40608-4

for Mickey

PART ONE
(Lucy)

i

Leonardo said it began when I was tapping my foot. We were sitting in the waiting lounge of the office of Doña Nora Reyes Morales de Mondragón, Honduras's Primera Dama. And on this day the First Lady had failed to show up for what had been my third scheduled interview at her request. Leonardo said, "When you tap your foot you are being very norteamericana," and rolled his eyes. It annoyed him when I tapped my foot. He shrugged his shoulders. "We do not live by the clock in Latin America." It was his standard reply when things did not go according to plan in Honduras, which seemed to be all the time. Doña Nora was launching her Plant-a-Tree-For-Nora campaign and Honduras needed a tree-planting campaign, which is why I returned a third time after having been stood up twice already in the attempt to interview her for my magazine. I looked out the window and counted with one hand the number of trees growing on the berm.

Leonardo said the mountains in his country used to be strong like a warrior. "Now they are like an old man who has lost his hair."

The Hondurans loved La Primera Dama. When she visited their neighborhoods she would touch their faces with her slender pale fingers on which she wore a diamond the size of a centavo, they couldn't help but notice. Those

1

delicious fingers with candy-coated fingernails stole the hearts of Leonardo's people. If anyone could rally them to plant more trees and be watchful about burning it would be Doña Nora.

But she didn't show up to talk about it and get it in print. So, after the tapping, I firmly planted my foot on the marble floor of her waiting lounge and Leo turned his head. I stood up, threw my backpack over a shoulder, and inclined myself toward the mahogany desk that carried the nameplate 'Eva Rosales,' Doña Nora's assistant. She was picking her cherry-colored candied fingernails and sitting on a cushion with tassels.

Leo also stood.

I leaned toward Eva Rosales.

Leo rolled his eyes a second time.

I reminded her that I was the chief correspondent for the premier Central American English-Spanish international news magazine *Los Tiempo* and said, "Doña Nora does not want this interview, does she?"

Eva Rosales looked at me queerly. "Yes. Doña Nora wants the interview."

"This is the third time she's called me to come and the third time she's failed to show up."

"Doña Nora wants the interview."

"She needs this interview more than I need to do it."

Leonardo groaned.

I said, "My career trajectory does not stand or fall on Doña Nora's Plant-A-Tree-For-Nora campaign."

Leo whispered to me, "When you start making comments about your 'career trajectory' it is time for me to save you from yourself." He leaned toward Eva Rosales from behind me. "Miss Lucy Shaw, she is very nervous. We are sorry. She has many responsibilities."

It annoyed me when Leonardo saved me from myself.

"Por favor," I said. "Tell Doña Nora that if I get the opportunity to reschedule, I'll call her."

Leo was disconsolate as we stepped into the elevator going down. "There are plenty of Honduran journalists who can write about the trees," I said. "Besides"—I turned my head, leveled my eyes and cocked my chin slightly in the way that bewildered him—"how many trees do you think Doña Nora is going to dirty her delicate little fingers to plant?"

I walked to my beaten-up Peugeot parked along the slope of the drive of the Executive Building parking lot. I always parked on hills to roll the car and pop the clutch to ignite the engine because the starter didn't work. Leo mounted his motorbike and did not wave as he began to pull away. I lurched into first gear after a steady roll and Leo slowed long enough to yell, "You drive like a cowboy."

I had arrived in Honduras five years prior to the events I recount here, fresh out of college, when I was hired by *Los Tiempo* to serve as regional reporter in Honduras. The magazine immediately sent Leonardo to me, assuring me he would be indispensable, and he has been. He's a jolly sort, soft-bellied and round-faced with longish brown hair he combs straight back. He is fair of complexion for a Honduran and has tried to grow a mustache, but it never took.

He wears the same gray polyester pants every day with three variations of a plaid button-down shirt. As a gesture of friendship when we started working together I gave him a leather satchel. He carries it everywhere.

Leo set me up in my small rented house on a balding hillside in a middle-class neighborhood of Tegucigalpa, Honduras's capital city. Depending upon the time of day I could lift my head and catch a waft of roasting coffee beans—my house was downwind from the coffee factory. Or, if the wind shifted, I might be choked by the smell of sewage or smoke from hillside fires. On good days or bad, I could pick fruit from the mango tree that shaded my front patio and, in spite of myself, I would stop to marvel at the fire-red blossoms of the flowering flamboyón tree along the curb. It bloomed only during the dry season and it seemed a miracle that such beauty could flourish when there was no rain.

Leo showed up every morning on his motorbike to deliver my mail. He knew where to get the best exchange rate for dollars and all sorts of other things a gringa such as I would have no way of knowing or ought not to know. He secured my driver's license and my *visas multiples* and made the necessary pilgrimages to government offices to stand in dark stuffy hallways with slow-moving fans in lines backed up to the street to render for me the bureaucratic obeisance required of resident aliens. He would stand in those lines clutching his satchel with that doughboy smile for as long as it took to obtain authoritative stamps on multiple copies of countless pages of endless documents that foreigners must submit to be legal.

Leonardo knew people. This is how he moved ahead in government lines.

As assistant and photographer—and self-proclaimed life manager in the tangle of necessities it took to get things done in Honduras—he also taught me how to start a car without a key. It saddened me to disappoint him about La Primera Dama.

Leonardo was right about this much: That visit to the office of Doña Nora was the last time I tapped my foot.

2

An unexpected assignment was waiting for me by electronic mail upon my return:

Posted: Tue, Mar 2, 1993 12:40pm
From: TiempLatam
Subj: Copán Tomb
Close: Mar 12
Lucy,

We've scheduled 200 lines on the archaeological discovery of a royal Maya tomb at Copán. The archaeologists are calling it the most incredible find yet. Why? What is the significance of the find and how does it compare to previous finds? When was the discovery made? We really want to run this, Lu. Go after great quotes from archaeologists Mario Lopez and the American James Fee. You know these guys, right?
Libby

I heard myself say, "Yes, I know those guys." I had been to the Maya ruins in Copán the previous year. *That*, in my way of seeing it, is when it really began.

The Copán ruins skirted Honduras's western border, a leisurely walk from the edge of Guatemala. The ruins were first discovered in 1839 by the explorer-archaeologist John Lloyd Stephens. Upon seeing them for the first time he wrote in his log, "All was mystery, deep, impenetrable mystery." He paid a local farmer fifty dollars for the land. For the subsequent hundred and fifty years Maya archaeology was slow going. No one could interpret the queer hieroglyphs emblazoned on ceramic vessels and carved into buildings and monuments. Odd and inexplicable three-dimensional vertical structures resembling god-kings, called stelae, had been strategically placed with the alignment of stars and planets. This led archaeologists to conclude the Maya had been a peaceful band of astronomer priests obsessed with stargazing. Decipherment progressed, as did basic archaeology. The discovery in the late 1940s of defensive ditches, implements of war, and murals and iconography depicting torture and human sacrifice forced researchers to override their initial optimism. They reluctantly accepted a different more evocative picture of the Maya.

At the time of that assignment the year before, I went to Copán because archaeologists James Fee and Mario Lopez had discovered what they thought to be the tomb of Copán's seventh king, Waterlily Jaguar. For these champions, finding the tomb of Waterlily Jaguar was "the most incredible find of their careers," though both Lopez and Fee tended to speak in superlatives about every discovery. This one was especially astounding in any case. A cache of ceramic vessels buried with the human remains were shockingly pristine and looked like they did the day they

7

were laid as an offering at Waterlily Jaguar's feet. Major media in the United States took enthusiastic interest and *Los Tiempo* sent me. I brought Leonardo. We flew out in a small plane chartered from a mission aviation agency my parents were affiliated with. My parents were linguists in the Amazonian jungle basin in Peru and missionaries were a small but well-networked worldwide tribe. I had access to small planes and reliable pilots.

On the day of the third aborted interview attempt with Doña Nora, having received Libby's email, I promptly called Leo and asked him to bring me the camera so I could take it with me on the assignment. He said he wanted to join me. I refused him. He was already inconsolable about Doña Nora, and who can blame him? How many Hondurans who grew up in a barrio such as the one Leo had, received the chance to photograph La Primera Dama? He would have been stood up ten times by the First Lady if doing so would have won the interview.

"I'm being sent to cover what the archaeologists think is the discovery of the tomb of Copán's founding king," I said. "You already know Mario Lopez will be no help and I do not expect James Fee to help either. I'm not sure any of the archaeologists will help me and I have no idea how I will get this story. I only know having an unneeded person along will only make it more difficult." Leo objected to being called 'unneeded,' for which I apologized.

Three events occurred on that previous trip, which conspired to cause misfortune that would befall me on my upcoming return visit. The first related to the Honduran press corps. Most national reporters in Honduras did not have planes to fly in on such as Leo and I did that day because of my missionary connections. To cover the discovery of Waterlily Jaguar's tomb, members of the national press suffered an eight-hour bus trip from Tegucigalpa to Copán Ruinas, the town near the ruins, and it goes without saying that the bus did not have air conditioning. These journalists endured breathing the diesel exhaust of slow-moving buses on bad mountain roads with wind in their faces and dust on their teeth. By the time they arrived at the archaeological park, their eyes burned, their heads ached, their stomachs had soured, and one can only imagine the condition of their hair. Their smart outfits and polyester suits looked like yesterday's news.

Leo and I, however, lighted from our plane on the grassy airstrip, crisp and spirited. We stood for a moment breathing deeply and drinking in the beauty of the deciduous forest that skirted the park, fresh breezes in our faces. A photographer from the news corps snapped our picture and the following day the leading Honduran newspaper ran our photo along with this clip: "While Honduran journalists rose very early and traveled by bus for more than eight hours to arrive at the Copán Ruins sweating like pigs and having the courage to hide it, Lucy Shaw from the international magazine *Los Tiempo* arrived in a private plane that made the trip in a matter of minutes, landed on the air strip beside the archaeological park, and, of course, was immediately attended to by the authorities." I won dubious national celebrity then as "the journalist with her head in the clouds."

That wouldn't have been so bad if it hadn't dovetailed

with the second conspiring event. This one involved Mario Lopez, the Honduran archaeologist who worked for the National Institute of Anthropology. After my story about the Waterlily Jaguar's tomb and pottery cache appeared in *Los Tiempo*, such as it was, Mario stopped taking my calls. The magazine gave it all of ten lines. This upset me as much as it did Mario, but he wouldn't sympathize. He had given me "the tour of a lifetime," as he called it, though I've already said the archaeologists tended to speak in superlatives. He felt indignant that a magazine of the stature of *Tiempo* would reduce the announcement of this incredible discovery to ten lines and a single small photo, which, in any case, made Leo proud. The affront was made worse by the story in the papers about the journalist's head in the clouds, which got twice as much copy.

The third event related to his partner in the tunnels, the archaeologist James Fee. As will be seen, he assumed the role of protagonist in past events as well as in those yet to come. But I am getting ahead of myself.

After speaking to Leo about the camera, I called Larry McCully, the pilot with the mission agency who had flown Leo and me the last time—the time I won 'national distinction'—and asked if he could fly me out again the next day, a Wednesday. He said he would check the flight schedule. Then he said, "Can't they send someone else? You know what I'm talking about."

He was talking about my history with James Fee.

3

I am the only daughter of jungle missionaries, along with a single brother Gabriel, named after the archangel. The Amazonian jungle basin was my childhood home and people have suggested subsequently, if not disparagingly, that the jungle "made me what I am." All my life and most of theirs my parents studied the unwritten language of a prehistoric Amazonian tribe called the Ninganahua with the purpose of giving them a written vocabulary, a dictionary, and a bible while enabling them to read it. My brother Gabe and I spent our childhood on a mission compound near Pucallpa, Peru on the outskirts of the jungle. My parents, along with two hundred fellow linguists and miscellaneous personnel, came and went to and from "the base" in Pucallpa after spending months in the jungle living in raised huts, sleeping in hammocks, eating yuca and drinking coconut water in the company of their respective tribes people. All the while they listened, turning an ear, and writing miscellaneous notes about the tones and allatones in speech patterns they thought they were hearing.

The Ninganahua, as was true of all tribes in the jungle, spoke a tonal language but had no written words. My parents spent nine months out of every year for forty years of their adult lives sitting with this tribe and deciphering lingual sounds in order to transpose it to a written form of their ancient stories, a dictionary, and of course, the New Testament. In so doing they saved the indigenous language. Along with the other missionaries who were doing the same thing among other tribes, my parents returned to the base after months in the jungle to update their translation work on computers and recover their health. Some forty-three tribes were hidden in the jungle basin, the Ninganahua among them. In the early days, the only way to get where they lived was by canoe—a seven day trip up river, a trek my parents made many times. More recently they have been able to come and go by means of a three-hour flight by Helio Courier over a carpet of solid green. Gabe and I joined our parents in the tribal village for eight weeks during the summer school break. Those days stand out as our most cherished and untamed. We were the pale, fair-haired, spindly birds among a flock of dark-crested quetzals, our Ninganahua playmates who possessed names like I Ate My Dog in the Remote Past. We lived and played as the Ninganahua children did, bathing in the river and peeing in tall grass. Once Gabe and I had to run from a jaguar.

This made me what I am.

People have asked me, when I moved five years ago from my college in Illinois to Honduras to take the position with *Los Tiempo*, if it had been a daunting cultural leap. I would tell them that the leap for me was moving from Peru to Illinois. I would break out in a cold sweat in Walmart because of all the choices.

During the school season, our parents would leave Gabe and me for months at a time at the base while they traveled to the tribe. We would stay in the dorm under the "supervision" of house parents.

Gabe and I got away with so much, we felt as if we were on our own, which, more or less, we were. He would take me on adventures, not of the sort one takes when one's parents are about, that is, calculated and circumspect. These adventures were uncalculated and out of control. Gabe was ten and I, eight, when he took me to the dusty airstrip at the local jungle airport. He found just the right spot at the edge of the field where we would lie in the grass waiting for an incoming Cessna to approach. When we heard its distant droning he would look at me. "You ready?" I would squirm and kick my bare legs and grab his hand. He said, "It's scary at first, Bu. Then it's fun." (As a two year old when I was born, he couldn't pronounce Lulu, as my parents called me. To him I have always been Bu.)

Bugs crawled in my underpants and grass tickled my neck. The incoming plane came into view, then dropped low. I would shut my eyes. I opened them just as its underbelly swept so close I thought I could touch it. Then I screamed. My brother threw himself over me and we rolled in the tailwind. Gabe clung to me in hysterics while tears rolled into my ears. "I told you it was fun, Bu."

The plane, the tailwind, the rolling, the tears, all came to mind when I thought about what it felt like when

James Fee rolled over my life.

He was the guide on my first assignment in Copán after the discovery of Waterlily Jaguar's tomb. The first piece I ever wrote about him, which *Los Tiempo* declined to publish, had been titled "Indiana Jones, He's Not." James Fee, applauded by Mario Lopez, refused to tear into any structure simply for the purpose of going for the prize, even if he knew—as he often did—that what lay inside could answer some burning historical or archaeological question. His philosophy of archaeology emphasized the long view and preserving the site over against invasively penetrating it as a gratuitous grasp for treasure. For example, James knows that Copán's fifteenth king, Smoke Shell, is buried within Structure 11, which has been left largely unexcavated. He knows it is there, he has said, because a glyph on the Structure says (as he put it), "Here, on such-and-such a date, was buried the body of the fifteenth king." But James will not go after it because, "to do it right would take ten years and I don't have ten years to give it right now."

He and his highly-trained contingent of scholars, diggers, artists and pathologists have spent countless hours— years, really—scraping, dusting, chiseling, dismantling, consolidating, rebuilding, restoring and reconstructing nearly every of the select mountains of Maya rubble they chose to penetrate, documenting every piece of every inch at every step of the way. He told me, "We could work on this scale here with two hundred workers for the next one hundred years and never solve all the problems and mysteries of the ancient Maya world. But if we do this little bit, and do it right, we will have, substantially, a more beneficial impact for resolving the unknown mysteries of the Maya, because the structures will be solid and intact for later archaeologists to work on."

James, by his own admission, has been deemed a maverick in the community of scholars and diggers. He has won the reputation among his workers for being meticulous to the point of exasperated guffaws and shaking heads. The work he orchestrates is more tedious in an already tortuously slow process. He won't cut down a tree where he doesn't have to. Conservation dictates his every decision.

At the same time, he insists that his approach has not forfeited the necessary investigative mandate of his finds. And, almost in spite of the meticulous conservative approach to his work, he and his colleagues have unearthed so many remarkable finds in recent years, he has already harvested a lifetime's worth of hidden treasures.

I came to Copán the first time to learn and understand more about the particular treasure they had unearthed in the form of the tomb of Waterlily Jaguar and its pottery cache. James Fee and I spent many hours together during that first visit climbing, sometimes four-limbed, over stone structures, and stooping and scratching through musty tunnels with sweat in our eyes and dirt in our noses.

In the late afternoons we would linger at the top of Temple 11 overlooking the ball court. We would sit under the Ceiba tree, the sacred tree of the Maya, until the sun was low and Pancho the spider monkey emerged for his feed. During these pleasant hours we chatted easily and laughed a lot.

On that trip we began to spend as much time after dark in restaurants and other watering spots in town. At James's urging I prolonged my stay by three days. He insisted, "you cannot understand the Maya at Copán in only a few days." After day five—the third extra day—my deadline loomed and demanded my return. Citing business at the Institute of Anthropology in the capital city, James drove me back to Tegucigalpa himself in his double-cab pick-up since Leo had returned already on the same plane the local journalists had written about. The truth of it is, James had little to do with the Institute's side of the operation, but I didn't know it at the time and accepted his generosity. He remained in the capital city for two more weeks and we saw each other nearly every day as our relationship blossomed into something neither of us expected. It culminated in a wrenching goodbye at the door of his pickup truck before his inevitable return to Copán. On a whim I asked if he would like to join me for my brother's upcoming wedding in Wisconsin six weeks hence. He said he would love to.

It might have been my family's unanimous relief that someone had finally captured my affections, or perhaps it was the other way around. Whatever the logic, the Shaws fell in love instantly with James Fee. You would have thought my father, Eugene Shaw, and James Fee were blood brothers. They knocked elbows and went on about things like, in my father's case, how the verbs "go" and "come" in Ninganahua were the same as they were Korean; and, in James's case, why the Maya at Copán identified with the bat. Yet if ever two people were hewn from different stone, these two were. Gene Shaw received a degree from a Bible college in Seattle, linguistic training from the mission's learning center in Spokane, and grew up in church hearing altar calls every Sunday. James Fee, son of pedigreed professors, earned his doctorate at Columbia where his parents taught, and if he ever heard a sermon, which I doubt, it didn't involve an altar call.

James and I attended the wedding of my brother together, when I met my brother's fiancée, Dottie, for the first time. At one point during the pre-wedding festivities, James and Gabe issued the challenge of a contrived version of men-versus-women in bocce ball and Dottie and I beat them handily. I have to say, I liked her after that.

At the reception my brother Gabe escorted me to the dance floor and held me as he had countless times over the years of our strange childhood. Both of us knew it was the last time we would belong only to one another. He looked at me and I looked at him and wetness rose into both sets of eyes. We had to stop the dance to dry each other's faces. At that moment our mother, Edith Shaw, was kicking a heel on the dance floor with James. Our mother, the straw-hat cotton-dressed jungle woman was as giddy as a prom queen spinning on the arm of that man. She wore aqua chiffon and it flared like a flower, her wrist angled oddly upon James's square shoulder. Her neck blotted purple the rest of the night, as happened during her unguarded moments.

James saw my brother wiping my tears, so floated my mother to the spot where we stood and finished the dance with me. A breathless toothy Edie Shaw turned to her wet-eyed son, took his hands and raised her elbow to turn him on his heel. That was when I told James he looked like Jesus. Anyway, I said he looked like how I pictured Jesus, with a thick beard, deep brooding eyes, unruly hair, good teeth. He laughed out loud. My Jesus, James Fee, brushed his beard against my face and carried me across the floor. I might as well have been floating in aqua chiffon.

When the time came for the reception meal, my father, Gene Shaw—James Fee's new best friend—walked around the head table and stopped behind him, hands on his shoulders. My father said, "This is our special guest, James Fee, here with our Lu." James glanced around self-consciously and kissed my hand. My father, squeezing his shoulder as a father would a son, then asked James to return thanks before the meal. Missionaries pray before meals. But James was not a missionary. He looked at me. Still holding my hand, he half stood, clutching his linen napkin, cleared his throat and respectfully declined.

Everything changed after that. James released my hand and returned it to my lap, excused himself from the table saying he felt overtaken with the flu, and left. I followed him back to the lake house where we had been staying, and lay with him all night, still in my white satin dress he had liked so much. He shook and groaned in sweats and fever throughout the night. It never occurred to me that the kiss on my hand would be his last.

We returned to Honduras as scheduled the following day, sick as he was. He slept through both flights, the first from Chicago to Miami and the second from Miami to San Pedro Sula. We retrieved our bags, navigated customs, and then he threw his garment bag over a shoulder. He leveled those Jesus eyes on mine. "We don't have a future. We might as well end it here." At that very moment I remember hearing someone's child yammering, Mami, mami, ¡dámelo! ¡Dámelo! and a man waving lottery tickets. James thanked me for the good time in Wisconsin, and I saw a Honduran woman in a tight black skirt and clicking high heels sidestepping us as she toted a wedding dress wrapped in plastic carried over her head. I remember thinking, Should I say You're welcome? James turned on a heel to walk away the same way he had turned my mother on her heel across the dance floor.

The missionaries would have been appalled to hear what came out of Gabe Shaw's mouth when I told him what happened that day at the airport.

My father and I spoke about it weeks later. He said, "Lu, we carry around the death of Christ."

I said, "It is a death sentence."

I was twenty-six when James Fee left me standing at the airport. Then, as a fresh wind, Larry McCully stepped into my life when I was twenty-seven. He told me he welcomed the turn of events that dispelled my "archaeologist fantasy," as he called it, and made a convincing case that, since he and I shared the missionary upbringing, it made for a compatible association. More to the point, he owned a scarlet macaw named Bart, whom I adored. I taught him to say, "Don't have a cow, man," which gave the bird something to say besides "I love you, Larry," taught to Bart by I don't know whom. However Larry McCully did not need to be told by anyone or anyone's bird not to have a cow and that he was loved. He carried himself with the swagger that befits the missionary pilot. His legs slightly bowed, chin up, his trimmed auburn hair brushing his collar, he was the kind of pilot you felt safe with. There was no place he wouldn't fly, including to Timbuktu, which he did, and later described as "a thirty-day's camel ride from nowhere." My poor mother couldn't hide her distress that there would be no more dances on the arm of James Fee. But she bore it like a missionary. In any case her demeanor alighted with the hope that a wedding may yet be in the offing for her jungle-reared and untamed daughter.

So when Larry called me later that same day, when I received the assignment to return to Copán, he confirmed our departure time for the following afternoon and reiterated that he was not happy about it. He made his case to come along the way Leo had made his. And I dismissed Larry's plea even as I had Leo's. He agreed to fly me out anyway, being duty-bound, as missionaries tend to be.

And so the moment had arrived when I needed to notify the archeologists of my imminent return to Copán. I sent a fax:

> *TO: James Fee, Project Director*
> *FROM: Lucy Shaw, Los Tiempo*
> *RE: Royal Tomb assignment*
> *2 Mar 93*

Am flying to Copán tomorrow, Wednesday, 3 Mar, to arrive around 2:00pm. Can someone show me the tomb?

4

We had been delayed two hours because a cloud of dust and smoke had settled over the capital city impeding visibility and stifling air traffic, as happened frequently during the dry season. At last, when visibility improved, Larry pulled the Cessna six-seater to the end of the runway, abutting Tegucigalpa's north highway by mere footage. Honduran military police stood biting whistles and waving stiff arms to halt traffic on the highway so we could take off. Larry turned the plane a hundred-eighty degrees and stopped momentarily at the farthest reach of the shortest runway in the Western hemisphere.

"You ready?" Larry McCully looked at me the way that endeared him to me. Dressed in his blue pilot's shirt, gold stripes on the shoulders, he righted his headphones and clicked buttons over his head. He glanced out his window, leveled the engine to a droning roar and, ready or not, we lurched. The rush of forward motion always brought tears to the edges of my eyes. "These babies just want to fly." He smiled like a boy scout.

In seconds we were floating over an ocean of shimmering corrugated tin roofs in the dusty hillside that was Leonardo's hometown, a squatter town. The surrounding mountains wore a collar of light, a sea of tin catching the sun's late shafts of luminescence.

Soon enough, Leo's slums gave way to velvet green mountains and I relaxed and shut my eyes. I worked over in my mind who might meet me when we landed at the ruins, now two hours late. The drone of the plane put me into twilight sleep. I thought about the fax I sent James Fee, the only communication we had exchanged since the moment he left me at the airport over a year ago now. I didn't expect to see him. Nor did I expect to see Mario Lopez, who nursed his grudge from the year before about those ten lousy lines in the piece for *Los Tiempo*. If anyone undertook the mission to show me around I imagined it would be Chloe Zorn, the freckled and resolute research assistant who, the year before, dutifully tagged along when James took me through the tunnels. I credit her for prompting my first encounter with James Fee. It happened after the initial press conference about the pottery cache found in Waterlily Jaguar's tomb. The archaeologists were escorting journalists to the site to have a look inside the tomb and see the pottery. But I dropped behind to hover with Mario Lopez, who was speaking off-handedly with a few reporters. I rejoined the group on the cusp outside the tunnel entrance where Chloe was taking journalists' questions. James leaned casually under a nearby tree. I insinuated myself to the front just as Chloe was saying, "Fray Diego de Landa was a sixteenth century Catholic missionary who burned all but four extant Maya codices. And, well, we all know what missionaries are like, don't we?"

I brushed the hair from my face and raised my pen. She pointed my way. "I grew up with missionaries. So tell me, what are missionaries like?"

Chloe tugged at her shirt and her cheeks flushed purple. James promptly emerged from under the tree.

"I'm sure this world would be a better place if all missionaries were like you," he said in his disarming and ironic tone. Laughter rumbled over the press corps. I asked no further questions. James came to me privately afterward and apologized. He said he hadn't meant to embarrass me.

I said, "I wasn't embarrassed. The world would be a better place if more missionaries were like me." His smile won me instantly.

The trip by air from Tegucigalpa to Copán is little more than an hour, though it seemed only minutes before Larry was touching my arm and pointing out the window. The ruins looked like anthills rising out of a lush green lawn. Larry banked right and we saw the shimmering snake of the Copán River. We dropped altitude and circled the Principal Group, the site core where the most commanding structures stood. I could see the tarp overlaying the face of the Hieroglyphic Stairway placed there by James and his crew to protect the engraved hieroglyphs from erosion. There was the ball court to its north. Then, to the south I saw the Acropolis—the mélange of temples and plazas that was James Fee's primary domain.

Larry and I looped around to land on the grassy strip

near the Visitor's Center. By this point in the history of Maya archaeology at Copán, epigraphers were able to interpret eighty percent of the glyphs, while James Fee and Mario Lopez, along with their accomplished coterie of scholars and helpers, had orchestrated so many shocking discoveries at that locals looked upon them as miracle-workers.

Larry touched down gently. Thoughts came to me of a brother and sister rolling in the tailwind. The landing was unspectacular, the kind Larry liked. "Any landing you walk away from is a good landing," he always said.

It felt like coming home. The previous year James had taught me what kings were buried under which structures, where not to walk to avoid the chichicaste plant that left rashes, and when Pancho the spider monkey would wander across the Great Plaza in search of food. In the year since I had traversed these grounds and tunnels, I had become the layperson's expert on Copán, a local celebrity in government schools where I would go and speak about the knowledge gleaned from my acquaintance with the "renowned archaeologists."

Larry filled out the flight log as I stepped from the plane. The breeze from the mountain caught my hair and out of a hidden corner of my memory I found myself thinking about Jack Thatcher, of all people, Gabe's best friend and mine when we were growing up in the jungles of Peru. Jack's parents worked with the Bora tribe in the rain forest to the north, near Colombia, while our parents did their work with the Ninganahua, south and east toward Brazil. Jack, Gabe and I had started a jungle band. We called it the Ningabors, a poetic (we thought) combination of the names of our respective tribes. (We initially thought of calling ourselves the Boranings but decided it sounded too much like "the Borings.") Gabe played guitar, Jack the bass. I played the seed pods because Jack said I could shimmy. Jack's family was musical and had resources, so we scheduled our practices at his house. Jack sat on his bed, the bass on his knee, and I sat beside him scribbling the lyrics. Gabe leaned on the bedpost near my feet fondling the strings of his guitar. Soon thereafter Jack and Gabe went off to college. During the first Christmas break, as Jack was returning home to the jungle, the small plane he took from Lima to Pucallpa dropped in a barren mountainside twenty miles outside the capital. Government officials found the fuselage and the five victims, Jack among them. They told his parents both legs had been broken. At the end of that sad Christmas holiday, before Gabe returned to school, Jack's parents, Wes and Billie Thatcher, asked us to come by the house. My brother was nineteen and I seventeen the day we stood in Jack's room with wet eyes and tight throats, along with Jack's parents, after he died. To our right we saw the photo I had taken of Jack and Gabe pointing to the divergent spots on a map of the jungle basin where our tribes were located. Jack was wearing his "Mr. Rescue" T-shirt and looked straight into the camera with that dimpled smile and shock of dark bushy hair that was forever falling over his eyes. The dried hibiscus blossom I'd given him from the Ninganahua village still hung on the corner of his mirror. I had pressed it in a book and laminated it. When I gave it to Jack he took it, kissed it, then handed it to Gabe. "Go stand over there," he said to my brother. Then he picked up his semiautomatic BB gun, told Gabe to hold it steady against the wall, took aim, and shot a hole in the upper left corner of the lamination while Gabe held it without flinching. Jack pulled the yellow ribbon from my hair and poked it through the hole he had just shot and tied a bow. Then he draped the dried flower over the corner of his mirror where it still hung. The hole from the BB was still in the wall. His bass guitar rested in the corner near the bed where we would practice. Wes Thatcher, bent and sad, went to take it and then handed it to Gabe. "Jack would want you to have this."

The emotion I felt standing in Jack's room that day captured in its essence the feeling that overthrew me as I stepped from the plane that day at Copán. With the sun on my face and the sweet smell of the valley, I couldn't tell then, even as I couldn't in Jack's room ten years before, which feeling was more true: the memories that had made the place sacred to me or the sadness that had taken it away.

A woman with dark sad eyes approached me carrying a basket on her head and asked if I wanted to buy vegetables. I was a soft touch when it came to women who carried baskets on their heads. I helped her lower it to the ground and bought a stalk of yuca. It reminded me of the Ninganahua women who squatted by their fires hacking the knotty bark with machetes. The woman lifted a tangled swathe of hair from the nape of her neck and brushed dandruff from her shoulders. It seemed to me she might have been striking once, with her angular Indio features and thick glossy hair. She looked to be in her thirties, though it was difficult to tell because of the peculiar kink of her neck that added years to her bearing. She wiped her hands on a dirty apron and handed me the yuca. "Are you here for the party?"

"Excuse me?"

"The party of the journalists."

I pulled lempiras from my pocket. "Yes." I handed her the money. "I am here for the party. How do you know about it?"

"I work here. I clean offices."

Larry by this time had grabbed my bag from storage and had thrown it over his shoulder. With a touch to the elbow, he prodded me. We both knew he had to turn right around and get back to Tegucigalpa before sunset since the airport's runway didn't have landing lights. The woman said, "Gracias," and smiled faintly.

Copán's Visitor's Center stood a few hundred meters from the airstrip. Its stuccoed double archways opened into a central courtyard commanded at its center by a scale miniature model of the ruins. The archaeologists' offices skirted the perimeter of the courtyard, including James Fee's. Larry dropped my bag at the information desk to knock on the counter. "Quién está?" He looked at me. "This place is deserted." A ceiling fan spinning tediously off-kilter had been the only evidence of human activity.

"Someone must be here."

"You notified them you were coming, didn't you?"

I had no patience for answering the obvious. I circled the courtyard and poked a head into James Fee's office. It stood in the corner between Mario Lopez's and that of the park's overseer, Virgilio Fuentes. His desk looked as it did a year ago, littered with books, papers, files and stone fragments. The lights were off. His chair faced the door. I turned away and shut the door behind me. "I'll take a cab to town and check in at the hotel. You need to get back."

"I don't want to leave you without anyone to help you."

"Since when has not having help stopped me from doing my job?" I took Larry's arm as we walked back to the plane. "I know how to get a cab. Besides, I don't want you wasting any more flying time." He hesitated before climbing into the pilot's seat. "I don't like the feel of this."

"You sound like my mother."

Larry McCully then surprised me when he curled an arm around my waist and kissed me. Missionaries tended not to make open displays of affection. "Call me when you're ready to come back. I'll come. Even tomorrow." He kissed me a second time and climbed into the cockpit. I watched as he switched on the engine, adjusted the headphones and followed the ritual of button pushing that so endeared him to me. He waved, was soon aloft, and the Cessna disappeared into the mountains.

5

I decided to get a cab and settle into my room at the hotel in Copán Ruinas, so returned to the Visitor's Center to retrieve my bag. I could not resist stopping to circle the miniature floor model of the Principal Group to try and locate where this new tomb might be.

My head cocked sideways, I lifted the braid off my neck, drenched with sweat. The miniature of the ruins brought to my mind the voice of the indomitable James Fee, whom I knew I would inevitably meet again. How many times had we walked together in the Great Plaza? I looked at the scale replicas of the stelae and could hear him saying in his archaeologist's voice, "These three-dimensional monolithic sculptures were commissioned by Ruler Thirteen, also known as 18 Rabbit. They are some of the finest examples of stone sculpture carved in the New World." My eyes passed over the miniature ball court and the Hieroglyphic Stairway and then the Acropolis to the south, and I could hear him reminding me that "all sixteen kings contributed their versions of temple structures to the Acropolis, often building one on top of another." How many times had he reiterated the Acropolis is the heart of Copán's sacred geography? How many times had he emphasized, in his animated yet disarming way, the temple pyramids for the Maya were the portals to the Upperworld and the Underworld where the gods and the ancestors dwelt? "The landscape and everything in it is alive with sacred power for the Maya," he said, "—every rock and tree, the sky and stars, temples, altars, stelae and plazas."

He prefaced his assertions with the words, "According to the inscriptions"—words uttered often and unselfconsciously from the mouths of all the archaeologists. And according to the inscriptions, the tomb they believed they had found, which prompted this trip, belonged to a nobleman named Yax K'uk Mo' who had arrived in the Copán Valley in or around C.E. 416 acting as leader and regent. This was a time known as the Classic period of Maya history, which fell between C.E. 250 to 900. At the time the land of the Maya stretched from the Yucatán, Chiapas, Tabasco Campeche and Quintana Roo in Mexico, through Guatemala and Belize and into western portions of El Salvador and Honduras. The Maya controlled more or less seventy city-states during the Classic period and at various points and in differing degrees these rival city-states made war against one another. For a time Copán was a mere chiefdom controlled by competing warlords. It remained disorganized and fractured so could not rally a notable defense against rival cities. After the arrival of the above-mentioned nobleman, who had come to Copán to establish this regal center, the Maya at Copán began to unify and flourish and became one of the few key locations among its major city-states.

K'inich Yax K'uk Mo'—'He of the Sun-Precious-Quetzal-Macaw,' was known also as 'lord of the west,' according to the inscriptions. In C.E. 426, ten years after he had been functioning as a tribal chief at Copán, Yax K'uk Mo' made a pilgrimage to central Mexico, the seat of Mesoamerican power, in a place called Teotihuacán. So vast was its beauty and mystery it had become known among the ancients through all those lands as the birthplace of the gods. Its tentacles reached throughout Mesoamerica and, during his pilgrimage there, Yax K'uk Mo' received sanction to establish his rule as king at Copán. With the authority at Teotihuacán, and having traveled east from Mexico back to Honduras for "a hundred and fifty-three days" (according to inscriptions), he thus became known as 'lord of the west,' and took his place at Copán as its first king and dynastic founder. Evidence suggests he fought a great battle. It is not known whether his accession to power occasioned it. Archaeologists do know in any case that he "rested his legs" in Copán, because that's what the inscriptions say.

Yax K'uk Mo's dynasty lasted approximately four hundred years, nearly to the end of the Classic period. Fifteen kings succeeded him. These subsequent kings, each in his own way, elevated and continued the transformation of this one-time tribal chiefdom into the premier regal ritual center it was destined to become. The final king was named Yax Pasah, who died in C.E. 820. Hieroglyphic inscriptions ceased in Copán in C.E. 822, and by 850 Copán had followed the pattern of collapse played out by all nearby rival city-states, though the Maya as a people survived and number in the millions to this day.

It was his burial place the archaeologists believed they had unearthed and that occasioned my return. I turned a corner cocking my head and pulling my sweat-drenched shirt from my chest, trying to locate the tomb in the context of the miniature.

Then, from the corner of my eye, I saw a figure emerge in the courtyard at the opposite side from where I stood. I looked up. A young boy appeared with sprouting black hair and ears that flared like firefly wings. From his size I would have thought him to be about age six, but his incoming front teeth suggested he was nearer to eight. He wore a moth-eaten Chicago Bulls jersey number 23 and his jeans rode high above his ankles with holes in both knees. He wore no shoes. I assumed him to be a beggar.

"Hola," I said.

"Hola."

"¿Cómo te llamas?"

"Paco."

"Paco?"

"Sí, Paco."

"Me llamo Lucy."

"Lucy?"

"Sí, Lucy."

He stared with no apparent intention to go or draw near or even to continue the conversation.

"Do you know Dr. Fee?"

"Sí."

"Do you know where he is? Or where anyone is?"

Before the boy answered, a voice arose from behind him.

"Over here."

James Fee approached and Paco turned to him. "Váyase," James said, and the boy disappeared. "This your stuff?" He pointed to my bag still by the counter where Larry had left it. "Do you want to put it in my office?"

"Your office?"

"While we go see the tomb. You want to go, don't you?"

"Now?"

"Why not?"

"All right. Put it in your office." He threw my bag over his shoulder the same way, a year before, he had thrown his garment bag over his shoulder as he exited my life, and flipped on the light in his office.

"It'll be safe in here. You want that?" He pointed to my backpack.

"I'll keep it."

I hadn't seen that face since standing in the airport at San Pedro Sula when he was saying "we might as well end it here." He wore the same blue cotton shirt I had seen many times, and the same sunglasses dangled from his neck with the same hemp twine. He pulled keys from the pocket of his jeans, the same hands, the same jeans I had seen—I can't count the times. One key over the next, those same fingers that slipped through mine when my brother said his vows. "Ah," he said, finding the right key.

I waved a hand. "I'll wait outside." He didn't look up. I

backed away and found a shady spot near the entrance under a tree nearby. I sipped my water. He had said "Ah" with the very same inflection he used the day he misplaced the tickets to the Cubs game he and Gabe and my father attended during our Wisconsin trip. We all rifled through our things in search of them when he found them in the pocket of his jeans, he said, "Ah." Then he threw me a kiss on his way out the door.

He approached me where I sat under the tree adjusting his baseball cap. "You ready?"

"Let's go."

He walked in leaning strides. The air was calm, the grounds empty and quiet save for the crunching of pebbles under our feet. We did not speak until, after a strained minute or two, I broke the silence.

"Why is it deserted?"

"We closed the park to prepare for tomorrow, the press conference, all that," he said without breaking stride. The sun was fading in the west. The guttural hooting of a Flycatcher echoed from the forest canopy beyond. We passed a hillock that hadn't yet been excavated and James sighed. "Too many places to dig and not enough arms and legs to do it." I had heard it many times.

We first came upon Structure 4, the smallish pyramid to our left as we entered the plaza. On we walked beyond the stelae ghosts of the Great Plaza, 18 Rabbit's prize redundancies sculpted in the image of himself. Across the lawn, James couldn't help pointing out the ball court on our right explaining, as always, that "kings and captives passed a hard rubber ball without the use of arms and feet, only thighs and hips," which I knew (had heard it many times). The ball game ritual simulated the movement of the sun and planets, which I also knew, and he added that "sacrifice was the inevitable consequence for the losers and kings didn't lose." Had he forgotten that other visit?

North of the ball court we passed Altar L. He cast a nod in the direction of the Hieroglyphic Stairway—"the ode to Copán and the great acts of the early kings. It's the longest single inscribed hieroglyphic text in the pre-Columbian world."

I stopped. He turned. I said, "Yes, yes. It stands 72 feet-high, 50-feet wide, has 61 steps and more than 2,200 carved glyphs. For all its grandeur, it was shabbily built and disintegrated quickly over time, revealing a half-hearted effort on the part of the king's laborers." I looked at him. "Am I hearing this for the first time?" I threw him the look that bewildered Leonardo.

He apologized. We walked on.

"So who brought you out?"

"*Tiempo* chartered a plane."

He adjusted his cap and slowed his gate. He folded his arms across his chest. "They have accommodating pilots."

I looked at him.

He elbowed me. "I saw you saying your good-byes."

Silence settled between us. We were moving to the rear side of the Acropolis, passing beside a raised wooden walkway where a *vigilante* stood guard. The few remaining workers were parking wheelbarrows and gathering shovels and buckets. They all waved and nodded as El Doctor passed by. Reaching the backside of the Acropolis, called the corte or 'cut,' James explained that the Copán River, over the years, had hacked off fifteen meters of the eastern face of the Acropolis "like a slice from a cake." He said it was "every archaeologist's dream" because inside the Acropolis is hidden four hundred years of successive accumulative building that the corte revealed and made accessible. A surface about a hundred feet high and five hundred feet long, it reveals floors, terraces, and stairways in a way that enables the archaeologists to visualize the sequential build up of Copán. The Acropolis, being Copán's "sacred mountain," that is, the epicenter of building of the sixteen kings' palaces, is comprised of temples, thrones and other significant buildings that had been used by Copán's ruling elite. In essence, the corte revealed a snapshot of the accumulation of superimposed structures, since the kings of Copán followed the pattern of demolition and burial of their predecessors' sacred places in order to build their own sacred place atop the ruin of the others'. It is here, at the Acropolis' penultimate layer, where the team found the bones they thought had belonged to Waterlily Jaguar. The recent digging into the lowest level, thus the earliest, revealed the tomb, they believe, of the founding king, which is why *Tiempo* sent me back. "Until we found this tomb, all knowledge about this alleged founding king came from sources subsequent to his reign," James said. "This discovery has added the necessary flesh to the bones of the story we were reading, written by Copán's earlier kings. Physical evidence of the existence of Yax K'uk Mo' means the historical documentation is true and that what we read can be trusted." We mounted a set of steep stone stairs. "Here we are." James pulled keys from his pocket and unlocked a barred door outside the tunnel entrance. Two steps in and we came to a second heavy wooden door secured with a pad lock. James was still explaining:

"This pattern of demolition, burial and rebuilding," he continued, "has been done at other sites, but in the process other structures were destroyed. Here the previous structures, more or less, are clearly notable. All we have to do is to hollow out the fill."

"I know this," I said.

He looked at me, jiggling keys. "About Don Gustavo?"

"Who?"

"Gustav Stromsvik, the beloved archaeologist"—inserting different keys to loosen the padlock— "He built a wall to defend the structure from further damage in the 1940s. He rerouted the Copán River. The locals called him endearingly Don Gustavo."

I said, "And every temple tells a story and the erosion presented an opportunity to hear the stories of all the kings that might otherwise have been too deeply buried to penetrate. You told me that."

"To penetrate *noninvasively*." He handed me the flashlight. "Hold this."

He leveled his eyes on mine, digging into his pocket for more keys, his shoulder slightly raised. Those eyes to me were the eyes of Jesus, death eyes. He pulled out a handful of keys and fumbled through them not once, but twice. Then he groaned. "I brought the wrong set." He pulled off his cap and wiped his brow with a shoulder. "I wanted you to see the tomb before the press arrive tomorrow.

"What time are they coming?"

He put hands on his hips. "Nine." He sighed. "I'll get you back here before then." He curled his eyebrows and looked at me with the familiar expression of part humor, part resignation—the same look he had given me when Dottie and I beat the men at bocce ball. "Nothing to do but walk back. Or do you want to go see the Ceiba tree on top of Temple 11?"

I had seen it before. But I didn't mind going and seeing it again. We meandered at our leisure south of the Acropolis to the area excavated by Illinois, the residential quarters of the kings, which I knew already and he didn't mention it. We climbed stone steps that led to the rear of Temple 16, the great and forbidding structure in which they had found the tomb of Yax K'uk Mo'. Then the site leveled out on to the grassy East Plaza.

"Did we go to the Jaguar dancing court the last time?"

Evidently in his mind there had been a last time after all.

"No," I said.

"Well let's go." He led the way across the East Plaza and stopped at steps flanked by sculptures of jaguars, each with an arm extended. He mimicked them. "They are beckoning people to the dance platform—'Come upstairs and dance.'" He looked at me, his arm out wide like the jaguars, then wiggled his hips. "They're kind of silly." I stared incredulously. He lowered his arm and adjusted his ball cap. "The jaguar was the most powerful of animals for the Maya. The priests made it their alter ego. But you know that." We moved up over rocks and roots to another stairway on the south side of Temple 11, the one-time reviewing stand of Copán's last king, Yax Pasah. He sat at the pinnacle to watch the ritual ball games being played on the ball court below.

James lifted a chin. "Smoke Shell, the fifteenth king, is buried somewhere in here," he said, meaning Temple 11, another redundancy, but he couldn't help himself.

I said, "There's a glyph that says 'Here on such-and-such a date was buried the body of the fifteenth king' and you're not going to dig it up because it would take ten years to do it right and you don't have ten years to give it right now." I looked at him and wiggled my hips. For the first time we both smiled.

Now atop Temple 11, I couldn't help wondering how I had gotten back to these ruins, to this temple under the Ceiba tree with roots bigger than a man, chatting with the one who rolled over my life like the tailwind of an incoming plane. James Fee stood atop the sacred mountain in this mysterious world of warrior kings—kings of the jaguar throne. When Venus arose they saw visions in blood spilt from their self-pierced member. They wore the headdress of the quetzal and raised the shield of woven mat and the scepter of the double-headed serpent. They anointed their thrones with the blood of their captives. And here I was again in this strange world. What did I know of jaguar thrones? Of temples carved from volcanic tuff? Clouds hung over the mountains to the north. The sun lent its final rays against an indigo sky spilling magic luminescence over the ball court. A storm was gathering in the west and a mist blew in. James leaned against the Ceiba tree, his arms crossed and a foot slightly raised, resting on a rock. The scraping and digging had ceased. Stillness hung over the ruins like a ghost. Pancho the monkey appeared on the Great Plaza, knowing the time he could emerge to frolic with the place to himself. A doe had stepped onto the plaza to graze and turned to lick the face of her fawn. "This Ceiba," James said—meaning the tree beneath which we stood—"has got to be a couple of hundred years old. We have a photo of it that was taken in 1885. It was the same size then, except for the root buttresses. They're bigger now." He faced the north. The breeze cooled the sweat from our faces. Butterflies gamboled in a lower tree about our feet, dancing little flames of saffron and orange. He said, "You'll still find Ceiba trees in town squares in traditional Maya communities in Guatemala and Yucatán." He paused. "They used to have a Ceiba in the plaza in town here. There are old photographs of it."

I looked over the Great Plaza as evening was falling. The mist descended, a deer was grazing and Pancho ambling. Butterflies floated and James rested his foot on a rock. I wondered how we had found ourselves here again under the Ceiba tree, I and the man who danced with my mother?

"We should go," I said. "It looks like it might rain."

We descended the stairs along the western slope. James stopped to comment on a different Ceiba, the twin, he called it. "Any one of the branches on that thing could be another tree. We don't have any photographs of this one from 1885. Ceibas don't have annual rings, so we don't know how old it is." I was thinking I might have taken his hand to make the descent. But he didn't offer it.

As we attempted to exit the park we were surprised to discover the exterior gate had been closed and locked. The guard, Don Berto Rodriguez, was not at his post. By this point a gentle rain had stirred and James looked at me. "We're locked in." Water dripped from his nose. "I'm going to go find Berto. You wait here."

I didn't mind the rain or the delay. James disappeared into the mist and I took the chance to breathe and settle myself. Seeing the temple structures, the ball court and Hieroglyphic Stairway, the stelae of 18 Rabbit, I heard myself echo the words of John Lloyd Stevens—all was mystery, deep, impenetrable mystery. I remained astonished at the work of the "renowned archaeologists." This aroused faint remembrances of something I thought might have been affection. Then I heard his words *This your stuff?*—James Fee's first words to me after a year of unresolved silence. I thought I would marry that man. My family did too, even Gabe. Thunder rumbled low from the north and the rain grew heavy, cooling my wet eyes.

A figure emerged from the trees behind me, almost as if a spirit. I soon recognized him as the old man, Don Berto, the guard James had gone searching for. He wore the same baggy pants I had remembered from the year before, still tied with the same tattered rope for a belt. His shirt hung loose and rain drizzled from the rim of his white woven field hat. He still had that withered look with puckered cheeks and toothless gums. I was fluent in Spanish but could not understand Don Berto to save my life because of his having no teeth.

"Don Berto. ¿Cómo estás? Do you remember me? I am Lucy Shaw."

"Sí. Sí," he nodded. "[Something] — [something] Señor Fee, a su orden, [something]. ¿Verdad?"

"He's gone looking for you. We're locked in."

"Sí." He pulled keys from his pocket. I thought surely that heavy load could drop his pants save for the rope belt. He fingered them achingly, one over the next with bony stiff fingers disfigured by arthritis. "Aqui está." He mumbled something I didn't understand. Turning the key he jostled the padlock. It sprung open.

"Berto!" James approached from behind.

"Asi es, Señor Fee." Berto pushed wide the gate and the two men chatted. I counted it among James Fee's innumerable and incomparable accomplishments that he understood Berto's toothless Spanish. James said, "I was worried something happened to you." Berto shook his head, responding in detail I did not understand. I heard only the words "I am the older by eight minutes, two grunts and a squeal." To my amazement James nodded in earnest reply.

By the time we returned to his office James and I were wringing wet. He always smiled when he was wet, I never understood why. Here he was again, smiling like the sunrise as he pulled my bag from the closet. "My truck is out here." He heaved my pack over a shoulder and we walked outside. "I'll take you to the hotel."

"I don't expect you to be taking me around," I said.

He ignored me. We landed in the front seat, my wet hair in tentacles about my neck, his dripping in streams down his forehead. "I'm assuming you want to see the tomb tomorrow before the crowd descends." He stretched his arm across the seat to back out, then shifted and pulled onto the road heading to town.

"I hadn't assumed that."

"What are you doing for dinner?" He jostled his wet hair.

"I hadn't thought about dinner."

We were driving toward Copán Ruinas, the colonial town nearest the ruins. Its stuccoed buildings were built along steep cobbled streets and it was less than a mile from the archaeological park. We crossed the bridge over the Rio Quebrada (river creek) and entered the center of town. James downshifted. The truck lurched. We crept up the hill and passed his small gated house on the right. Up another block, then left and down, we pulled up at the entrance of the hotel where I was staying, its double doors opened to a welcoming courtyard. "I need to go home and clean up." He pulled my bag from the rear seat. At this point I attempted to thank him for the ride and to make general inquiries about the next day's schedule at the tomb. He cut me off. "I'll meet you at the hotel restaurant at half past seven." James had a way of overthrowing my earnest and modest intentions.

6

I found James Fee in the hotel restaurant a few hours later and he had already ordered three beers. "One for you, two for me," he said. In the background the Chi-Lites were singing Have You Seen Her? and he raised his glass. "To Yax K'uk Mo', the Maya king who brought Lucy Shaw back to Copán." He sank half his beer in the first swallow, then settled and leaned back in his chair with his hands clenched behind his head. "So how are your parents? How is their work?"

"The Ninganahua New Testament is in Korea being printed as we speak." This surprised him since the last he saw them the translation process had been set back. "They still have the dictionary to finish. But they will be dedicating it this May out at the tribe."

Talk of my parents inevitably took us to awkward remembrances, back to Wisconsin and the occasion of my brother's wedding when the Shaws fell in love James Fee. And when, for the first time in his career as an anthropologist and archaeologist, he saw something of the work of the linguist missionaries he hadn't before understood. Everyone at that time, including I believe James himself, thought that Lucy's wedding would follow on the heels of her brother's. The strain of the moment found relief from a man at the bar who was declaring to his drinking companion, "My name is Julio Cabrera Cabrera. I am a very brave man!" I don't remember what the friend of Julio Cabrera Cabrera said in response. The server returned with fried platanos and I tucked a loose strand into my braid. James rubbed his beard, and rested a cheek in his palm. "So tell me about the pilot."

The pilot. Dear Larry. The man in my life who fixed things. I wanted to tell James how Larry fixed my washing machine. How he took the motor apart and found wood chips "the repair people" had jammed inside to secure electrical connection and how he had then promptly marched down to the repair shop to demand the new motor they had charged me for, which they surrendered, and how he then installed it and got the machine to work again. I wanted to tell James how Larry flushed out the two-foot iguana that had come up from my toilet. And how, after the screams, Larry had grabbed it. But it squirmed back down and so he dumped in a half gallon of bleach and it floated up a few days later bloated and rotting, and Larry fixed that too. I wanted to tell James how I thought I would marry Larry because sometimes I would collapse into tears behind the wheel of my car because I couldn't find a hill to park on and how marrying Larry would mean getting a car that didn't have to be parked on a hill and could be started with a key. How marrying

Larry would mean I would no longer have to live on the same corner where the neighbors were robbed at gun point by four men who poisoned the dog, jumped the fence, broke down the door, tied them up and pillaged their home while, bound and gagged, they looked on. Marrying Larry would mean I would not have to fear my dog would be dead when I returned home, or that my bedroom had been plundered and my passport stolen along with my stowed-away cash. I wanted to tell James that marrying Larry would fix my broken life.

Instead, I said: "Can we start over?" I touched the napkin to my mouth. "Thank you for offering to show me around and explain your remarkable discovery. Though I would think it is a job better suited to a research assistant, say, Chloe Zorn. That is, unless she is no longer your assistant and has become your lover." I placed my napkin to my lap and held my ground. He lifted his beer smiling faintly.

"Okay. No more questions about Sky King."

"His name is Larry."

"No more questions about Larry." He leaned toward me. "And, no, she's not my lover—not that she doesn't want to be."

I leaned toward him. "Fortitude on top of brilliance. Is there no end to this man's virtue?"

And so he who dusts rocks with soft-haired brushes had again met she who taps her foot on marbled floors in waiting lounges. He who coaxes beauty from the dirt was sparring in concert with she who drives like a cowboy. James Fee and Lucy Shaw spoke no further of romance, though it seemed to hover somewhere beyond our reach. We focused instead on the reason I had come, the discovery of the tomb of Yax K'uk Mo'.

"To review," James said —he enjoyed reviewing things. He placed his hands palms down on the table, face-to-face with me, Julio Cabrera Cabrera behind us and the Chi Lites still keening. "You already know the last four years have yielded a cornucopia of discoveries." He was assuming his National Geographic voice now. "The tomb we found under the Hieroglyphic Stairway in 1989 we were sure belonged to Ruler Twelve, Smoke Imix God K. They did a *National Geographic Explorer* on it." He sipped his beer and signaled for more chips. "They were filming and we were all saying it has to be the tomb of Smoke Imix, Ruler Twelve. He reigned for sixty-seven years, the longest-lived king —you knew that, right? Everything pointed to its being his tomb. The stratigraphy, the pottery. The Hieroglyphic Stairway is dedicated to him. Glyphs everywhere on it bear his name. The tomb is near the geographic center. It contained forty-four vessel offerings, ten painted pots, and nineteen spiny shells. It had a child sacrifice. It had to belong to a king. Who else could it be?"

"Was it a captive?"

"What?"

"The child. Was the child a captive or did people sacrifice their children?"

He smiled dryly.

"There are no first-hand accounts." He paused to sip his beer. "We don't know if these children were given up voluntarily or not. We've estimated that the kid was about eleven years old and had bad teeth, we know that. He was probably the child of a commoner who was sacrificed to accompany the king on his journey to the Underworld." He leaned back and folded his arms. "Anyway, the preliminary conclusions drawn by the physical anthropologist about bone fragments contradicted the theory that the tomb belonged to Smoke Imix. The physical anthropologist said the bones didn't show the wear and tear of arthritis or other evidence of aging you would expect to find in an older individual. So he concluded the remains belonged to a person between thirty-five and forty years old, which eliminated Smoke Imix who lived into his seventies. We've deduced that the tomb must have belonged to a son who never lived to take the throne."

"So the initial conclusion was a misfire."

"I prefer to see it as deference to the opinion of the physical anthropologist." He drained his beer and the server brought our dinners. "My gut was telling me it was the tomb of Smoke Imix. But I also knew the physical anthropologist knows the bone. And the person who knows the bone was telling me something else. So I respected my colleague's opinion. That's what we went with.

"Then, last year in March," he said, still reviewing, "we found the tomb we thought belonged to Waterlily Jaguar, the seventh king, or one of his sons, the eighth or ninth king. Between them, the sons ruled less than ten years. Very little is known about them. They are our 'putative kings.' "

And on it went—a soliloquy about Waterlily Jaguar's tomb and the discussion of "putative kings"—catchwords for me that held other associations.

"Mario called it an 'incidental find.' "

"What?"

"Waterlily Jaguar's tomb. Tombs can be incidental finds. At the time we had been tunneling through the slabs and stairways of the Acropolis to separate the architectural forms of the various city levels—"

—"You're using your National Geographic voice"—

He paused "—and when we came to the center, we stumbled onto a stairway. So we cut an axial trench through it."

"What's an axial trench?"

"Cut along the axis. I told you that." He rolled his eyes. "You're a journalist. You're supposed to remember these things. Archaeological methodology tells us this is where you generally find offerings and tombs."

"At the center."

"Didn't I say that?"

The server asked what more we needed. James thanked her and waved her off. "We didn't anticipate finding a tomb during this operation and we never expected to find the kind of ceramic offerings we dug up. From the archaeological standpoint it was a shocking find. These were *al fresco* vessels made without the firing process that fixes the paint to the ceramic. The colors were as bright as the day they were put there. That was last year's big news."

Taken as I was with last year's big news—Waterlily Jaguar, the so-called putative kings, and *al fresco* pottery— I felt the inclination to dig out my wallet. He moved on to talk about the "tantalizing clues" associated with the discovery of the tomb of Yax K'uk Mo' when, as if from heaven, a ruck-faced gringa floated to our table. Fifty-ish with pinkish eyes, she wore a billowing red skirt and orange sunflower earrings made more alarming by the red bandana wrapped tightly over her graying red hair. "James Fee, of all people," she said. Then confusion erupted. She touched her pale cheek to his thick beard. I stood, digging out my wallet. James also stood, clutching his napkin. The gringa put a hand on his shoulder. I placed some money on the table. James said, "Lillian. It's been a long time." Then he turned to me. "Where are you going?"

"Lillian DeWine," she said smiling with lipstick on her teeth. She extended her hand.

"Lucy Shaw." I returned her handshake.

"Lillian works with the Lenca Indians in Belén, south of here," James said. "I haven't finished telling you about the tomb."

"Catch up with Lillian." I turned to leave. I had reached the restaurant exit when James called to me.

"What's your room number?"

I showed two hands, four fingers each. His expression suggested he wasn't sure if I meant room forty-four or eight. But he figured it out. Soon afterward I heard a knock at my door, room number eight, and James Fee stood in the glow of the courtyard lamp, light glinting off his sweating brow.

He looked like the Maya sun god. "My name is Julio Cabrera Cabrera and I am a very brave man," he said with a grin. I joined him on the bench in the courtyard outside my room, a spot we had shared other times in differing circumstances. In those days James might have draped his arm across the back of the bench and twirled my braid between his fingers. I might have dropped my head to his shoulder. We might have reposed in silence for time we had no inclination to measure. This night however arms stayed close to chests, all heads erect. "I thought we would go to the tomb in the morning before the workers show up," he said.

I looked at him. "Why are you doing this?"

He looked back. "I want a good story." He tossed a pebble into the garden.

I preempted the silence. "How was your chat with Lillian?"

"She wanted to know about my father. She studied under him."

"How is your father?"

"I haven't heard from him in over a year."

Duncan Armerding Fee, distinguished in his field of study of the Lenca, had spent summers in Central America with students and occasionally brought his son along. He had hoped to arouse in the young James Fee a similar allurement to the study of the Lenca. Instead his son's enthrallment with the Maya proved a disappointment to his father. They did share, in any case, separate interests in Honduras's respective indigenous people groups. Duncan Fee had an astonishing library with volumes numbering in the thousands. While other boys chased rabbits and climbed trees and played cowboys, the young James Fee probed his father's library stacks and read verticle bindings of his father's books. He especially fancied books with name Fee on the spine, of which there were many. He didn't have to crane his neck to read them—Fee. Fee. Fee. Fee. Fee. Fee. Fee — his little head bobbing up and down. James told me that night outside my room at the hotel that Duncan Fee's research and eccentric imagination had more recently been seized by a fascination in the Artemis cult of ancient Ephesus and as a result he had been traveling in Turkey for the past year. They had had no contact between them.

James yawned and lifted his cap. He turned his head my way. "Can you be ready at 5:30?"

"Why so early?"

"The workers arrive at 6:30. That will give us plenty of time."

"Then we'd better call it a night."

He walked me to the door of my room and leaned a shoulder against the frame. The lamplight bronzed his face and I dug into my pocket for the key. He said, "Are your parents inviting outsiders?"

"What?"

"To the dedication. Are they allowing any outsiders to attend, or is it only for family?"

I dropped my key. "I haven't asked them." He retrieved it. "Why?" He placed it in my palm.

"I thought it might be interesting to go. Their translation work doesn't sound that different from our trying to decipher glyphs. I'd be interested in seeing what they've done."

"Ask them," I said. He said he might.

I have sometimes wondered if it had been better to have shared all the precious moments I experienced with James Fee, along with that single shattering one, or not to have shared any moments at all. I would like to think that the good moments with the single shattering one were the better of it, though it would be dishonest not to concede that, in the end, it bestowed to me a kind of madness. But journalism and madness aren't so far apart and life went on for me. Larry helped. Leo taught me to start a car without a key. I moved forward. Yet here I was again at a hotel room door in Copán Ruinas standing shoulder to shoulder with the bronzed-face sun god who had loved me once, then left me just like that. Now he was asking about my parents' dedication ceremony at the jungle tribe. Was this to suggest we might meet again in the world that made me what I am? Are we to meet in the jungle, James and I, where Gabe and I grew so attached to one another we couldn't breathe without the rhythm of the other's breath? Where my parents grew old bringing a written form of an obscure language to people who would just as easily use their New Testaments to wipe their rear ends?

I said goodnight and retreated to my room. I showered and, keeping my shoes on, sat on the bed in indecision. I always kept my shoes on, even if I arose from my bed in the middle of the night. The single time I did not, and subsequently stepped on a cockroach, was all it took to establish this pattern. My hotel room was dimly lit, as were all public places in Honduras that subscribed to a seemingly unwritten law warranting a single forty-watt light bulb sufficient to give ample light in any single room. Songs of crickets and cicadas arose through my window and I debated whether or not to keep the light on, fearing it would attract bugs. The window was little more than an alignment of glass louvers that had no screen. I knew I ought to go to bed, given the early start the following morning. But I also knew it would be impossible for me to fall asleep readily and that I might as well make good use of my sleeplessness.

During my trip to Copán the year before James had supplied me with more journal articles than I could read, at least for that assignment. I brought them along on this trip and decided to start flipping through them. I also pulled files and notebooks of my previous interviews with various archaeologists I had kept from the year before. I passed over the article titled "The Ritual Dances of the Popol Nah." No interest in reading "9 Ahua House," nor "The Early Classic Elite Residential Complex," nor "Political Office and the Ah Holpop." I stopped at the article titled "Sacrificial Burials."

I read that three human sacrifices had been unearthed in the residential section at the south end of the Acropolis where Copán's ruling elite had lived. The first belonged to a young person who had been buried face down, his lower legs drawn up behind him with his arms crossed and folded under his chest. The placement of his appendages suggested he had been tied and bound, which meant he had been a captive. The second victim was a large male with healthy bones whom they found buried on his stomach. His arms and legs had been dismembered and tied in a bundle to his back. There were no cut marks on the bones, so experts speculated the victim died as a result of torture that included dismemberment. The third human sacrifice was small, the bones slight, probably a child. Noble families, the article concluded, sacrificed humans as a matter of course in the rites of dedication that attended the construction of new buildings.

I had interviewed Randall Bowman from Illinois, who oversaw excavations at the residential complex. According to my notes, he told me then that the residential area had been the living quarters of the high nobility near the end of the dynasty, including the brother of the last king. Bowman's findings dated around C.E. 822, the year hieroglyphic inscriptions ceased at Copán, and included a rich assortment of Late-Classic painted pottery. He called it "the garbage of the rich," as I had written in my notes. The area also yielded, in contrast, an abundance of coarse tools for polishing, cutting, and grinding, which he had said were the implements used by the working class. The mingling of the garbage of the rich along with the implements of the working class, according to Bowman, suggested that social ferment was underfoot in the dynasty's final stages.

I had written in my notes: "Residential area taught much about Maya human sacrifice," quoting Bowman. "The Maya ruling elite felt they had the right to sacrifice people. It was part of their understanding of the power of blood and the need for ritual," he had said. When it came to the power of the blood rituals, I came to understand, there was a marked distinction between blood sacrifice as embodied in animal sacrifices and sometimes human victims, and the flesh-piercing blood ritual known as letting blood. The latter was performed by the Maya kings after days of spiritual preparation that included fasting and self-intoxication. The king would pierce his genitals, dripping the blood onto bark paper, and then burn the bark paper in an incense burner. The ancestors, who after death had become gods, would then appear to the king in a vision in the smoke. By letting blood the king invoked the power of the gods and conferred its benefits to his mortal constituents. "This went a long way in protecting his position," Bowman had said, according to my notes.

He had explained that the other blood rituals—human and animal sacrifice—nourished the Maya gods so they could continue to sustain the physical universe, the rising and setting of the sun, the movement of the planets, the seasons. The blood from human sacrifice fed them so they could keep the rhythms of life in motion. Captives caught in battle frequently satisfied this purpose. Many went to work in fields as slave labor. But some were kept alive to be humiliated and tortured before being dispatched for ritual sacrifice. Bowman had also said the "iconography played it up," meaning the images of sacrifice on vessels and carvings embellished the extent of this practice. Though he conceded "all Mesoamerican societies did a lot of this." The dismembered robust male found buried in the residential complex had been one such prize. The strong bones indicated he had been well fed and the jade teeth in-lays meant he had possessed wealth and status. He probably had been a high-ranking warrior.

This reading only accelerated my pulse rate and I had to stop. I threw cold water on my face and made an attempt to sleep, which eluded me as I knew it would. In darkened and lonely thoughts in the twilight of sleep, I saw bones of a young person buried face down, legs drawn up and arms bound and crossed under his chest. Then I saw James Fee with his arms around me, fingers playing with the strings on the back of my dress. I saw a warrior's bones, arms and legs, dismembered and tied in a bundle to his back. Then I saw two strong bodies, his and mine, swimming in the lake, arms and legs bundled together under the water. I saw the slight-boned offering of a child, given up because of his weakness. I saw myself, soft-boned and weak, first before my brother Gabriel, a man of the strength and the highest of angels, and then before James, who rolled like thunder over my life. I was remembering the morning James and Gabe met. They looked at one another, shook hands, smiled with the crows feet of one pointing to the crows feet of the other. The dark-bearded sun god with brooding eyes and a sunrise smile had met the fair angel with eyes like ice and hair like the wind. As their hands and their eyes met I saw only then how the one would deliver me from the other.

I never pretended to be holy. Gabe and I were not holy. The dress I wore to Gabe's wedding appalled the missionaries, my mother among them, with its dipping bust line and plunging back where spaghetti-string straps criss-crossed precariously. James called it a "very bold dress," white, satiny, with a slit up the leg. He saw me in it for the first time after he had been outside the guesthouse, where we stayed for my brother's wedding, getting directions to the church from a cousin of mine. We were running late because of complications related to that dress and he walked back into the house agitated. He yelled up the stairs, "We gotta go, Lu!" He hadn't seen me where I stood in the kitchen writing myself a note. Then, with a turn of his head, he saw me, my arm bent slightly in alignment with my pen, the dress catching the late afternoon sun. He pulled off his sunglasses. I looked up. In the next breath he had lifted that writing arm and pressed my palm to his cheek and kissed it. "Mi amada bella," he said. I felt the stiffness of his collar on my face and he smelled of cologne. Then, as if by magic, he slipped his fingers through the strings on the back of my dress. I whispered, "Pull the strings to get the prize."

I don't know why he didn't. My beautiful beloved, he had said. I tossed in my bed and wondered if frail bones sacrificed won the blessing of the gods. Or were they destined to be only the food for the gods? He told me I looked like a moonbeam in that dress.

In time sleep finally overtook me. It seemed only a minute later when I heard a knock at my door. James Fee had returned for the private, early morning tour of the tomb of Yax K'uk Mo',

"I need coffee," I said.

"We'll get it when we come back."

7

On any given day in the small colonial town of Copán Ruinas, old men carrying burlap sacks over stooping backs might shuffle along alleys or walkways of the main plaza. Women in flat shoes and tight skirts might carry baskets on their elbows or heads. School children in crisp uniforms might huddle in packs passing secrets. But this day, on the morning James Fee fetched me for an early look at the tomb, the streets of the town were still. The cobblestone fluoresced under a shining moon and all was quiet except for the plaintive crowing of a lone cock.

We drove to the grounds in silence, that is, until I said, "I'm assuming you brought the right keys."

"Aren't you the one who hates stupid questions?"

We parked on a nondescript gravel road on the grounds that was inaccessible to public visitors. I heaved my backpack over my shoulder while James pulled his flashlight from under the seat and led the way, as he always did. We followed his light through the dew-soaked grass beyond the Great Plaza, beyond the ball court and the northern edge of the Hieroglyphic Stairway, to the corte and the eastern face of the Acropolis.

We climbed the steps where the day before we had been forced to turn back and came to the first locked doorway. "Hold this," he said. He handed me the flashlight and fished in his pocket for the key. The first lock sprung loose, as did, thankfully, the second lock bolting the interior door two steps in. Then down we went on a moist dirt path that felt as if it was leading us to the center of the earth. "Stay close," James said. Going deeper in and farther down, he switched on lights where he could, thanks to a primitive system of wires and loose bulbs jerry-rigged by the archaeologists. But the flashlight was our surest guide. The pathway through the damp underbelly of Temple 16 dipped here and undulated there and I kept a hand on the jagged wall. The air grew more stifling and I quickly lost track of the twists and turns.

James turned left. I followed close behind him and felt a descent. "I can't see where I'm going," I said. He slowed and cast the light's beam to my feet. We came to a metal door, still descending, and could no longer stand erect. "This way," he said. He stooped and hopped down a few steps. "Be careful." He pointed out two boards loosely covering a hole in the path, then turned left, still stooping, and down two more steps, notches carved into the rock. He lent me his hand. I navigated a final steep step. "Now we go up," he said. "Watch this." He directed the light to a gaping hole in the path. We then had to heave ourselves up onto a ledge, the way you pull yourself from a swimming pool. He said, "You got it?" We were both winded. Sweat poured from our faces. I felt dirt beneath my fingernails from clutching the wall.

At last we had come to the tomb chamber. His voiced strained, he started giving instructions. "I'm going to stand here." He crossed a trench at the tomb's outer entrance and handed me the light. He groped to turn on a light bulb that revealed a plastic tarp draped over the buried remains. James shifted his weight to lean on a knee in order to pull away the tarp. "I'll get this out of the way," meaning the tarp, and he swept it in a single motion.

In the face of sudden shock human response shows itself in what feels like slow motion and a lack of sound. Yet, at the same time, I knew and could hear in an oddly otherworldly way, his yelp and my scream and I saw James reeling. When the moment of initial disorientation settled to clear-headed awareness, we found, hanging over the stone bier of Yax K'uk Mo', a dead body suspended grotesquely in a hammock hung from parallel poles. It had been positioned as a Maya sacrifice, arms crossed and bound in front and it legs bent backward and tied behind. Most shockingly, it had been painted blue.

James recovered from his backward fall and rallied himself to take a closer look. He instantly recognized the body as Don Berto, the guard who had opened the gate for us the day before when we had been locked in. Berto was wearing his signature baggy pants, the rope belt, and mud-caked boots. His blue face bore his familiar toothless puckered visage. The blue substance used to paint him streaked down the temples of his white hair almost like shampoo. He hung there dead as stone.

"Get your camera," James said. My lungs tightened and I started to heave. He stepped into the trench to approach the bier. He turned and barked. "Lucy, give me your camera. Hurry."

I labored for every breath and couldn't control the shaking of my hands. But I managed to open my backpack and grope for the camera, dumping all contents, and mumbling "camera, camera." Once in hand, I passed it to James who tossed me the lens cap, which I did not catch. He started snapping photos of the body from every angle, the flashes of the light discharging explosions of blue.

"I'm going to be sick," I said.

"Not now, Lucy." He inched closer to the body. "Come here. Get behind me and hold my belt. I need shots from below, for his face, but I can't get close enough without damaging the tomb. You'll have to counter-balance me so I can lean."

"I need air." My eyes were wet.

He turned to face me. "Look at me. Look at me, Lucy. You can do this. I need you. Now hold me." He turned to face the tomb and told me to put my hands on his belt. "Do you have me? I'm going to lean in. You can't let me drop. I'll screw up the pots. You got me?"

I answered with groans and focused only on the belt. I leveraged him from behind, by the belt, tugging his waistline, pulling, pulling, while he leaned down and in, closer to the body, grunting and heaving. He snapped and snapped, first shots of a blue face, then blue flaking arms, then blue hands, then bony knees poking through ragged pants. When James exhausted the film he recovered his balance and gave me the camera. He told me I could release his belt.

I do not recall how we managed to retrace our steps down that deep ledge, over the hole in the path, and up to a landing where finally I collapsed. "I'm going to be sick." James rooted around and found a discarded cement bag and held it for me. "Try and breathe. Take some water," he said. He rolled up and tossed the bag and squatted nearby. I rested my head against the wall. He pushed back my hair. "We've got to get out of here. Can you walk? I'll help you." He lifted my pack and held the flashlight three steps ahead of me.

"I can't see anything."

He slowed and put the light closer to my feet. "Here. Watch the boards." We were stooping. He pulled my hand. "Steps here. Come on." The tunnel was opening up. The air became cooler. Down another path, we passed a wheelbarrow loaded with rope parked in a nook. The increased oxygen quickened us as we neared the entrance.

"We're almost there," he said. I saw daylight.

Outside the tunnel entrance, we both collapsed on the landing entrance, stunned and sucking air.

He took off his baseball cap and wiped his brow with his sleeve. "I've got forty journalists coming this morning."

"Why would anyone want to do that to that old man?"

James glanced around. "I need you to do something for me. Take this film." He pulled it from the camera and pressed it into my hand. "Go to the lab and give it to Carlos. You remember Carlos? You said he looks like an Ottoman sheik. He gets to the lab around seven. Don't say anything about what's on it. Just give him the film and tell him I want him to process it, double prints. Can you do that? You're a journalist. You can do anything."

"Shouldn't we call the police?"

"I'll deal with the police. The workers will be showing up soon. I'll send one of them to get the police and we can get the body out of here. Can you stand up?"

He took my hand to help me up. I leaned against the wall, his hands on my shoulders, and the next thing I knew I was smelling the sweat on his face and feeling his beard against my cheek. "I need you to be strong, Lu. You can do this." He rubbed my back. "You ready?" I wasn't, but that was irrelevant. He pulled me from him. "Take my truck. You remember how to get to the lab?" He dug the keys from his pocket. "Give the film to Carlos. Then wait in my office. I'll meet you there when I'm finished here."

"If you fail under pressure your strength is not great"—a proverb my brother Gabe used when we young to coerce me into joining him in whatever outrageous adventure he had concocted for that day. Gabe always appropriated proverbs to accommodate his plans. For reasons I don't understand, when I approached the driveway gate at the lab, only to find it locked, the favorite of all of Gabe's proverbs came to me: "Blows and wounds cleanse away evil, and beatings purge the inmost being, Proverbs twenty verse thirty." Gabe would have jumped the gate. He would have injured himself, experienced equal measures of bodily pain and euphoria, and bid me to follow him. Absent of his inspiration at this moment, instead I waited listlessly in the truck, my hands loose on the grimy steering wheel, my face turned to the sun. Yet I felt neither the sun on my face or my hands on the wheel. If I felt anything, it was the pain in my head for want of the coffee James and I never returned to retrieve. When I closed my eyes I saw blue. I saw baggy pants with skinny legs folded backward tied with ropes. I saw white hair. And knots. I saw a gaping jaw with no teeth. I opened my eyes. Then I smelled James in his truck, his sweat, his hair, the dirt from the tunnels, oil and vinyl and newspapers and petrol.

A Nissan pick-up pulled up beside me. I lifted my head, promptly recognizing the driver. Carlos Gutierrez, lowering his window, smiled at me with that come-get-me smile accentuated by his perfectly sculpted mustache.

"Do you remember me? I'm James's friend, the reporter with *Los Tiempo*, Lucy Shaw. I came to one of your baseball games last year."

"Of course."

"James asked me to bring you something." I held up the film.

"Come with me." He pressed his horn and a guard appeared to open the gate. At the top of the drive where we parked, Carlos touched my elbow to lead me to his office.

I remember very little about this visit. I remember he leaned against his desk, cross-armed, and that I stood near him, to his right, handing him the film cartridge saying, "double prints." He turned his head to me.

"These are?"

"After you develop them you will know. You and James and I are the only ones who will know."

He patted my cheek as a father would a child. "I have to process these before I can know our little secret, mi chiquita?"

"Asi es, mi chiquito," I said.

"And my friend, James Fee, where is he now?"

Then, as if awakened from a sleep, I stiffened. "He's in a mess. He'll tell you about it." I waved a hand and glanced around. "What time is it? He's waiting for me. I need to get back."

"It is too early in the day for mysterious secrets, mi chiquita." He dropped the film in his front shirt pocket. "No te preocupe. Tell my friend he will have the prints in an hour."

For all the disorienting numbness that had otherwise overtaken me that chaotic morning, the single point of clarity I clung to was keeping with the plan. James told me to wait in his office. So I made haste and fretted to think I had kept him waiting.

I hadn't. He wasn't there. I sat at his desk and dropped my head in my arms and felt the breeze of the ceiling fan against my tired face. I don't know how much time had passed before I heard a commotion in the courtyard outside. I lifted my head. The door opened and I brushed back my hair. Mario Lopez walked in, his shirt open two buttons down revealing a gold crucifix swallowed by a swath of black chest hair. A corpulent man followed him, along with two heavily armed Honduran militias. The officer was dabbing sweat from his jowls.

Mario, James's partner in the tunnels, was tall for a Honduran, his eyes narrow and dark. He bore an edginess about him that was made more pronounced by his sullen brow and angular chin. He wore his thick dark hair combed back in waves behind his ears.

"Mario," I said, surprised. "What's going on?"

"Lucy, these people want to talk to you." He introduced a wheezing and lumbering Osvaldo de Soto, chief of police in Copán Ruinas, known by the locals as El Gordito.

"You are Lucy Shaw?" he said, awkwardly approaching me, one leg in front of the next. His two armed officers remained a tortured half step behind him.

"Yes."

"Were you at the royal tomb earlier today?"

I looked at Mario. He gave no signals of reprieve. My stomach rose to my throat. "Where is Dr. Fee?"

"Please answer the questions," said El Gordito. "Were you at the royal tomb earlier today? As you know, there has been a dead body found there."

"I was there with James Fee. He was showing me the tomb. That's when we found the body."

"Is that the only time you have visited the tomb?"

I looked at Mario a second time. A second time I found him at loss for consolation. "Why are you asking me these questions?"

"Where were you last night?"

"James took me to the tomb but it was locked. He

didn't bring the right key, so we left. Later we had dinner at the hotel."

"What did you do after dinner?" I imagined Gabe reciting Proverbs twenty verse thirty and pictured him sanctifying El Gordito's inmost being with a heel to the shoulder blade. "I went to bed."

"Was Dr. Fee with you?"

"Mario, what is this about?"

"Lucy, answer the questions. It is best."

"Miss Shaw, we found this under the funeral slab inside the tomb. It has your name on it." He dangled from his swollen fingers a plastic bag containing a gray film cartridge with 'Shaw' written along the side.

"Can I see?" There was no denying it was my film. And the more I explained, the worse it sounded. "I brought a camera and kept it in my backpack and James wanted to take pictures and asked me to get the camera and was yelling at me and I was about to get sick and he told me to hurry up and I dumped everything and handed him the camera and he threw me the lens cap and I didn't catch it."

"You are staying at the hotel across from the plaza?"

I sighed. "Yes."

"Some workers said they saw your light on late into the night, into the morning, in fact. We saw notes and articles about human sacrifice on the floor by your bed."

"You went into my room?" Turning: "Mario? Can they do that?"

"Why would you be reading about human sacrifice? Why were you up until the morning hours?" El Gordito wiped his neck. Mario stood in retreat. "I am afraid we have to take you with us," said the police chief. I looked at Mario.

"There is nothing I can do, Lucy."

"Can't we wait for James? He'll be back any minute. He can explain everything. Mario, don't let them do this."

"Lucy, please. You are only making it worse. It's best if you go with them. I'll talk to James when he returns." He closed his eyes and spoke to the officers. "You do not need to shackle her. She will cooperate."

"Please come with us. Bring your papers," said El Gordito.

Bring your papers was the last thing I heard in the world as I knew it then. The last thing I saw was an ink drawing effigy of Yax K'uk Mo' hanging on the wall. He looked to me like Bart Simpson with that silly half smile and goggled eyes. K'inich Yax K'uk Mo' in his bird-winged hat and saucer lips was saying Don't have a cow man. I pulled my passport from my bag along with my carnet and my driver's license, treasured documents that Leonardo had won dearly for me waiting long hours in slow moving lines. Like that, they were gone. I had no documents. No rights. No Leonardo. No Larry. No Gabe. James Fee was my only friend and he hadn't kept with the plan. I kicked my backpack under his desk. Don't have a cow, I heard Yax K'uk Mo' say as we walked out the door of James's office. We pulled away from the Visitor's Center in an army truck, El Gordito clutching the dashboard with his fat fingers.

8

The door to my cell looked medieval, thick and forbidding, with only squared slots allowing the entrance of narrow shafts of light. It closed behind me. Wetness came into my eyes when I heard inside my mind the words, "You ready?" Gabe spoke them moments before the tailwind rolled us. Larry, before the Cessna lurched down the runway before lift. James said them too before leading me into tunnel pathways to the center of the earth. Who could ever be ready for such moments? Who could be ready for this? I was not ready when these men took me to places that brought tears to my eyes. Nor was I ready then as I faced captivity in a rank and gloomy cell with a rusted cot, a soiled mattress and a toilet system I did not understand. The guard, who introduced himself as Alfonso, explained that it was a canal cut into the corner of the concrete floor that drained to the courtyard on the other side of the wall. I was not ready to think about how not to pee in that corner. How never to pee again for the rest of my life.

For all the years James lived in Copán Ruinas he had never visited the jail. So when he arrived and Alfonso led him first to the courtyard in the back behind the front offices, James looked exceedingly perplexed. "Where's the jail?" he said, and Alfonso lifted his chin. They stood together in the sun of the back courtyard, James and Alfonso, looking toward a darkened nook where old bed frames and fouled mattresses lay in a heap. On either side of the nook were opposing concrete-block walls, each with a medieval door, one to the right, the other the left. The sign over the door on the right read Celda A, my cell. The other door read Celda B.

James saw my hand draped through a slot in the door. He came near, stunned, looking up and down trying to see me. There were no lights or windows in my cell and his eyes hadn't adjusted to the dark. I saw him clearly. He turned to Alfonso. "Why is there no light?" Alfonso lifted his chin in the direction of a single bulb above the bed frames and piled mattresses outside the two cells, the only source of light for both. He said, "If we give them a bulb inside they break it."

James squatted near my hand, his eyes slowly adjusting. My hair fell in my face and around my neck and my clothes reeked. "My God, Lucy." He looked around and sighed.

"They went through my room," I said. He shook his head. "I have a headache." At that moment we heard a commotion arise from the front office. El Gordito had made an appearance. James paused and turned his head that way.

"I hear Gordo. I'll be right back."

I listened attentively to the exchange that ensued between James and Gordito.

"I can vouch for her. She had nothing to do with this."

I heard the squeak of a chair.

Gordito said, "We found evidence that points to her."

James said, "I know what you found. She was with me when she dropped that film cartridge. I took her to the tomb this morning. We discovered the body together. She got sick. I can show you the bag with her vomit."

"Did you take her to the tomb last night?"

"You already know I did."

"You did not have the right key?"

"That's why we returned this morning."

"Why did you feel Lucy Shaw had the right to see the tomb before other reporters?"

"We're friends. It was a favor."

"Were you with her all night until you returned to the tomb in the morning?"

"We had dinner together. Then I sat with her for a few minutes outside her room."

"How do you know she didn't leave later and return to the tomb? Workers say her light was on late into the night."

I heard James sigh.

"I've got forty journalists arriving this morning. Do you think I'd be here now if I had doubts?"

"As much as I would like to satisfy you, Dr. Fee, I cannot. Until I have evidence that points to someone else, what little evidence I possess points to her. If you want to talk to her do it now. We will move her to the capital when we finish the paperwork."

"Give me a day," said James.

"I am a man under orders," said Gordito.

"Is there a fine to be paid to keep her here another day? I'll gladly pay it."

The conversation paused. I heard a drawer open and the movement of papers.

James said, "That covers the next twenty-four hours. Agreed?"

"Twenty-four hours. I promise nothing more," said Gordito.

James returned, embattled, and squatted by my door. "I've bought us some time. You're not going anywhere for twenty-four hours."

He took this to mean good news.

I asked why he had not kept with the plan, emphasizing that if he had been at the office as he said he would, Mario would not have allowed Gordito to haul me to the jail. He explained what transpired after I left for the lab.

He had sent the first worker on site to go for the police, at which point Mario arrived. Mario, seeing James's obvious distress, asked what was going on, and James descended with him a second time into the tunnels. Before entering the tomb he had attempted to prepare Mario for what he was to see by describing Berto on the poles, Berto bound, Berto painted blue and the soapy smell that mingled oddly with the sweat and urine. James also attempted to explain what had happened that morning when he and I first found the body. Mario stared at him blankly.

He responded (as James put it), "We have a sacrificed watchman in the tomb of Yax K'uk Mo' and *Los Tiempo* saw it? That's just great." James told me he defended my presence to Mario by attesting to his need of my camera, as if this would comfort me.

"What did Mario say?"

"He said he didn't trust any journalist, especially one from *Tiempo*. He said, 'All journalists are wolves.'"

Upon seeing the body Mario said instantly, "Whoever did this understood Maya human sacrifice." James said it certainly narrowed the suspects. When the two of them left the tunnel and stepped into daylight they saw the lumbering Osvaldo de Soto—El Gordito—laboring up the stairs to the tunnel entrance. Then, a summit meeting spontaneously convened and the three tacitly agreed that word of a murder at the Copán Ruins served no one's advantage. James made his case for removing the body quickly, since death scene photos had already been taken and the earnestness of his expression, his perfect Spanish, and reassuring tones won approving nods from El Gordito. In any case, he told me, "Gordo wanted to see the crime scene" and both James and Mario were stricken with the thought of trying to get him through the narrow twists and crevasses of the tunnels. Gordito dismissed all pleas to dissuade him. In deference to James's two previous trips to the tomb, Mario agreed to take Gordito in, a decision, James said, both Mario and Gordito later regretted.

On site workers entered the tunnel to remove the body. Once inside the tomb they positioned themselves in opposing corners and, grunting, heaving, scraping their feet, they extricated Berto by the poles that suspended him. James said the workers labored impassively. They wrapped Berto in a blanket and retreated with the poles on their shoulders while "Berto swayed like a bell without a clapper," he said. The bamboo had been cut adeptly to negotiate the angles of the turns.

By this point, he said, all thoughts of the plan, as he had outlined it to me, had evaporated. James hadn't shown up at his office because, he explained, he borrowed Mario's truck to deliver the bad news to Don Berto's family. The Rodriguezes lived outside of town in a hillside barrio called Brisas de Olancho, a typical mountainside neighborhood amuck with pigs and horses and chickens wandering the rutted unpaved roads while ribbed-racked dogs lay in the shade of doorways. James said he spoke with Yamileta, Berto's niece, who, as he approached, was draping wet clothes over a bamboo fence. He broke the news by saying, "We found your uncle this morning on the grounds. Someone killed him."

"Who's we?" she said. James explained how he had taken a visiting journalist to see the Hunal tomb, as the archaeologists call it, and "that's when we found Berto killed and left inside." Yamileta stepped over twisted balls of wet clothes in buckets at her feet and asked James if he suspected who might have killed her uncle. He said it would take a while. He asked to speak to her father, Berto's brother, and Yamileta said he was sleeping and she would tell him the news later. James assured her the Project would cover costs for the burial since Berto was killed on the site. Yamileta wanted to know what other costs might be paid to them. James said the government would take care of Berto's pension, but it may take a few weeks. He said he offered to help her with paperwork. He told Yamileta, upon leaving, that Berto was a good man and that everyone with the Project was going to miss him. He then told me that Yamileta said, "Maybe your friend killed him. The one who went with you to the tomb." James told me he responded that he didn't think so.

When he finally returned to the Visitor's Center after that visit, he parked Mario's truck near his, where I had left it. There, the little boy Paco informed him of the unpleasant details of my detainment, not overlooking Mario's lack of helpfulness. Paco didn't know people's plans, but somehow he managed to know everything else. "El Gordito says she killed the watchman," Paco told him. "Señor Lopez told her to go with Gordito."

James returned to his office to find Mario pacing nervously. The subsequent exchange, details of which I pressed for relentlessly, was not congenial. Mario asked James why he took "that girl" out there and added emphatically that I was "nothing but trouble" and that James should have known that. James asked Mario to explain what had happened with Gordito, and Mario told him about the film cartridge and the articles about human sacrifice they had found in my room, as if rummaging through my room was beside the point. The cartridge and the articles, for them, Mario said, had built the case in their minds that I had returned to the tomb without James late at night for the purposes of my story, got caught by Berto, and so killed him. Mario said, "You yourself said she does what she has to do to get a story." At that point James turned to leave to come to the jail. Mario reminded him that the press conference would be beginning soon.

James seemed satisfied to have purchased my twenty-four hour confinement for three hundred lempiras, a bargain at six-point-three-nine to the dollar. That came to forty-seven dollars. It did not feel like good news to me.

"Listen," he said, "this press conference is about to start. Let me get through that. I need to think about this. I'll be back." Then he departed as abruptly as he had come.

He left his little friend Paco to keep me company. The boy squirreled around into a ball outside my door, his knees poking through the holes in his jeans. He pressed his face to a slot in the door. "Do you want food, Miss Lucy?" For the first time I saw the fire in his topaz eyes and the delicacy of his cheekbones. I moved my face close to his.

"Where do you live, Paco? Where is your mother?"

"I don't have a mother."

"Do you have a father?"

"Sí, I have a father."

"Do you live with him?"

"Mr. Fee lets me sleep behind his house."

"You live with Mr. Fee?"

"He has a bodega behind his house. He lets me sleep there sometimes."

"But where is your father? Why don't you live with him?"

"My father does not want me to live with him." He lowered his eyes and pulled threads from his jeans. "Do you want mango, Miss Lucy?"

"Paco, look at me." He lifted his eyes. "I have a job for you, something more important than bringing me mango." He nodded. "I need you to be my eyes and ears at the press conference. Then come back and tell me everything you saw. You shall be my assistant and that is a very important job. Will you do that for me?" Again he nodded. "When I get out of the jail I will buy you school supplies and new jeans. I will tell your father you are a fine boy." He seemed pleased with his assignment. I told him I trusted him to return to me well supplied with helpful details.

So Paco left and I made the necessary mental adjustments to face twenty-four hours in darkness and squalor. The nose accommodates to foul smells, and ears to irritating sounds such as the grinding motor of a laboring fan, or shoes scraping dusty linoleum. The eyes make strange pictures in dark places. I could not see the man in Celda B, though I felt an inexplicable bond with him. We were two ghosts that had been swallowed in parallel darkness. I actually, sincerely, posed the question, *So what are you in for?* He said that on the day of his wedding he shot his brother-in-law. I asked why. He said, "He humiliate me." He said his bride accused him of being drunk when he arrived at the church and she refused to hear vows at the altar from a man who was drunk. The priest took her side. "I would never come drunk to the house of God." I pictured him crisply outfitted, his tie askew, his face flushed with rum and stubble of a beard. He told me that the priest, to test him, had him walk the aisle and back "and if you do not fall down, I will marry you." The man in Celda B continued, "I walk. I do not fall down." I imagined his bride at the altar, eyes wet, lips curled down, wondering if he would walk. I pictured the priest conferring the vows to a wet-eyed bride now having second thoughts. I imagined the smell of rum on her new husband's breath at the exchange of the kiss and celebratory gunshots mixed with mariachis. "I got drunk later," he said. "That is when my brother-in-law humiliate me. He said I am the son of a whore. I am a bad shot when I am drunk. That is God's gift to me." Then the ghost in Celda B shuffled his feet in a way that signaled movement to the peeing corner.

"Who you kill?" I heard a zipper.

I hastened from my spot near the door and retreated to the mattress along the opposite wall burying my face in my knees. "I didn't kill anyone."

"Jails are filled with innocent people, gringita." He zipped.

"I'm accused of killing a guard at the ruins. It's complicated."

"I once work in the tunnels with el Señor Lopez on the Rosalila. I work also with El Doctor on the Papagayo," he said.

"El Doctor?"

"On the Papagayo. El Doctor is always the first one into the tunnels." He moved to his bed and sat for a moment in silence. In time he spoke. "My ancestors, they come to me in a dream last night, gringita. They tell me it is time to plant my corn. But I am here in the jail. Who will plant my corn?"

"Do ancestors speak to relatives who are drunk?"

He said, "Gringita, that is when they speak the loudest."

9

By the time Paco returned I had grown accustomed to the dark. He found me sitting on the metal bed frame, my hair in tangles and my legs cramped and bleeding from scratches incurred by loose springs on the cot. He was unfazed by my condition and rendered his report of the morning's events chattily, as if we were sitting in a cool breeze under the Ceiba tree. He said first, "It is a bad day for Mr. Fee." I moved closer and sat cross-legged on the floor where he squatted on the opposite side of the door. He clutched two slats with his little hands. Our eyes met again through those slats, his sprouting hair piercing the dim light.

"Why is it a bad day for Mr. Fee?" I asked. This was his report: When James returned to the Visitor's Center for the press conference he seemed agitated. His mood worsened when reporters overtook him as he entered, asking things such as, "Who actually made the initial discovery, Dr. Fee?" and "Did you know ahead of time you might find the tomb in this location, Dr. Fee?" and "Is it the greatest discovery of your career, Dr. Fee?" Paco mimicked these people with unselfconscious animation. James prodded the journalists to the conference room where, Paco said, Mario Lopez stepped to the podium. He lifted a hand to settle the crowd while James leaned along the side wall, arms folded and legs crossed.

Mario said that it was an exciting day for everyone at Copán. "The deeper we go into the mysterious world of the Maya the more surprises we find." Mario had finished saying, "Today we are going to tell you about what we believe to be the discovery of the tomb of Copán's first king, K' inich Yax K'uk Mo', " when a reporter interrupted from the back. Paco said he asked, "Tell us—where is your friend, the writer with her head in the clouds?" which, according to Paco, unsettled Mario. "He put his hands like this." Paco placed his arms akimbo. Mario ignored the questioner and solicited serious inquiries from other journalists, of which there were several. Then Mario concluded his remarks by inviting those who were feeling adventurous to walk with him to the site core after the conference and he would take them inside the tomb. He said, "It is not an easy walk. Your clothes will get dirty. But the decision is yours." He turned to Mr. Fee and asked if he wanted to say anything. Mr. Fee said no. Then someone in the crowd said to James, "Where is your friend Lucy Shaw? We have been waiting for the plane."

Mario deferred the podium to James, who at that point, according to Paco, "went like this." The boy stood, straightened his elbows grabbing two slats of the jail door as if sides of the podium, with hunched shoulders and a lowered head. James said, "Thank you for coming."

"Then what did he say?"

"The same man stood—the one who asked about you—and said he was Ricardo Fernandez from *La Tribuna*. He asked Mr. Fee if he remembered him. He said he met Mr. Fee and Lucy Shaw at the American Ambassador's house the year before."

At this point James looked stricken and stood at the podium a broken figure. He shrugged in a worsening mood. Of course he remembered the reporter, but he didn't say so from the podium. They had met the year before, when James had been in Tegucigalpa during those few weeks when our relationship blossomed. Ricardo Fernandez —"Ricky"—as I called him, was the man who had prompted our first fight. It was our last night together before James's return to Copán and we both felt unsettled. The American Ambassador held a cocktail party in James's honor, since the distinguished archaeologist so rarely made it to the capital city. James was thus obliged to attend. Ricardo Fernandez was present, as were many members of the Honduran press, as well as others in the cultural elite. Upon our arrival, James became immediately distracted by social obligations, which left me to fend for myself. I stumbled onto Ricky sitting alone on the balcony outside the main sala sipping a beer. He asked me to join him, which I was happy to do. This did not go unnoticed by James Fee who, at that moment, was being held hostage at the grand piano in a conversation between the chief of Honduras's Forestry Development Corps (COHDEFOR) and the overseer of the National

Supplier of Basic Products, (BANASUPRO). With dramatic flourishes they were discussing that season's fires and crop loss. "Since the beginning of the dry season there have been nine hundred fires," said the COHDEFOR chief. The BANASUPRO overseer replied, "And now we have a lack of beans!" Philip Mondragón, El Presidente, otherwise known as husband of Doña Nora whom we've already met, joined the group and added an impassioned plea. "We must convince our compatriots we are making a great effort!"

About that time Ricky and I were sharing journalists' stories and were buckled over in laughter. He was slapping a knee pleading, ¡Bastante! ¡Bastante! Back at the piano, the Archbishop, who had joined the group and was standing next to James, was explaining that the Virgin of Guadalupe cried blood again and that the lab tests confirmed it was human blood but hadn't determined the RH factor. "We don't know if it is a hoax or a revelation." In the meantime, Ricky and I, still laughing, exchanged high fives when James excused himself from the grand piano and approached me from behind looking spare and distraught. He said, "You're needed at the piano for a religious discussion." I took his cold limp hand and pressed it to my cheek. "This is Ricky Fernandez, *La Tribuna*," I said. "I told him you might be willing to give him an interview sometime." I turned to Ricky. "This is James Fee. You know who he is."

My missionary's opinion about the blood-weeping Virgin proved a disappointment to James. He escorted me to the grand piano where someone—I don't know who—asked what I thought about it. I said, "Well, yeah, it's weird." Then the Ambassador approached, a kindly diminutive man I had met on other occasions. He had shining eyes and a peach-faced complexion and was so endearing that he emanated the feeling that he was your friend. I said, "How are you, George?"

He returned a bewildered gaze. "Fine, thank you. How are you?"

James and I were walking to his truck later that night when he said, "You called him George." He slowed his leaning stride and looked at me.

I said, "He's such a nice man. I didn't think he would mind me not saying 'Mr. Ambassador'. "

"His name's not George. It's Bill." Our conversation only deteriorated from there. "And what kind of answer was that about the Virgin—'yeah, it's weird'?"

"His name's *Bill*?"

James unlocked the door to his truck. "He's the Archbishop, for God's sake, Lucy. Couldn't you have come up with something more —theological?"

"I didn't ask to be brought into that conversation."

"And I didn't agree to an interview with your friend, Ricky what's-his-name. You and Ricky were the life of the party."

Paco described how James stood stiffly at the podium clutching both sides with whitened knuckles. Ricky Fernandez said, "The Honduran press is a small world, Dr. Fee. There is little that gets past us."

James looked up and answered dryly, "It's all I can do to keep track of Copán's dead kings. I'll leave it to you hounds to keep track of your own reporters." Then, according to Paco's account, James waved off further questions, patted Mario's back, and slipped out the door.

Paco said that as James walked away from the press conference he was met by Carlos Gutierrez in the Visitor Center courtyard, photos in hand. "Your pictures," said Carlos. The two men retreated to James's office and closed the door, which required that Paco improvise. He prowled around outside until he found a spot beneath a window that lent unhindered access to sights and sounds from inside James's office. He described in great detail the ensuing exchange. Carlos dropped into the chair opposite James and landed his crossed feet atop James's desk. Tossing the photos onto the desk, he said, "A mouth open like the maw to the Underworld. A few rotting teeth. Thank God his eyes were closed."

"Lucy Shaw and I discovered him this morning," James said, plucking a stone fragment from his desk, tossing it hand to hand. "They found a film cartridge on the floor of the tomb with her name on it. It fell out of her backpack when she grabbed her camera for me. They think she did it. They locked her up."

"No me digas," Carlos said.

Carlos, now upright, listened as James recounted how officials had likewise found the article on human sacrifice in my room. "And then it got messy." Carlos asked about the body. "I mean—" he threw a nod toward the room filled with reporters. James confirmed the body had been removed and was at the coroner. He said the police found the film cartridge when they investigated the site. Carlos said, "So what about Lucy?" James told him the price he paid to buy Gordito's passivity and retain me for twenty-four hours. "Well, my friend," Carlos said, "we will have to solve this mystery within twenty-four hours. Who are the suspects?"

Paco recounted in startling detail the following exchange. "Let's start with Lucy," Carlos said, and James shook his head. I had met Carlos the year before when James and I attended a game of his Little League baseball team called Los Relámpagos. Baseball was Carlos's first love and his team reciprocated the devotion. Carlos knew the names of all players, their batting averages and on-base percentages, and spent half of his free time driving them to and from practices. Los Relámpagos made it to the play-offs the three years Carlos coached them. He had tried repeatedly, and in vain, to get his good friend James Fee onto the field to coach third base. It had become a local outrage among unmarried women that Carlos Gutierrez preferred coaching baseball to cavorting with them, what with his being a dead ringer for Omar Sharif.

Carlos said, "Why eliminate her as a possibility?"

"She's the daughter of missionaries, for God's sake." He sighed. "They don't murder people."

"Worse crimes have been committed to win the nations for Christ," Carlos answered.

James said he eliminated me as a suspect not because I grew up in a missionary family but because he knew me, to which Carlos responded, "She was in love with you.

Do you remember? She prolonged her stay here last year at your insistence, my friend. You lingered in the tunnels. You drove her back to the capital city in your own truck. You stole your first kiss."

"*She* stole it," James protested. Carlos demurred. "Cómo no. And then you heaved, that's right."

The heaving, noted by Carlos, referred to the first kiss of a blossoming romance that will forever be associated with a wet mango and violent retching. On the road a few hours outside Tegucigalpa, James and I had stopped to stretch our legs at a fresh market. He found a table outside near the aviary with toucans and wild turkeys and well hidden behind a flowering hibiscus. I bought a ripe mango. Finding him at the table, I lifted it to his nose. "Perfect," he said. I pulled a damascene pocketknife from my backpack, a gift from Gabe after his semester in Spain. We straddled the bench facing each other. I peeled the mango in the spellbinding way the Ninganahua women taught me, in a single, drawn-out, spiralling slice. It was a juicy mango. I sliced wedges and dropped them with the tip of the knife into James's mouth. I wiped his beard and he inclined himself my way. Then without forethought, I initiated the first entwining of our lips. The kiss didn't last long and he seemed to enjoy it at the time. I excused myself to wash my hands and upon my return found him buckled over near the truck retching in dry heaves. He asked me to drive. For the next two hours he slept while I pondered first kisses, hounded by the sense that dry heaving oughtn't to be associated with the picture. When finally I pulled up to the outer gate of my house—James still sleeping—I had worked myself into indignant resolve never to see him again. I determined to make my escape into my house and lock the front door, leaving him as he was, asleep in his truck. But my suitcase had gotten caught between seats in the back and I couldn't extricate it delicately. I decided to leave it and walk away. At that point, he awoke, attended to the suitcase and pulled it free with ease. He said he loved the mango and asked me to dinner.

". . . so you attend the family wedding and dance with the mother," Carlos continued, Paco mimicking his "ay yai yai." Carlos shook his head. "You end your love affair and leave her at the airport. Badly done, my friend. I say it with love. One thing you will never get from me is a lie." Carlos clasped his hands behind his head. "Maybe now she is ready for revenge."

James then said, "Someone who thinks of sex as theological does not commit murder." Still tossing the stone from hand to hand, he added that I wouldn't be interested in revenge because I've got a new boyfriend. Paco stopped. "Who is your boyfriend, Miss Lucy?"

I waved a hand. "It's irrelevant. What else did they say?"

Carlos smiled. "Lucy thinks of sex as theological?" He paused. "I take it you two never smelled the roses?"

"Theology complicates it."

Carlos said, "Indeed."

"Can we move on?"

"Think about this, Fee," Carlos said. "If Lucy Shaw sees sex as theological, maybe she also sees murder as theological. Her religious sensibilities make her the

89

perfect suspect. Berto was sacrificed, after all."

James told Carlos to cross me off the suspect list and, on any other day, I might have found this consoling. "Who's next?" he said.

"Mario."

James gaped. "I give you only love, my friend. Someone has to say it." Carlos suggested that perhaps Mario had been jealous because James commands the media attention, the influence of government officials, makes great shots for *National Geographic*—"a gringo," Carlos said. "An outsider and one who is more handsome than he is, that is your cross. Maybe he wants to compromise your position."

James asked Carlos to explain how sacrificing Berto Rodriguez would accomplish that. Carlos said, "If I didn't know you better, I'd say you were stupid.

"You are wrong to look upon this crime only as someone sacrificing Berto, God rest his soul." He crossed himself. "Someone sacrificed Berto and planted his body the day the journalists were planning to come. The timing was not lost on whoever did this." Paco imitated Carlos pulling at his mustache. "Of course they did not anticipate James Fee would show up beforehand, discover the body, and remove it without the press knowing about it. That was a miracle," he said. "Do you believe in miracles, Fee? Most Columbia Ph.D.s don't." Carlos leaned back. "Whoever put Berto in the tomb did it with the intention of humiliating James Fee. I tell you because I love you."

James said, "That still wouldn't explain Mario."

"You are a stubborn man." Carlos explained that it had

been James who was scheduled to present the discovery to the journalists and that "instead of unveiling his magnificent discovery James Fee uncovers a sacrificed body dangling over Yax K'uk Mo'. It would have been a moment of great humiliation, yes?"

James said Mario loved the ruins as much as anyone and that even if he felt jealous of James Fee he wouldn't damage the thing he loves out of spite. Carlos then said, "Chloe." James groaned. "She's in love with you. It's not your fault. Another cross." He waved a hand. "She was pursuing you, that was obvious. The *Tiempo* reporter comes to town and steals your heart. Chloe loses hope. Then suddenly you return from the family wedding a free man. Chloe's hopes are renewed. Still you will not give in to her advances even after all this time. How many hearts do you plan to break before you become an old man? Lucy comes back. Chloe gets crazy." Carlos said, "Someone went to a lot of trouble to paint him blue and hang him up. Whoever did it had more than murder in mind."

James responded, "Which also suggests that whoever did it had a degree of physical strength, and that eliminates Chloe. It couldn't have been easy getting that body through the tunnels." Carlos said, "But once he's on the poles gravity does the rest and there he dangles over the tomb. That's it."

James scratched his beard and rocked back in his chair. Carlos rubbed his chin. Then he stood and walked to the window, momentarily alarming Paco, who skirted aside to elude discovery. Carlos turned and waved a finger, saying, "What about the guys from Pelanque?

Maybe they are upset that Copán gets the magazine covers for once."

James laughed out loud. "What do they care? They got the cover of *Time*." Carlos returned to his chair.

"Maybe Berto owed money to someone. Maybe he had enemies. Maybe a worker had something against him."

James shook his head and sighed. "Berto didn't have any enemies. He had no teeth. He didn't talk much and he's older than dirt. He couldn't provoke anybody."

"Why a sacrifice? Why today?" said Carlos. "Whoever did this seems to have been going after you, my friend, not to hurt you so much as to damage you. Maybe that it happened to be Berto is beside the point."

"Other than the fact he had the key." James groaned. "What am I going to do?"

"Has the family has been told?"

"I went this morning. I told Yamileta, Berto's niece. Berto lived with her and his brother, her father Ramón."

"How did she take it?"

"Fatalistically. She accused Lucy."

"Why would she accuse Lucy?"

"Why would anyone do anything that has happened here over the last twenty-four hours? This whole place has gone crazy. Now Lucy is in jail and tomorrow they are going to take her to the prison in the capital. Once she's there, God knows when she'll get out. People rot for years in that prison just waiting for a trial."

Carlos said, "No te preocupe. We will find it out." James asked Carlos if he had seen anything odd in the pictures. Carlos laughed. "Apart from a body painted blue bound with ropes hanging by poles? No."

"The clothes, the hair, the teeth? Any marks? Bruises? Cuts? Gunshot wounds?"

"Nada. The journalists know nothing, of course?"

James said, "If we can make it through the day, we're home free, at least when it comes to the press. Then it's local news and nobody in this town will do anything to hurt the reputation of the ruins."

"Yes, I don't think so," Carlos said. He glanced in the direction of the door. "They are breaking up. Go with Mario. Take them to the tomb. James Fee can satisfy them. Do you want me to go with you? Do you want me to visit Lucy? Tell me what you want me to do."

"Let me know if you come up with ideas"—though the idea of visiting Lucy in Celda A had seemed a good idea to me.

10

Alone in my prison time moved in and out of the world I pictured, that of listening to James speak with the visiting journalists. He would have said something like, "the ancient Maya left tantalizing clues." I pictured them standing outside the tunnel entrance, as I myself had the year before when Chloe commented about missionaries. Probably only half of those who came for the press conference would have made the trek to the site core. Of those, only a handful of hearty souls would have ventured into the dank meandering underbelly of the temple. I pictured the sun on his back, the breeze in his face, and Chloe's entrancement standing at his side, eyes fixed on him. The furthest thing from his mind would have been the one journalist who was not there. In such moments, it was all about the Maya. Thoughts of wet mangoes and first kisses, airport exits, or even jail cells would not have entered his mind. James was the master of usable quotes. I pictured tape recorders held to the mouth of the expert, journalists scribbling notes and raising pens, and James adjusting his ball cap in casual volley with them. I imagined the ease with which he and Chloe would explain in plain language the "implications" of the lost world they so meticulously reclaimed from the bowels of a hidden earth. I imagined he would have been using his National Geographic voice.

He returned to visit me in the jail near dusk. By this point I had settled into a dark corner on the floor near the door to capture the last glimpses of daylight. Unlike Paco's casual response seeing me there like an animal, James grew alarmed. In the dark on the floor, I was sharing space with cockroaches and scarab beetles. The metal from the rusted bed frame scratched my legs. My face was drawn, my hair in every direction as if the braid itself had surrendered. "I brought you food," he said. I moved nearer to the door.

"I can't eat."

"You have to eat." He pulled a tortilla from a tea towel, rolled it, and pressed it through a slat. "Take this." I forced myself to eat, though it felt dry and pasty in my mouth and I couldn't swallow it. "Drink some water. You're going to dehydrate." He tried to pass a water bottle through an opening in the door, but it wouldn't fit. He yelled for Alfonso, who responded quickly. James asked Alfonso if he could sit with me inside the cell. The guard opened the door.

Squatting next to me he opened the bottle and tipped it to my lips. "Why is your mattress on the floor?"

"I couldn't decide between sitting on the mattress with

lice and pee stains, or on the floor with cockroaches and scorpions. I picked the best of all possible worlds. I threw the mattress on the floor and decided to sit on the bare bed frame, but it scratched my legs. So I've ended up on the floor with the cockroaches. You get used to it." He tipped the water bottle a second time to my lips and I sipped. "My eyes hurt. My headache is making me sick."

"Let's get you back on to the bed." He held my elbow to ease me back on to the metal bed frame. I sat at the head of the frame, knees to my chest and my head against the wall. "I used to fear cockroaches would crawl into my hair if I leaned against the wall like this. Then I thought, how bad could it feel?"

He sat at the other end of the bare frame, elbows on his knees, and tossed his baseball cap on the portion between us. "This is my fault."

"Why is it your fault?"

"I told you to give me your camera."

"And you weren't nice about it either."

He looked at me. "What can I do for you?"

"Coffee would help."

"Do you want me to call anyone?"

"My parents need to know. You could call them."

"It will upset them. Maybe you should wait."

"Their number is in the notebook in my backpack. I left it under your desk in your office. They need to know."

"Do you want me to call Larry?"

Oddly, Larry had not been on my mind, though I knew of all people, he would have come to try and fix this. "I'd rather him not see me in this situation. Do you remember my assistant Leonardo?"

"I remember him."

"He should know. Maybe the magazine can do something. His number is in the notebook."

"Call your father. Leonardo. Not Larry. Get coffee. Do you want a blanket?"

I closed my eyes momentarily. "You don't have to manage this, James." I looked at him. "The sooner we figure that out the easier it will be for both of us."

Images of Jack and Gabe and Larry and Leonardo passed before me, people far away or forever gone who could not help me now. The only friend I had was the man at the end of my prison bed who had once slipped his fingers through the straps of my dress and did not pull the strings. I sat at one end of the bed clutching my knees. He, at the other end, clasped hands pressing his thumbs together, both of us swallowed in shadows cast by the single dim bulb in the hallway. We sat in silence. Then, after a time, words arose I cannot account for. "Do you remember me, James?"

He turned his head and looked at me. "Yes, Lucy. I remember you."

"So you remember Wisconsin?"

"Yes."

"And the wedding?"

"I remember everything."

"You remember my dress?"

He laughed, almost yelped, and shook his head. "I remember the angle of the sun through the window and the way it made that dress shine on you." He smiled. "It was a very bold dress."

I pressed my fingers to my eyes. "Thank God one of us exercised sound judgment that day." He played with his cap. I said, "I had an English professor, old Dr. Goodrich—but we called him Goody. I may have told you about him. He said one time that words spoken in deep love or deep hate set things in motion in the heart that can never be reversed." I paused. "Do you remember our last night in Wisconsin when you got so sick? Do you remember how I lay with you all night, still in that dress, the lilacs wilting in my hair? I was telling you how my family loved you, and how I loved you. I was saying how I would take care of you." He looked at me. I looked straight back at him. "I'm not embarrassed by it." He moved his eyes to the floor. The prisoner in Celda B let out a snore. "You never turned back to me. To this day I don't know if you heard me."

He paused, then looked at me. "What else did Goody tell you?"

"That I constantly violate the four uses of the comma. That I should never use 'like' as a preposition." I smiled, remembering. "And he said sometimes God manifests his sacred purpose even through the profane. That Goody." James picked up his cap. I pressed my face to my knees. "I want you know that when I said those things that night, I was speaking them in deep love." I leaned my head back and sighed. "I don't know what became of that dress. We left in such a rush the next day, I must have thrown it somewhere. It never ended up in my suitcase."

"It was a lovely dress." I leveled my face to see him looking at me. "You were beautiful in it."

"Then we each have something to take with us."

He stood up and adjusted his cap. "You take cream in your coffee, no sugar, right?"

ii

The only way I can bring myself to understand what happened next was to try and put myself inside the mind of a Maya warrior king. All kings at Copán were warriors in the tradition of its founder, Yax K'uk Mo'. Portraits of all the kings appear on the Hieroglyphic Stairway, built by Ruler 15, each one bearing a shield to signify his combat prowess. Maya kings fought battles the way any king would have, to gain political territory. But, as was the case for everything in the world of the Maya, warfare also carried divine significance and the king was its heavenly agent. So war was a ritual. The blood of the captives taken in battle became food for the gods.

"The gods had to be nourished by the most sacred and precious substance they knew," James told me once.

For the Maya, only human blood was worthy of the divine transaction. It is what perpetuated the cycles of life.

Since the king was the bearer of divine power, the conduit of supernatural agency, it meant that he mediated between these two worlds, the one who kept the rhythms of life in motion, the rising and setting of the sun, the movement of the planets, the seasons and perpetuation of new life. None took this mandate more seriously then one king in particular, that is the indomitable 18 Rabbit. He acceded to the throne after the sixty-seven-year reign of Smoke Imix God K, the beloved king whose bones James thought had been found under the Hieroglyphic Stairway. James hailed 18 Rabbit as a "patron of the arts" because under his dominion the Maya at Copán reached new levels of artistic and technical sophistication. The king had commissioned the stelae in the Great Plaza, most of which are various versions of himself. They became known worldwide as the culminating expression of Maya's "high relief and fluid style" that became the hallmark of sculpture in Copán. (When James was making these "patron of the arts" comments to me one of his guides whispered, "18 Rabbit was a very proud man.")

The stelae of himself, along with everything else that attended Maya kingly rule, 18 Rabbit undertook to perpetuate his supernatural authority in the minds of his mortal subjects. Thus, in keeping with the effort and to celebrate his kingdom's unrivaled prowess, around 738 he constructed a new ball court, which for the Maya at Copán, had been its third (and final) version.

James told me that 18 Rabbit may have been on a journey in search of captives to sacrifice for its dedication when, to the shock of all the Maya kingdom, he was ambushed and captured by a rival Maya fiefdom called Quiriguá in Guatemala. Soon thereafter they ritually beheaded him. The death of any king could turn the world of the Maya upside down. Who would keep the planets in motion? Who would serve as portal to the gods? But the demise of 18 Rabbit, which James called "a seminal event" for Copán, was all the more shocking because this seemingly invincible king was felled by a weaker fiefdom. His death threatened to collapse altogether the underpinnings of Copán's political and religious life.

And in an inexplicable way, the impact and disorientation of the ambush and ritual beheading of 18 Rabbit can be likened to what happened to James later that day, after he left the prison with the promise to bring me coffee. He was ambushed—not unlike 18 Rabbit—in a way he never saw coming. And, like 18 Rabbit, it diminished him. It turned his world upside down and my world too.

I learned of it as follows.

I had determined that if it was my last act on earth, I would not pee in the canal carved in the corner of my prison cell and the time had come to test my resolve. I called to Alfonso with the intention of asking him to use the toilet in the office. The weakness of my voice, however, along with the aggravating grinding motor of an oscillating fan, made it impossible for him to hear me.

The man in Celda B walked to his door. "Tzch tzch."

Alfonso responded, "Diga."

"The lady calls."

Alfonso appeared. He hesitated, as any guard should when confronted with a special request from a prisoner. Yet he seemed kindhearted, his jutting teeth evoking a boyish tenderness.

The man in Celda B said, "She can't hurt anybody.

Let her use it." Alfonso unlocked my cell door and I proceeded to the outer courtyard and then the hallway where even the dim fluorescent lighting stunned me. The guard's bathroom had little over the canal in my corner, but it had a door and I thanked God for his miracles. In slow steps I returned to my cell where I found Paco sitting in a ball on the floor outside my cell door waiting for me. I settled myself on the floor of the other side, the prisoner's side, and pressed my face near the slats of that thick door. "Have you been crying, Paco?"

He burrowed his chin into his knees. "Do you want me to bring you mango, Miss Lucy?" His lips curled downward and I reached my hand to touch his face. "What's wrong?"

"It is a bad day for Mr. Fee."

"What do you mean?" He looked away. "What's the matter, Paco? Did something happen?"

"Mr. Fee made a mistake."

"What mistake did Mr. Fee make?" He didn't answer. "Paco."

He wrinkled his eyebrows. "I saw him kissing la puta."
"What?"

"He got coffee and it was on his desk and then the lady came and sat on his lap. She kissed Mr. Fee."

"The lady?"

"The lady in the tunnels—esa putita."

"Chloe?"

He shrugged. "Mr. Fee got your coffee and the lady went to his office and closed the door and was kissing Mr. Fee. I knocked on the door. Mr. Fee came and walked with me. I asked if he was going to do sex for the whore and he told me not to talk like that." Paco looked at me with wet eyes and spoke with a crack in his voice. "He did not do sex for her, Miss Lucy."

After an awkward and stunned silence, Paco explained the series of events as they unfolded after James visited me in the jail. Paco said he saw James heading home before returning to his office to make my phone calls and get me the coffee. He seemed agitated. He brought Paco home with him and made him lunch. Paco, curling a tortilla, looked at James and said, "I feel God's power." James looked at him. "It hurts me," Paco said. The maid, Brigida, patted Paco's head with a splayed palm and said "Paquito is the Holy Spirit now." She had made the tortillas and red beans, but left the frying of them to James. He had his own combination of sautéed bacon and onions and garlic and chilies. As Brigida poured the boy grapefruit juice, Paco said to James, "Miss Lucy prays."

"Yes, I know."

Paco asked James if he was praying for Miss Lucy to get out of the jail. James said he wanted Miss Lucy to get out of the jail and was trying to get me out, "if that's what you mean."

Paco said, "That is not what I mean. I am praying Miss Lucy will get out of the jail."

James said, "Good."

Paco said, "I am praying Miss Lucy will take care of you, Mr. Fee."

That is when James rose from the table and said it was time to go.

Paco and James returned separately to the archaeological park, James in his truck and Paco on foot—oftentimes surer and swifter than wheels. As James approached his office at the Visitor's Center Ricky Fernandez caught him in the parking lot. "Can my photographer take our picture? You and me?" James managed a smile. Click. "One more." Click. Click. Slight retreat. Click. Ricky said, "I am sorry Lucy Shaw did not make it to the press conference. I would have liked to have seen her again," he said. "If you see her, tell her I said so, will you?" James said he would.

Still agitated, he left for the snack shed to buy me coffee. He walked wearily to the serving window and found it closed, but heard voices. So he rapped his knuckles on the window.

"Can I get a cup of coffee? It's James Fee."

Paco heard him mumble, *Now she wants coffee.*

"Con leche?" the server asked. James nodded. There were no lids and, according to Paco, James soon discovered neither were there disposable hot cups. The server put the hot coffee in a plastic cup, the kind for cold drinks, and if his mood wasn't sour enough, he burned his fingers trying to carry it, which prompted an effusion of expletives that left the girl behind the window shocked and embarrassed. Returning to his office Paco heard James mumbling, *Who does Lucy think she is?*

At this point he heard a knock on the door and looked up. Chloe Zorn stood breezily in his doorway. Paco didn't use the word "breezily," but that's how I pictured it. James replaced my journals to the backpack.

"Hey," she said. "Where've you been? I haven't seen you since the press conference."

He said, "What a day."

She walked in and stood behind him and started rubbing his shoulders. She congratulated him. "You got through it. No one had a clue about what happened."

"That feels good." He shut his eyes.

"You need a beer," she said.

"I need a nap." He dropped his head to his arms on the desk while she rubbed his neck and shoulders. "You're tight," she said. "What have you been doing all day?"

He said he didn't want to talk about it. She wanted to know if there was anything he did want to talk about. He said no. She asked if he wanted her to close the door. Paco didn't know what he answered because at that point he left his perch outside the window.

Chloe's hands were working their magic. I pictured James mumbling something like, Who is Lucy Shaw? A troublemaker! Lucy always argues. I could not deny these imperfections. Chloe's fingers were having their way and I pictured him grumbling, She'll marry the pilot. Missionaries stick to their own kind. Why did she come? Why did she contact me? Why did I take her to the tomb? Now she is in jail and Chloe is seducing me.

I don't know if he mumbled such things. I only know I cannot bring myself to think about the otherwise inexplicable exchange that took place next in any other way.

Paco interrupted with a steady knocking at the door, which jolted them. Paco heard Chloe say, "Don't answer it." The knocking did not stop and Chloe, kissing and pleading, continued to urge James: "Don't answer it. Whoever it is will go away."

The knocking did not go away. James must have seen the sprouting black hair through the frosted glass. He yelled, "Go away, boy!"

The boy did not go away.

Paco heard James groan. "He's not going." He stood up and gathered himself and waited while Chloe gathered herself. Then he opened the door. Paco stood glaring at him with eyes like fire, tear tracks tracing lines down his dirty face. He gulped and heaved.

James kneeled and put his hand on the boy's shoulder. "What's the matter?" Paco didn't speak because of the gulping. James put his hand on his head and led him across the courtyard to the conference room. "You shouldn't be hanging around like this. You don't need to know everything that's going on," he said.

"You forgot to take Miss Lucy her coffee, Mr. Fee."

James pulled a tissue from his pocket and kneeled to meet him face to face. "Here. Blow your nose." Paco wiped his nose and then used the same tissue to rub the tears from his cheeks. "You're right. I forgot to take Miss Lucy her coffee. I failed. I'm sorry."

"Take it to her now."

James stood up. Chloe had not emerged from the office. He looked at the boy. "I need a few minutes. Then I'll take Miss Lucy her coffee."

Paco said to me, "That's when I asked if he was going to do sex for the whore. Mr. Fee asked where I learned to talk like that. He said he didn't want me talking like that. I asked him if he was going to do sex for the whore. He said 'Those are dirty words. I don't want to hear you talking like that' and I said 'Then we are both dirty, Mr. Fee.' "

Paco said James brushed back his sprouting hair and promised he wasn't going to do anything dirty. He kneeled again. "Do you believe me?" Paco nodded.

Nothing else happened between the two. James zipped the backpack and picked up the coffee, now cold and separating, and told Chloe he had to go. He asked her to forget it happened—such a foolish thing to ask of a woman.

So we return to 18 Rabbit, who —at the pinnacle of his reign—was ambushed and beheaded. He never saw it coming. Maybe for James unrest arose because of the smell of urine in my cell. Or maybe it was because I mentioned words spoken in deep love. Maybe it was Paco looking at him saying he felt God's power. Maybe it was the garlic in his eyes when he fried his red beans. Maybe Maybe Maybe. Maybe it was the sadness that fell over us when we sat on the rusted bed frame. Or maybe it was Ricky Fernandez. Who knows? But during that disorienting time we each found separate versions of madness, and his version ambushed him and caught him off guard and he lost his head the way 18 Rabbit lost his head because of his own version of madness.

"Look at me, Paco." I pressed my forehead to the door. He looked at me with fire eyes and I looked at him with icy ones. "Are you going to see Mr. Fee?"

He nodded.

"When you see him—Look at me, Paco."

"Miss Lucy?"

"When you see Mr. Fee tell him not to bring the coffee. Tell him I don't want it."

A tear dripped off the tip of his nose. "He will bring you the coffee, Miss Lucy."

"I don't want it. Tell him not to bring it."

He wiped his face with the back of his wrist. "Do you want mango, Miss Lucy?"

"I don't want anything. Tell him I don't want anything. Now go. Tell him."

12

Berto had been sacrificed in this world of madness and, oddly, the thought of it helped me keep my head. It made sense in a way I can't explain. I had not moved from where I sat when Paco had come with his dirty wet cheeks to tell me the news about Mr. Fee's "mistake." I sat, eyes closed, remembering the wet eyes of that little boy, wondering why he did so much and cared so much for gringos. And I saw the blue dangling body of a toothless Don Berto. Darkness settled over the courtyard outside my cell. All was shrouded in shadows of silver and gray. A chill came over me.

I did not know the time, nor even the passage of time, when I felt the touch of a cold hand upon my arm. I opened my eyes to see the appearance of orange and red billowing before my hazy eyes. I thought I was hallucinating. Then I heard a voice, a siren, saying, "I brought you soup." From the red and orange slowly emerged the face of Lillian DeWine. She was kneeling at the cell door, her skirt puffed like a parachute and sunflower earrings bobbling. She poured soup from a thermos to a foam cup and slipped it through a slat in the door. "Drink this. You don't look good, dear." I took the cup in both hands.

"How did you know I was here?"

"This is a small town. Everyone knows about Berto. Not so many believe you did it. Sip again." She paused, then smiled tragically. Her skin was fair and pale, a little bluish, and her smile betrayed the lipstick caked on the edges of her teeth. "Yet, my dear girl, here you are in this jail. You are in the world of Maya, and in the world of the Maya nothing is what it seems."

She continued, "Do you know about the Maya cosmos? There are secrets hidden there that carry meaning in this moment. Shall I tell you about it?" I didn't answer. "Picture a square bed sheet. The four corners are the four cardinal points. Now picture four heavenly creatures— dragonish of a sort, but with a human aspect. They are holding each of the corners. The creature on the northern corner is white; the one on the east is red; the one on the south is yellow; the one holding the western corner is black. Are you picturing it?" I closed my eyes and nodded. "Now picture not one, but thirteen sheets, one on top of the other, all of them rising upward in the thirteen levels of the Maya Upperworld. The heavenly dragon creatures are the sky-bearers, called bacabs. They hold the corners of the thirteen levels of the Upperworld." She inclined toward me. "You'll be interested in this." I turned my head. "The book of the Apocalypse talks about four horsemen in heaven. Their horses are white, red, black and yellow, just as the bacabs. Four angels hold the four corners of the earth holding back the four winds. Isn't that interesting? How would the ancient Maya come up with that never having read the bible?

"Anyway," she pulled an earring, "rising out of the middle of the thirteen levels of the Upperworld is a Ceiba tree. You know the Ceiba is the sacred tree of the Maya, the tree of life. Well." She interrupted herself. "Take some more soup, dear. You need the nourishment." I raised the cup to my mouth and slid it back through the door. "Look over there and try to see the shadows cast by the moon. Over there." She pointed toward the courtyard. I saw only buckets and metal drums dimly lit by the evening light. "How brightly she shines tonight," she said. "But soon she will fade and disappear. The Maya goddess Ixchel is the moon weaver. Have you heard of her?" She didn't wait for my answer. "She appears in the western horizon like the birth of a child once hidden in the womb. She grows in brightness and becomes a half moon, a gibbous moon, a full moon. Then she fades with the approaching sun in the eastern horizon until she is hidden again behind the sun's light. That is death." She paused. "Then rebirth! The cycle begins again. Women are the givers of life. We are the moon," she said. "And moonweavers too. For, you see, Ixchel also weaves. You know the huipil?" Again, she didn't wait for an answer. "It is the blouse covering Maya women wear, full of beautiful colors and intricate brocade designs." She refilled the foam cup. "When the Maya woman weaves the huipil she is telling the story of the Maya universe. The huipil is a map of the sacred universe that brings rain and grows the corn. It is the world of her dreams.

The huipil is her power. It is shaped like that square sheet, like one of the levels of the Upperworld. Sometimes she is the weaver sitting at her loom, her legs tucked tightly beneath her as she focuses on her task. Sometimes she is the spinner at her wheel forming the cloth for her huipil. Spinning you see, does not demand the same concentration as weaving. The eyes of the spinner roam about. Her hands and legs are loose and free. Sometimes she loosens her blouse. Sometimes it falls on her shoulders and shows a little breast. Ixchel the spinner invites the glances of men.

"When the Maya woman slips on her huipil, placing it over her head, she emerges through the opening as the great Ceiba at the center of the Maya universe. The Maya woman stands at the center of the universe woven from her dreams. So you see? She is a woman, a shining moon-weaver, and she holds the Maya universe in her hands. Nothing is as it seems in the world of Maya."

She paused and sat up stiffly pressing her hands to her lap. "I am forty-eight years old and have run out of dreams." She smiled faintly. "My companions are the Lenca. I have written my books. I understand what the Lenca have lost and what they have kept. Barely four hundred words remain from their oral tradition. They still practice the staffs of Moses, but that is Catholic." She looked at me. "I am a competent anthropologist." She paused.

"How old are you, dear? Do mind my asking?"

"Twenty-seven."

"I was in graduate school studying under Duncan Fee when I was your age, twenty-seven. He was as handsome and winsome then as his son is now. You know what I'm talking about." She sighed. "I fell in love with him. You know what I'm talking about there, too." She shifted her weight. "Do you know how I chose my field of study? Duncan Fee needed a research assistant. I set my life's course around that man's need for office help.

"Duncan Fee believes human beings are ruled by animal instincts. He believes that a man's primal instincts require physical satisfaction from more than one woman. It's programmed into them, he says. He calls such satisfaction 'extra-pair copulations'. I never knew his wife." She hesitated. "Have you heard she's not well?"

I hadn't heard. James had not mentioned it. Lillian went on to explain how James Fee's mother, Jane Blackman Fee, had contracted an especially ferocious form of meningitis on one of her field trips researching the Chibcha. The Chibcha tribe had dwelt in eastern Honduras and predated the Maya. Jane Fee would joke with her archaeologist son that, because of that fact, she had one up on him. Her bookshelves did not contain the innumerable volumes her husband's did. Only a single vertical binding carried the name Jane Blackman Fee. Instead of writing she spent most of her time traveling the jungles in the east, making it a personal mission to help contemporary Hondurans reclaim their Chibcha heritage. Christopher Columbus stumbled upon the Chibcha and thought they were Maya, she says. He described them in one of his logs as "coming from the land of Maya." But Jane Fee insisted that " 'coming from the land of Maya' and being Maya are two very different things." The Chibcha were especially strong in metalworking and she was quick to point out that this set them apart from the Maya who did not use metals. After the meningitis, Lillian said, she recovered, but was not the same. "There were strange episodes when she would walk the streets of New York in her night gown, knocking on doors of drug houses looking for her son James, whom, she said, had been born through immaculate conception." Her husband Duncan Fee in the meantime was traveling in Turkey researching the Artemis cult, leaving his ailing wife in the care of Jane Fee's sister.

"When I was his research assistant I never knew James," continued Lillian, "that is, until later when we both ended up here in Honduras. I saw him only once during his childhood. A handsome boy then, in a boyish way, as he is handsome today in his mannish way." She described the single episode when she saw James Fee as a young boy. He happened to come to his father's office unannounced and walked in on what Duncan Fee would have called extra-pair copulation research. "He didn't see my face," she said. "To this day he doesn't know it was I who was with his father that day."

A tear rolled off the tip of her nose. "The look on that little boy's face horrified me. I felt such shame. I tried to tell Duncan about what I felt seeing that boy's face. Do you know what Duncan said? He said, 'What we are doing is strictly biologizing. It is unhelpful to see it as anything more than that. He's a boy. He'll understand it soon enough.'" She passed a wrist across her wet cheeks. "James stopped coming to his father's library after that. That's when he started playing outside, which was a good thing,

I suppose. That was how he discovered his love for archaeology."

I remembered vividly when James described that summer to me. We had been hiking in the Cloud Forest on a day during his visit to the capital city. He had rested a blanket over pine needles and I lay on my back, he on an elbow nearby. He touched my face and then ran a finger down my chest to rest it on my heart, which was beating like a storm. He said, "Who has claimed this heart?"

"There have been only two—before you—and one died." That was Jack. The other was my brother Gabe. I believe James Fee made up his mind right then he would conquer Gabe Shaw. (James Fee and his battles.) Then, a little while later, our places on the blanket reversed, I on my elbow and he on his back, I wanted to ask the same thing, but held my tongue. I didn't really want to know how many women had owned his heart. Instead I asked about digging. That is when he described the summer Lillian was referring to, when James was ten. Instead of climbing bookshelves in his father's library he went outside. He dug up an arrowhead in his back yard, turning it front and back, mystified by who could have chiseled its fine edges and symmetrical flared tips. His research led him to conclude the arrowhead must have belonged to a Lenni-Lenape warrior. That was the summer when that little boy became a Lenape hunter, a great warrior who carved tips of his arrows and used them in battles. That summer he discovered the power of discovering with human hands worlds hidden beneath the dirt.

"I understand why Duncan told me what he did about

human behavior," Lillian continued. "But I have come to disagree. Human beings are more than animals. No." She shook her head. "More is required of us. When he drew those conclusions he didn't factor in guilt. Guilt is a human phenomenon. He didn't factor in love either, another human phenomenon." She smiled faintly, blinked, and paused. "There's an old gypsy proverb, 'You have to dig deep to bury your father'."

Lillian put a cold hand through the door and squeezed my arm. "James is still digging, dear." She pulled a crumpled tissue from her waistband and dabbed her eyes, then smiled. "I have run out of dreams. But it is not too late for you." She squeezed my hand a second time. "We are Ixchel. We are the moon. We rise again. We raise our heads in the center of the universe we ourselves have woven in our dreams. You are too young to give up your dreams." She gazed at me through the little opening in the door, her eyes pink and shining. "Sometimes the weaving Ixchel is demure. But there are times when she must be bold, like the spinner. She changes like the moon, you see. In the world of Maya nothing is as it seems." She gathered her skirt. "I must go." She stood and turned to leave, the red and orange fading into the shadows. Then, like a bolt, she returned and kneeled, her skirt as a cloud. "James Fee is not his father."

13

My old professor and friend, Goody, told me once that we are closer to the truth in the world of our dreams than in the real world. At this moment, I would have liked to ask Goody what he meant by that. I wondered what Lillian meant when she said Ixchel wove the universe of her dreams. What is real about the world of our dreams, Goody?

In that dark night my dreams were overthrown, like a fire rising in my throat and over my cheeks and around my eyes and out my ears. Then the fire settled and smoldered inside me in some place I could not locate because everything hurt.

Cockroaches crept about my feet, needling antennae against my socks. Clouds covered the moon and rain started to fall. Water poured in rivulets down the drain in the courtyard. I pondered our differing claims, James's and mine. I was a writer who kept my nose to the wind and my head in the clouds looking for the narrative behind the story. James was the archaeologist, who kept his nose in the dirt where the story rose up out of material earth he himself displaced. I looked high. He looked low. The dirt kept him pinned to earth where betrayals seemed mere optional readjustments.

These thoughts took me to remembrances of Sebastian, the Ninganahua village chief, who betrayed my parents many times. I remembered the time he invited the Catholics to come and build a church for the tribe despite the fact that my parents had established one already, meeting in the school they had built. Sebastian was angry with my father, as he often was. So when a priest pulled up by canoe to the riverbank and asked Sebastian if his tribe wanted a new church, he saw it as a means to hurt my father. At the time my parents were staying at the compound in Pucallpa and did not know what the priest was doing. The building crew moved into our hut and the Catholics built a very good church with lattice under trimming and a shiny corrugated tin roof that did not leak. The workers were getting ready to pour the concrete floor when Cuscobundi, second in command in the tribal hierarchy, mentioned that members of the tribe would be gathering at the church for their singing services. The workers asked, What singing services? That is when it became known to the Catholic missionaries that the Shaws—Protestants—were living with the tribe several months a year, transposing their indigenous language into written form and translating the New Testament. Without a moment's delay the workers gathered their tools and shovels and set off in their canoes. They never did pour the concrete floor.

When my parents learned of Sebastian's duplicity

it marked the first of many times my parents retreated alone so my mother could cry. They usually went down the river in the canoe. On that particular occasion, when my parents returned to find their hut in disarray, I watched from high on the ridge as my parents walked down the steep path to the river. My mother wore a blue cotton skirt and sleeveless white blouse and my father, the same cotton work pants he always wore, the same white T-shirt and baseball cap. I sat alone in the grass on that ridge, knock-kneed and pulling up grass, watching my mother clutch my father's arm, tripping and sliding all the way down the ridge to the river's edge. As Edie Shaw settled on the floor of the canoe she dropped her safari hat into the river. My father grabbed it before it floated away. He faced her, sitting on a slat of wood, while a Ninganahua man pushed the canoe with a pole. My mother cried with her face in her hands. My father leaned and touched her shoulder. The Ninganahua man lifted the pole and the canoe went forward. I saw my father turn his head to listen to her, his elbows on his knees. It always unsettled me to see my mother cry.

Then Gabe called. Abu! Abu! You're going to get chiggers! He came running to me—I saw it all so clearly. He was twelve and I was ten. I had never given a minute's thought about the chiggers in that grass, though my mother warned me constantly. Gabe took my hand and we ran home the way we always did, racing and holding hands. He took me out of the chiggers, though it was too late. I had bites up and down the insides of both legs. I cried for days because of the itching.

Gabe and I used to listen from our hammocks when Sebastian beat his many wives. They always ran away when he beat them. Then Sebastian would get in a canoe and go up river looking for them. Gabe used to say he was so busy chasing his wives up and down the river he didn't have time to be chief. When Sebastian would find his wives he would bring them back then beat them again for running away. Outsiders were not supposed to get involved in tribal affairs, but our father and mother put dressings on the wives' wounds anyway.

My parents endured Sebastian's insults many times. He would drink and Cuscobundi wouldn't allow him to lead singing services. Cuscobundi would tell him before the assembly that he could not be a respected leader because of his drinking. Sometimes Cuscobundi would lead small gatherings in Sebastian's hut and read the portions of the New Testament my parents had translated with the hope that "the Owner would drive his words into Sebastian's innermost." Sebastian would respond, "Why couldn't the Owner send us a good linguist?"

One night as Gabe and I slept in hammocks, I saw my parents step outside to look at the stars. Gabe always slept easily, no matter what. I couldn't sleep that night because I heard my mother crying again. I peeked outside and watched as she pressed a crumpled tissue to wet eyes, her neck blotching the way it did when she cried or laughed or danced. My father held her hand and my mother was praying, her lips curled downward, If we're really supposed to be here, Lord, please cause a star to fall. They opened their eyes and looked at the southern sky filled with diamonds of light. And at that very moment a star passed over the night sky, as if it had been made to order. My mother sobbed. They prayed again. This time my father said, Lord, would you send me too a shooting star as a sign of your encouragement? They looked up and this time there was no star. He smiled at my mother. 'I guess one star is all we get.'

Yet for all Sebastian's insults and betrayals, alone in that prison that night, I could not recall a single occasion when my father spoke a harsh word against him.

I have never woven a huipil and I could not conceive of the dreams I would weave.

14

I was unable to move. I didn't want to move. I began hearing voices and this consoled me. I closed my eyes and saw Gabe standing with my father and me at the graveside of a Ninganahua woman called Nobody. She died of Whooping Cough in the epidemic that killed fifteen babies in the tribe. Before she died Nobody had whispered to my mother, When I die tell them not to burn the house. Tell them, don't throw all the good things in the river. Jesus is going to take me to the next life. Tell them it is okay to wail, but don't wail too long. The men had already thrown her hammock in the river. They had burned her hut. They feared the spirits of the dead and didn't want Nobody's spirit returning to them in the dark. They were covering her body with dirt when the Ninganahua man said, It is dark where she is. Our father said, It is dark where her bones and flesh are. But where her spirit is, it is light and will never be dark. I was holding Gabe's hand. I whispered to him, Why did they throw Nobody's hammock in the river? Nobody didn't want them to throw the good things in the river. Why didn't anybody listen to Nobody?

I heard a whisper. "Amiga. I am Carlos." I turned my stiff neck to see him sitting cross-legged on the floor on the other side of my door. "You don't look well, mi chiquita," he said. "The journalists, they did not learn our secret. So much for the nose of a reporter, eh? Now you must be saved."

I looked at him blankly. "Who's going to save me?"

"Of course our friend James Fee blames himself. I try to tell him there is nothing gained by blaming himself. But he doesn't answer me." Carlos hesitated. "Some people in this town call him a hero. Did you know that?" He looked at me with those fawn eyes that made him as handsome as a sheik. "But he will tell you he is not a hero." Carlos paused. I said nothing. "You are interested in the bible, yes? And I am interested in the bible. So here is another secret we share." He slid closer. "You know the story about Abraham, when God told him to go the mountain and sacrifice his only son Isaac?"

"I have read it, yes."

"Do you understand it?"

I closed my eyes. "In as much as anyone can understand it."

"Let me tell you, mi chiquita, that if James Fee had been Abraham and had been asked to perform that test he would have failed."

"He would have failed by not going to the mountain? Or by going to the mountain and then not offering his son?"

"He would have gone to the mountain. But he would

have spoiled the story." I looked at Carlos. "He is not a coward. He is not afraid of danger. He would have gone to the mountain."

"The whole world knows James Fee is not a coward."

"But there is a courage faith demands that he does not possess." The rain fell gently against the tin roof, spilling into puddles and rivers that flowed into the drain.

"James finds his truth in the dirt. Sometimes it fools him. But Abraham mounted his mule, chopped the wood for the fire, traveled three days looking toward the mountain, and then drew the knife on his son. It is absurd." Carlos pressed his fingers to his eyes. "Then—after all that, God said, 'Forget about it.' Abraham made the journey and raised the knife to his son." He looked at me. "It doesn't make any sense."

"What time is it?"

"Eleven thirty."

"It's not meant to make sense," I said.

Carlos hesitated. "Of course it is not." He said, "People come to these ruins and see the monuments, the temples, and hear the birds and see the beauty of the valley. To them it is as if they themselves are discovering a world no eye has seen. It is the world James Fee has reclaimed from the bowels of the earth, stone upon stone, for them. And you come and see it and nothing surprises you. You see these ruins the way you see everything."

"I don't know what you mean."

"You walk in the Great Plaza and hear James explaining the stelae of 18 Rabbit, and you say, 'It is his vision of life after death.'

"You walk by the Hieroglyphic Stairway where James will say, 'It is the ode to the great kings,' and you say, 'Maybe it is their attempt to reach heaven.'" Carlos shook his head. "You're not wrong, mi chiquita, don't misunderstand." He shrugged. "James, he doesn't understand you. But he is awakening to his love for Lucy Shaw and it terrifies him."

"You said he would ruin the Abraham story. And so he has."

"And yet all the powers of heaven and earth have not enabled him to renounce you." He leaned on his elbows and inclined himself to me. "I am not a good Catholic but I believe in the holy Son of God. The Maya taught me that. They have shown me there isn't enough human blood in all the world to satisfy the gods. They are telling me the power of the sacrifice cannot be found in the blood of humans sacrificed by human hands." He paused. "The warfare between cities increased toward the end of the dynasty, did James tell you?" I nodded. "The Maya city-states all over the lowlands fought their civil wars and took captives. Did they send them to the fields to work? No. They cut off their heads and put them on sticks. For what? What did they gain from all that blood? The gods were not satisfied. All sixteen kings took their place on Altar Q—the first king handing the scepter to the last—and that was it. The dynasty of Yax K'uk Mo' collapsed. That is why I believe in the Son of God. It was God's blood spilled. It is God's madness, like Abraham's. The story of Abraham is absurd because his madness was his only hope."

"So now you are a theologian?"

"I am not a theologian. I am Carlos Gutierrez, twenty-eight years old, and my companions are Los Relámpagos, fourteen baseball players, that is, when I am not picking through bones and teeth of dead kings. Abraham had only a few pieces of the picture, mi chiquita. For three days Abraham climbs the mountain. He is at war with himself. He is thinking, 'God has promised me a nation will rise from my loins. In my old age, in Sarah's old age, we are childless. Yet, she conceives. Here is the child of the promise. His name is Isaac. Then God tells me "Go lay him on the altar and slay him." ' Still Abraham walks. He goes to the mountain. He walks with the little he had. He looks up to the mountain, not down at the ground where his feet met the earth. There is a difference." He touched my arm. "The contradiction is resolved only by walking, mi chiquita. It is madness. But sometimes madness is your only hope."

15

A dog barked over voices echoing in the night. Darkness settled over me and I felt pinned to the cold concrete. At the same time I felt oddly afloat. You are somewhere. You are nowhere. I wondered if angels could see us. Below the dim light of a waxing moon and above the rain as it slowed, radio music clamored from the street. I lifted my eyes and there was Goody sitting in my cell, in the opposite corner. When angels come it is left to us to see them and we rarely do, he said. He wore his signature seer-sucker shirt and crew neck sweater and his disheveled white hair, as always, looked like an unmade bed. The desire to belong to another person is an expression of the desire for home, our real home, he was saying. It's a kind of homesickness, you see. Goody? My dear, if I could lead you there I would, and if you could take me there I would give myself to you in an instant. Dear heart, the deepest prayers we speak use silence for their tongue. I hear your silent pleading well. Then he was gone.

The head can rest and legs can float. Shut your eyes

and find your home. Lean back your head and let your arms hang low. Find your rest. You float. You rise. Gabe said, They're pressing the button, Bu. People push the button only when they're going to die. We were clinging to each other in the hammock. Torrential rains caused the river in the jungle to rise. You have a problem, Gene? Wes Thatcher's voice was barely audible as we heard it on the other end of the short wave radio from the base. My father had pushed the distress button, which meant Wes knew someone in the jungle faced an emergency. Pray the Lord would stop the water from rising, our father said, we're inches from being swept away. The current had already pulled many huts into the river. Our hut was newly built and the poles went deep so it was holding. Cuscobundi brought his wife and children, Juna and Jaime, to our hut. Cuscobundi said to our father from his canoe, Our house is beginning to tilt. Can we come to your house? Their children were the same ages as Gabe and me. The four of us curled into the hammock together. We sang a Ninganahua song.

> Min imi foni. Cruzhuun afa
>
> Min imi foni. Cruzhuun pacuni.
>
> Aicho Ifo Jesus non mia fanaishoin.

My mother read from the bible. When you pass through the waters, I will be with you. When you pass through the rivers, they will not sweep over you. Let the rivers roll.

Sometimes it hurts more to live than to die. Living is dying, dying is living. Hey. Write that down, Bu. That's good. I saw Jack sitting on the springs of my prison bed the way he would sit during band practices. The Ningabors weren't fit for this world, Bu. We were sanctified. His bushy hair fell over his happy eyes and he still had that dimpled smile. He was wearing his Mr. Rescue T-shirt.

Why did you leave us, Jack? Was it is because you weren't fit for this world?

This world's all you got, girl. You'll find your way. Gabe too.

Gabe's married.

Did you expect him to play back up to your shimmy the rest of his life?

They said your legs broke. Did you feel your legs break?

My mind became clear and I thought of the perfect words for a song. It's the Ningabors. It's that good.

Gabe and I stopped singing after you died.

I want you to sing, Bu.

I'll never sing again.

I'll give you the words, you and Gabe.

Then there was silence.

16

The coffee mug only just fit through a slat in the door. He slid it through, the handle-side first, then reached an arm through another slat to pull it around on the floor near my bare leg. The light fell checkered white and black from shadows of the moon cast through the slats in the door. Steam rose in curls. He had made it hot.

He sat outside my door cross-legged, like a Maya king. His face was dark, his eyes half-mast. He rested his head on the door. I heard a whisper. "I brought you coffee, Lu." I closed my eyes. I felt his hand touch mine as it lay across my lap. He curled my fingers inside his. "Who am I, Lucy?" I didn't move. "I'm sorry. Sorry for everything." He caught sight of a cockroach near my foot and swatted at it twice with a bare hand. I did not move. "I know it's too late for the coffee. I wanted to bring it anyway. It's all I've got, Lu." A dog barked. A motorbike roared up the street. He touched my arm, then removed his hand. I didn't open my eyes. He knew, as I did, there was nothing for him to do except to go back home.

17

Why did I call the United States Ambassador George when his name was Bill? Why did I call him by his first name when I should have called him Mr. Ambassador? I don't know how to dig an axial trench or why *al fresco* pottery stays bright over a thousand years of darkness. Why did Jack's plane drop? Why did Larry's bird Bart like the sound of my voice? Why did my mother wear dresses in the jungle? Why is Julio Cabrera Cabrera a very brave man? Why did Duncan Fee go to Turkey? Why does Lillian wear red and orange?

Do Virgin statues weep blood? Why did the man in Celda B humiliate his bride? Why did his bullet miss its target? Why did God tell Abraham he would build a nation through his seed and then tell Abraham to sacrifice his son? How did Abraham summon his boy? How did he arise that day and mount the mule? How did it feel to ask Isaac to carry the wood for the fire? How did it feel to walk three days and see the mountain? How did Isaac feel when he carried the wood and walked on alone with his father? What was Abraham thinking as he carried the knife? What thoughts possessed my father upon hearing James's voice? Did James comfort him? Did my father console James? Did my father call him 'son'? Can power arise from a dead body painted blue?

I am sinking. My legs pull me down into where it is dark, where coldness and wet and hopelessness and exhaustion are beyond the reach of prayer, beyond remorse, without a will to care, nor fear, nor even to possess sadness. Sweat covered my face. Strange dreams, silent pleading, cockroaches and madness all came to me in the darkness of that long night.

When I die do not throw all the good things in the river. Gabe, hold my hand. The waters sweep over me. I use too many commas. Aicho Ifo Jesus non mia fana-ishoin. Where is my brother? It is a kind of homesickness, you see. They press the button when someone is going to die. Where is my father? Why didn't anybody listen to Nobody? I will be with you when you pass through the waters. Do angels see us? Abraham had a few pieces of the picture. Abraham's madness was his only hope. You have cast Your shadow over me. I lie in the dust. I sink into the ground. My tongue is dry. I do not see You. Gravel fills my mouth. My spirit has left me. My life passes in the shadows. The dead cannot lift up their hands to You.

18

Morning light dispelled shadows of the night and I awoke to find myself seated where I had been all night, on the floor near the heavy door that closed the world to me. I felt numb and turned my head only slightly to feel my neck crack. I opened my eyes. That is when I saw the mug near my leg on the floor. The milk had separated and risen as a skin to the top. I leaned and adjusted my back, then picked it up and brought the mug to my lips. The coffee was cold. But I drank all of it in successive swallows, resting then the empty mug on my lap with both hands. I did not move for another half hour. Then, like a wind, my headache lifted.

Paco appeared at this timely moment, as he tended to do. I revived enough to see him squatting by the door where the sun broke through. He poked a boney arm at me and tugged the skin of my elbow. He held a soft warm tortilla in his dark little fist. "I bought them from the lady on the street," he said.

When I asked where he got the money, he shrugged. "I

begged."

I finished two tortillas before I knew how hungry I was. I ate another and could have eaten more.

He pointed to the mug. "I told you Mr. Fee would come."

"Yes. He came."

"You drank his coffee."

"Yes."

I thanked Paco for the tortillas and gripped the door to pull myself up. "I am old before my time, Paco." I groaned. "I need to lie down. My back hurts." And so I walked achingly to the bare metal cot.

Finding relief without a headache I managed to doze. In fact, I must have fallen into a deep sleep because the next thing I heard was the sound of keys. I opened my eyes and saw Alfonso pulling open my door. Leonardo stood triumphantly behind him, his satchel clutched under an arm and a smile wide enough to swallow his face.

"I bring you greetings from Doña Nora Reyes Morales de Mondragón."

I sat up. He pulled a paper from his satchel and waved it. "Doña Nora says it is time for you to come home." Oblivious to all aches and stiffness, I lurched and he handed me the paper. I couldn't read it for my blurring eyes and trembling of my hands. I saw the presidential seal and that Nora Mondragón and el Presidente Philip Mondragón had signed the letter. I deciphered the words "liberación"—"exoneración"—"alivio"—and "al punto." Freedom. Exoneration. Relief. Immediate. Leonardo was all smiles and I clutched him. "I love you, Leo!" He reciprocated in awkward patting, smiling in his sheepish way, as I sobbed on his shoulder. Alfonso and the beleaguered bridegroom looked on in bewildered amusement.

"Vámonos. El Presidente and Doña Nora signed everything. Let's get your documents."

Paco must have overheard my cries of relief, for they sent him running. Alfonso remitted my documents with that buck-toothed kindly smile and seemed genuinely relieved to render me my freedom. I thanked him for his generosity of spirit and joined Leonardo, who was waiting for me out front. The brightness of the morning sun made me flinch, but I made the adjustment. In a matter of only a minute, as we made our way to the center of town, I saw God's miracles in every passing thing. I saw it in the man sitting cross-legged on a bench on the corner. His mustache turned down with the lines of his mouth. A miracle! I saw the miracle of birds in the trees above us and in the clouds hanging low over the mountains surrounding us. I saw the miracle of school girls shuffling their back packs and darting flirtatious glances. Another miracle: women with baskets on their heads! That morning, the smell of smoke in the air, the morning dew, the sidewalks and men on benches and birds in trees and in trees themselves. Blessed normalcy! Such sheer delight even my exhaustion could not dispel. I live! I wanted to kiss the door of the community house as we passed it. How lovely are the flowers in its iron flower boxes, red geraniums robust and asserting such hope. It is the picture of all good things. The bells rang more clearly and the birds pitched their songs more sweetly. The mountains stood grander and the clouds more at rest. I would have kissed the man on the bench and say, Turn up thy lips, old man! You live!

But Leo would have stopped me.

We walked and Leo clarified how it came to pass that he secured the document from Doña Nora. He said that James had indeed called him and explained my predicament. Leo then went immediately to Doña Nora's office— "a place we know well"—he looked at me grinning. "And for once, La Primera Dama was there. Of course Eva Rosales remembered Lucy Shaw." He threw me a knowing look. "As luck would have it, Eva Rosales happens to think Dr. Fee is very handsome and asks many questions about him, which I can answer because of our tours last year. She always wants the opportunity to meet James Fee"—a sideways glance—"and as soon as I mention his name, Eva Rosales is very helpful about your predicament." He smiled at me and I rolled my eyes. "I explain that Dr. Fee tells me the police took the wrong person—you—and this won no sympathy with Eva Rosales. But she asks if Dr. Fee himself can come and present the case to La Primera Dama and I tell her it is a very good idea and that I would tell it to Dr. Fee. But, I explain, Lucy Shaw is soon to be moved to the capital and I ask Eva Rosales if she can present the case to Doña Nora without the presence of Dr. Fee since we are without much time. She asks if she ought to speak to Dr. Fee on the phone, and I say again this is a very good idea." He tilted his head and smiled again. " 'But' I said, 'Dr. Fee is very difficult to reach. He is always in the tunnels.' I ask her if she can present the case to Doña Nora without speaking to Dr. Fee. Eva Rosales says she can." Leo shook his head. "She explains the situation to Doña Nora who then escorts me to her office. Her black beaming eyes became the picture of tragedy. She explain me to wait while she speaks to her husband, El Presidente. So I wait in Doña Nora's waiting lounge for three hours. I began to fear it would be impossible to get a bus to Copán that night." He looked at me. "I was tapping my foot. You are a very bad influence on me.

"Doña Nora returns at eight o'clock that evening. She tells me her husband made calls—I do not know who he called. She does not tell me that. Then she hands me the document. 'Tell Lucy I will schedule an appointment when she returns so we can talk about the trees,' she said.

"I caught the last bus for Copán Ruinas at eleven o'clock and arrived at eight this morning. I slept. I am all right. A little sore." He put his hand on my shoulder. "So, I am telling you, Lucy, Doña Nora wants the interview."

When we arrived at the hotel I possessed no thought other than to get to my room for a shower and to sleep. I asked the attendant behind the front desk for my key. He looked at me blankly. "You have been checked out, Miss Shaw," he said.

I blinked. "I haven't checked out."

"Dr. Fee was just here. You might still find him outside, but I don't think so. He said he was in a hurry." I gaped and turned, staring at Leo. Then I turned again to the attendant behind the desk.

He smiled. "He checked you out a few minutes ago. Your bill is paid."

"He took my things?"

"He was carrying a suitcase. Could it have belonged to someone else?"

I turned. "Leo?"

Leo stepped up to the counter. "I will get a room, Lucy. Don't worry." He waved a finger. "You can rest in my room. I will go to the ruins and take pictures. I will get an explanation."

I needed to sit. I found an old wooden chair hidden behind a potted palm, and dropped there, out of sight. With my head in my arms, the elation of freedom began to evaporate in the capitulation to all-out exhaustion. I perceived dimly the glimpse of a maid swiping a dingy mop across the red tiled floor. I heard a guest ask the front desk for a towel for the pool. The phone chirped. People greeted one another with kisses to the cheek. Hola. Hola.

"Are you Lucy Shaw?"

I looked up to see standing over me a friendly-faced Honduran in a straw cowboy hat. He had bright black eyes, a bushy black mustache, and smiled and bobbed unselfconsciously. "My name is Raúl." He removed his hat and held it to his chest. "I am here on behalf of Mr. Fee. Mr. Fee asked me to tell you that he checked you out of this hotel."

"I've discovered that."

"Mr. Fee has taken your bag to his home. He would like me to take you there so you can rest. He said you will be more comfortable there."

"Mr. Fee didn't say anything to me about it."

Raúl smiled and dipped. "Mr. Fee told me you would say that. Mr. Fee told me to tell you he understands why you say it." I turned, looking for Leo. "He said to tell you he will talk to you about it when he returns."

"Returns from where?"

"Mr. Fee is attending the funeral of his friend, Don Berto Rodriguez, the watchman who died in the tunnels. That is why he did not come here himself. That is why he sent me. He wanted me to tell you that."

"I need to talk to my friend." Leo was leaning over the reception desk, a key dangling from his finger, when I tried to explain in a jumbled sequence Raúl's mission. Leo looked as confused and skeptical as I was.

Raúl approached. "You are Leonardo? Mr. Fee told me to bring you with Miss Lucy to his home to show you where Miss Lucy is staying." He bobbed. "He said that after you see where Miss Lucy is staying, I am bringing you to the tomb while Miss Lucy rests, that is, of course, if you want to see the tomb, which I'm sure you do. Everyone wants to see the tomb. It's incredible."

Leo and I exchanged pondering looks. We agreed, in any case, that this change of plan was consistent with the way James Fee operated. In the end, perplexity gave way to fatigue and we followed Raúl.

19

James's maid Brigida greeted me at the door smiling, "Señorita," signaling recognition. She pointed me to the bedroom and bathroom, highlighting clean towels and fresh sheets, and she patted the bed—James Fee's bed, where, evidently, I was intended to sleep. I saw my suitcase in the corner. Then she led me to the kitchen and lifted a basket of fresh tortillas that she had left on the counter for me. She pulled out a pitcher of freshly-squeezed grapefruit juice from the "refri," as she called it and Leo waited at the door with Raúl. I looked at him helplessly. "I am too tired to do anything about this right now. Go with Raúl. Get some good pictures." I told him I would be calling my parents then shower and go to bed. "I'll call you when I get up. We'll figure out what to do then."

Leo kissed my cheek. "Get rest, Lucy. I will be back."

Before he left I pulled my backpack from the kitchen table, pulled out the camera, and pressed two film cartridges into his palm. "Don't drop these." He smiled. I hugged him. "You're my hero, Leo."

There I was, standing in James Fee's bedroom, looking into the mirror where a beaten-down fallen ghost looked back at me with sunken eyes and hair like field grass. What forces conspired to bring me to this moment? The maid knocked gently and entered. "I have for you sleeping clothes."

"Sleeping clothes?"

"Señor Fee ask me for you to prepare your sleeping clothes." She held in her arms a folded, freshly ironed bundle of white.

"I have my own sleeping clothes."

"Señor Fee ask me to tell you that you want these. He tell me to have them ready for you." Unmoved, she held out the folded white bundle until I took it. I recognized it immediately as the sleepwear I had brought to Wisconsin. I couldn't fathom how it had ended up here. I looked at Brigida. She said, "Mr. Fee say if you are hungry there is chicken and rice in the *refri.*"

By the time I sank as dead weight into those crisp clean sheets it was approaching 10:00 a.m. I slept for the next twenty hours, with one life-altering interruption. But I'm getting ahead of myself. Sleep carried me away amid the sounds of horse hoofs on cobblestone, a shoe repairman yelling ¡zapatos!, the peal of motorbikes, children kicking around a soccer ball, and a young man calling "¡Doña Hilda!" Then I heard no more. Sleep came quickly and soundly. I was powerless under the weight of my exhaustion.

I arose only one time several hours later, when I heard Leo's voice from the kitchen.

"Casillero del Diablo, a good wine. Chilean." It was evening; the clock read half-past seven. I had been sleeping for nearly ten hours. I heard James say, "I think she is going to sleep through the whole night." Then I heard the sounds of forks on plates and the lifting of glasses. Leo said, "You are a cook as well as an archaeologist." That is when I put on my robe and made an appearance, startling them both.

"Lucy." Leo stood and kissed my cheek. "Dr. Fee made you dinner but you did not wake up. So he gave up on you and offered it to me. Here. You take it." He lifted his plate to me.

"I'm not hungry, Leo."

James pulled out a chair and I joined them at the table, though he and I didn't exchange words. "Have some wine, Lucy," Leo said. "It is Chilean. Muy rico." James pulled a glass from the shelf and filled it half full, the way he knew I took my wine.

"How do you feel, Lucy?" Leo asked.

"The bed felt good anyway." I registered the laboring and grinding motor of the refrigerator—a sound I knew—and, forgetting myself, said to James, "I thought you were going to get that fixed." He didn't answer. I registered a dog barking on the street and the gentle wind from the fan above our heads. The surroundings were familiar to me.

"I am asking Dr. Fee about the investigation of the watchman, but he doesn't want to talk about it. So he was asking me how long we work together, Lucy. Has it been five years?" Leo smiled and turned a jolly face toward James.

"She works me hard. She is a hard woman, but you know that." He sipped his wine, then attacked his plate with self-possession. I lifted my face to catch the breeze from the fan, then turned to face James. "No word on Berto?" He shook his head. He paused. "I don't want to talk about that right now."

I turned instead to Leo. "Did you get photos today with Raúl?"

"Some very good ones." He nodded. "Lucy, pásame la crema?"

James changed the subject and asked Leo how he learned English.

"The Nazarene Church," Leo said. He explained in ex-cruciating detail how, when he was a boy of fourteen "or maybe I had fifteen, I don't remember," the Nazarenes sent a pastor to his neighborhood, which was, at the time, a squatter town outside the capital. The pastor built a church and told the community that anyone who joined the church would be able to enter the co-op and get a better price on corn and beans. Leo was telling James that the Nazarene Church brought gringos to the barrio to teach the locals how to read and write.

I felt heat rising in my face and pressure mounting behind my eyes. I passed Leo the cream. James pushed away his plate and responded, "So that's how you learned English?"

"That, and from the television. People in my town sac-rifice many things to get a television."

I tried to focus on the books on the shelves behind the dinner table to steady my spinning head.

I recognized the titles as those that James had pulled and lent me for my research. *Aztec and Maya Myths*, Karl Taube. *The Maya Scribe and His World*, Michael Coe. Leo said, "We are an invasion community. My people live in crisis all the time. With television they can go to another world." He was waving his fork. Leo said, "We are campesinos who came to the city to find jobs. So we come and we find first a piece of land on a hillside, then drive stakes into the ground and start building houses. They are made of cardboard at the beginning. We are waiting to see if anyone claims the land.

"No one claimed the land in my neighborhood, so we elected a governing council and raised the flag of the liberal party to support us in our fight for legitimacy."

"Leo," I interrupted. "I am going to get my things. We need to go."

"In a minute, Lucy. Have some more wine."

"We need to get back to the hotel, Leo. I'm ready, after you eat."

James commented about the church being responsible for the condition of the poor. "They conquered these people. They oppressed them."

Leo, sipping wine, responded, "There is little evidence to contradict your conclusion, Dr. Fee. People say it would be better if the Spanish never came to the New World. But if the Spanish didn't come, we would be speaking Dutch or Portuguese or Arabic. And if Colón had not reached these shores in 1492, someone else would have in 1493 or `94." He said, "They might not have brought Catholicism. But they would have come. They would have brought their diseases and their swords." He paused, oblivious to me. "There are many cruel people in the world, Dr. Fee. That is not a mystery. The mystery is why there are also many good people, people who help you—the way the Nazarenes taught me to read. They taught me that it is better to work than to steal. Because of that, I am able to find work with *Los Tiempo* who gave me the opportunity to work with Lucy. She makes me work hard. But her hardness makes me strong. Lucy introduced me to Bartolome de Las Casas. He was a good Catholic. Right, Lucy?"

"Leo, we have to go."

"Bartolome came to the New World and defended the Indians. He is a hero of mine." He sipped more wine. "Lucy helps me understand that not everyone who wears the name of a Christian is a conquistador." He looked at me. "Lucy, five minutes. Drink some wine. It will help your stomach."

Leo, still circling his fork, sighed deeply and went on to explain the time, a year ago, when four different families emerged to claim the land on which his squatter village stood. "Not one. *Four.* Remember, Lucy? The entire colonia rose up and set fire to tires and blockaded the highway. The police threw tear gas bombs. But the families are still in their homes. Lucy wrote about it. She got tear gas in her eyes on that day."

James looked at me. Color drained from my face and I had broken out in a cold sweat.

"Are you all right?"

"I need to lie down," I said.

Leo wiped his mouth with his napkin and they both stood.

"Wake me before you leave, Leo. I'm going back to the hotel with you." I lay on the couch, not wanting to miss Leo's exit, and dropped my head onto the pillow. I heard Leo speaking of farm people who had come to the city—"they know only how to plant corn." I heard James carry his plate to the sink. Leo was saying, "My mother used to rise at four in the morning to grind the corn she boiled the night before. She fried the tortillas and then caught the five-thirty bus to the city. My sister, she sold the tortillas and with the money my mother earned as a maid she bought more corn and more firewood and more kerosene and made more tortillas. The dream of the big city."

I drifted in and out of dreams, dreams with women holding babies in a rustic church. I heard an echo in the distance that sounded of Leo's voice. She looked like a flower sitting there on the bench in her summer dress. The only gringa with all those Honduran women. The pastor told the people to embrace one another. But no one came near to me. I stood alone with no one to embrace until a crooked and toothless old woman with stringy gray hair approached me. She put her arms on my shoulders then pulled me to her. After that every woman in the church came to me wanting an embrace. They didn't think a gringa would want to be touched by them.

In my dreams I found myself standing by a deep and peaceful river with swift-running water. James stood with me along its bank. We stood together looking at the river. A wind arose and the water began to rise. It began to churn and swirl and form white caps. James and I stood in the wind watching the water as it pitched and foamed. Ninganahuas came to the riverside and began being blown into the water by the storm. The swiftness of the current was carrying them away. I looked at James. It is Nobody. He said, Who is Nobody? I said, Nobody doesn't want the good things thrown in the river. James looked at me. You can't help her. She is going to drown. If you go in the water, you are going to drown too. Don't go, he said. I said, I have to help her. He said, Don't go, Lucy. Stay here with me. I looked at him. Then I jumped. James stood on the riverside and watched me swim with the current. I was trying to reach Nobody. Her head bobbed up and down in the waves. Sometimes the water pulled her under. Sometimes she came up again. James stood on the riverbank and watched while I kept swimming. The water carried me down river. I bobbed up and down the way Nobody was bobbing up and down. I was trying to reach Nobody. James called to me. I looked back and our eyes met a last time and then the water took me farther down the river until I could no longer see him. I went under. Lucy! I could not answer. I could not look back. The water carried me. The dreams of that night brought darkness over me as with a rushing river. I groaned. My flesh felt cold. My heart raced and I couldn't breathe. "Lucy." Where am I? "Lucy." I am not in the river. I have not been carried away. I pulled on a blanket. I saw a square bed sheet, its four cardinal points rising in the hands of angels. I am rising. I feel the breath of the angels on my face. I am the Ceiba tree. I am at the center of the universe.

I am weaving in my dreams. I am the moon.

"I am putting you in bed."

I felt hands beneath me. I felt hands playing with the linens about me. Abraham was great by virtue of his madness. What is comparable to Abraham's journey to the mountain? The Holy One asked Abraham to believe what he did not understand.

I hear myself whisper, "K'inich Ahau."

He answers, "What?"

I open my eyes and sit up straight. "K'inich Ahau, sun god of the east, full of light and fire and steady rising."

"You're having a dream, Lucy. Try and go back to sleep. We'll talk in the morning." I feel a touch to my hair. I turn and look at him. He drops to his knees beside the bed and brushes his fingers against my cheek. I hear myself say, "K'inich Ahua marries the white goddess, the new moon, mother of rain and rivers, waterfalls and floods." My hands are on his shoulders. "The mover of tides." I curl my hands around his neck. "First mother, full of shadows, keeper of the three stones."

"Lucy?"

I am wrapping him in my legs and pulling him close. "She of the rainbow, consort of K'inich Ahau." I am kissing his face. "He of the generations descends to the jaguar throne." He is kissing my face. "The bride and the groom point to one another. The right hand seals the marriage."

He of the Generations wrapped his hands about the waist of She of the Rainbow and began kissing her neck, and I felt wetness in his eyes. "Why are you crying?" I am holding his face. He weeps and I am kissing his tears. "She of the Rainbow, the portal, points to her husband, lord of fire." And now we are moving. "He points to the goddess of water, goddess of the moon. Its finishing comes into being. She enlarges. She fills the evening with light. They take! They point! To the Upperworld! To the Upperworld!"

And so that moonlit night, She of the Moon, weaver of dreams—her nightshirt a jumble—wove her own dreams and his dreams too.

20

I awoke the following morning to the sound of a ringing bell dangling from a vendor's cart outside the window. I didn't know where I was. Am I in the prison? I looked at a clock nearby and saw that it read five-thirty. Then I remembered, dimly. I began to recall glimpses from the night before. I assessed objectively that I had not been dreaming when the white goddess pointed to He of the Finishing, her husband; when She of the Moon made vows with He of the Sun, K'inich Ahua before the jaguar throne. They had done things.

I rose, dressed, and left the bedroom quietly. I sat momentarily at the kitchen table where, the night before, Leo had waved his fork speaking of Bartolome de Las Casas. Where was Leo? Why did he leave without me? I pleaded with him to take me with him.

It took two cups of coffee before my head cleared enough to realize I must go immediately. I must take the first bus back to Tegucigalpa with or without Leonardo. I grabbed only my backpack, abandoning my other things, and left the house. Outside, in the gated courtyard, I found the front gate locked and bolted with a padlock that could be opened only with a key, which I did not possess. I was locked in. In that moment I felt of being forever and always locked in.

Standing in the courtyard, powerless to escape, I saw on the corner table the bonsai tree I had given James a year before, its leaves withered and the pot cracked. Only a single small patch of green remained amid all that withering death. I wanted it to live. So I picked it up, my eyes wet and my nose running, and pulled it from the broken pot. Cutting wire through blurry wet eyes, I transplanted the struggling tree to another unbroken pot and pruned the dead branches with my damascene knife, the same knife I once used to peel a mango. Then I collapsed in a ball by the gate, my face in my knees, and sobbed. A stray dog sniffed at me through the iron bars. I cursed the gate and the dog too. I cursed the ground I sat upon. The world was not a better place with a missionary like me.

I pressed the blade of the knife against the translucent skin of my wrist. What are those white ridges? Tendons? Which are the veins? Arteries? Are those blue tentacles inside my skin little rivers mighty enough to drain the life out of a person? I wondered if it hurt when a knife pierced the flesh. I thought it would if you went slowly, as I would, since I am coward. Then I thought, If you go fast you would probably not feel as much pain. I thought, But what if I use the knife, cut my wrists badly and not die? I would probably only cripple my hand so I could no longer write. I then abandoned thoughts of cutting the wrists and wondered if instead the length of the blade might reach my heart. If I plunged it there and if I scored a direct hit, the blade, which is narrow, might at best puncture the heart. But it would not strike a mortal blow. My heart would bleed and bleed and struggle to keep pumping, until finally it would collapse and give up. How do people know what to do amid such quandaries?

I sat on the ground of my prison, the bonsai transplanted and the dog sniffing other trails, and dropped my head in my knees. It felt like the worst day of my life. I had lost all sense as to how to measure such things, and then I felt a hand upon my back. I looked up. James was kneeling and turned me to face him. He hoisted me to my knees and he held me, knee to knee. After a minute he whispered, "Your father is on the phone." I stood without answering, brushed the gravel from my pants, and went inside. He followed.

My father asked all the things any father would ask a daughter who had spent a night in prison after confronting a murdered man in an archaeological dig and then being accused of the crime. "What are your plans?"

Plans? I told him I planned to stay in Copán only long enough to complete my story. After that I had no plans, I said. Maybe I would visit them in Peru. He asked, as he always did when we spoke on the phone, if I wanted to hear the scripture verse he had read that morning. And, as I always did, I said yes. " 'I am being found by people who were not looking for me. To them I have said, I am here.' That's from Isaiah, Lu. Chapter sixty-five, verse one." We said our good-byes and I handed the phone to James.

"He wants to talk to you." I heard only James's part of the conversation, and that only in broken sentences: "No, we haven't talked . . . Yesterday . . . She hadn't told me that." They said their good-byes and I loaded my backpack.

James leaned against the kitchen counter, his legs crossed, sipping his coffee. I sat at the table, my backpack in my arms. "Your father told me you were planning to leave today."

I didn't answer.

"Lucy, why are you planning to leave today?" He slid into the chair beside me.

My throat tightened. My face felt hot. I stiffened. "I need to get back to my real life."

"What's your real life?"

I pushed hair from my face and wiped my eyes with my wrist. "I need your keys. I can't get out."

"What's going on?"

"I have a story to write. I'm a journalist. That's my real life." I stood up. "I have two hundred lines to write. I need quotes. I've seen a lot of things on this trip, but I haven't seen the tomb. I'll rephrase that. I haven't seen the tomb without a dead blue body hanging over it." I held out my hand. "Can I have your keys?"

"I'll take you."

"I'm not asking you to take me."

He sighed. "I don't want you going there alone."

"I am not a prisoner anymore. Doña Nora set me free. Have you forgotten? You can't keep me here."

He stood. "You don't you remember anything about last night, do you?"

I turned away, then back again. "How much do you require? Must you take everything? You've made the missionary Jezebel. Take a bow for the jaguars." He stood motionless. I went to the bedroom to collect my things. I stopped to face him before closing the door. "Do you want to know what is the worst of it? My family still loves you." I shut the door behind me.

Without asking for or receiving permission James followed me. He found me kneeled on the floor piling things into my suitcase. He sat on the edge of the bed, elbows on his knees and shook his head. "I am glad you are here with me, even if it is the end."

"Oh. It isn't the end. The end happened in an airport."

He nodded and sighed and turned his face to the window. "Hope fails sometimes, Lucy." He looked back at me. "What a story, huh?"

"You'll get a copy when it's published."

"I mean our story." He paused. "The one you will write about us someday. I am wondering how it will end. You've always been bent on resolution."

"Resolution doesn't always make for the truest plot."

He stood and dug into a pocket and pulled out his keys. He tossed them onto the bed. "I wouldn't keep you here against your will." He lowered his head. "Lucy"—he hesitated and cleared his throat—"I couldn't face another lifetime being a disappointment to that man, Lucy." He opened the door.

"Your father?"

"No." He faced me. "Your father."

The sun poured through the louvered glass window

breaking into shards of light that pierced the place where a minute before he was sitting. I wasn't sure in that moment how the story would end. I wasn't sure if the story even had a script. I wondered if the story was somehow bigger than the script.

"I'm going to make scrambled eggs," he said. "After breakfast we can go to the tomb. I'll give you your quotes. Whatever you want." He shut the door behind him.

My eyes burned. I went to the washroom to splash water on my face. He may make me insane, but he wasn't going to make me old before my time. I pressed a towel into my eyes and found my cream that softens puffiness. I powdered myself. I painted my lips and combed out my hair and tied it in a ribbon and let some of it fall. There was a knock on the door and it opened slightly. "The eggs are ready." He did not look in. I lifted my head. I breathed deeply. I went to breakfast.

"You look pretty," he said. I didn't respond. I opened my napkin to my lap.

"Do you want salt? I didn't salt them," he said.

"Yes, please."

"Juice?"

"Yes, please."

"Are you going to marry the pilot?"

"His name is Larry."

"Are you going to marry Larry?"

I salted my eggs. "No."

We did not speak after that. My stomach ached, but I forced myself to eat. I would not give him my appetite. I would not let him take my ability to do my job.

"You're not eating much. You haven't eaten for two days. You must be hungry," he said. I carried my plate to the sink. He stood and carried his plate. I wondered what to do next. Walk to the door? Get out of the way? Turn around? Do the dishes? Cry? Hit him? Run? Grab the knife from the drying rack and run it through my heart, or his?

"I'll do these," I said, meaning the dishes. "You go get dressed."

He left and I did the dishes. I was swift and decisive with dishes. I finished them in no time. My chest tightened and my heart skipped a few beats. I thought, What if I drop dead? Then I thought, Don't die. Don't give him that.

I sat on the couch preparing my notes and flipped through the photos James had taken of Berto dangling over the tomb the morning we had found him. I recalled James snapping and snapping and here before my eyes were images of that bad dream: Berto's signature baggy pants, his rope belt and mud-caked boots, his toothless puckered cheeks and the blue streaking down the temples of his white hair. His face was dead as stone, his knees bony and arms flaking with blue. And those hands.

James appeared, refreshed and spirited and I gathered the photos into my sack. He joined me on the couch and saw in my notebook where I had written the day's assignment at the top of the page: Yax K'uk Mo'/James Fee/Final interview. Then he sprang from the couch and adjusted his ball cap. "You ready?" How was I supposed to answer that? He shoved his trowel into his back pocket.

We did not speak as we drove to the park. I did not return his glances. He pulled to the spot where we had parked many times before and he looked at me. He then grabbed the flashlight and slid out of the truck while I sat motionless. He walked to the passenger side and lowered his head to my window. "You coming?" I did not move. He leaned patiently against the truck tossing pebbles at a tree. He leaned a second time in my window. So I grabbed my pack and went forth to join him. He closed the door behind me.

I do not remember the steps we trod as we made our way across the path we had walked together so many times. Shadows from the rising sun summoned strange stone figures, these lost kings, whose mantles and scepters and dreams of immortality had long been carried off by time. They left such tantalizing clues. James went on and on in his matter-of-fact way about things such as the Long Count and baktuns and stable bone isotopes and mineral signatures. He conveyed it all in such a spellbinding way. What tireless unrelenting force of the universe conspired to bring us together, back to this place of ghosts and lost dreams?

We were circling Altar Q and all discussion turned to the passing of the manikan scepter and the baktun completion. "What Yax K'uk Mo' started, the other kings built upon until the will of the ancestors deemed their kingdom would stand no more." That is, until James Fee reclaimed it from the ages.

The dew still wet under foot, we stood on the west face of the altar directly in front of Temple 16 where Yax K'uk

Mo' was buried.

"Altar Q is the key to understanding the place of Yax K'uk Mo' in the Copán dynasty," James said. He pointed out that the west face carried the image of K'inich Yax K'uk Mo'—the first king—handing the kingly scepter to Yax Pasah—the last king. "It is a symbolic gesture legitimizing the final king's reign as well as the reign of all the kings in between. It links them all to the founder." He spoke as he always did, so easily and authoritatively. I took my notes as I always did as well, with similar ease and authority. "The hieroglyphic inscription on the top of Altar Q says that this is the stone of K'inich Yax K'uk Mo'.'"

We circled it and James lifted his cap, replaced it, and folded his arms as he highlighted the four squat pillars upon which the altar rested. "These pillars imply a funerary location of someone buried in the Acropolis. You'll see on the burial slab when we go in the four cylinders support it the same way." He paused. "The implication is"—James frequently used the phrase—"since it is placed in front of Temple 16, one of the most massive structures on the site; and since it mimics a burial slab; and since it indicates it is the stone of Yax K'uk Mo'; we took a pretty good guess that Temple 16 was the funerary temple of the founder. Altar Q was *his* monument. So we tunneled in." In his mesmerizing way, James went on to explain the baktun completion that marked the reign of Yax K'uk Mo'. "A baktun is a four-hundred year cycle calculated with a 360-day year in the Long Count." The Long Count was the Maya calendar system, the way they kept track of linear time. "The Maya estimated time began in 3114 B.C., which initiated the first baktun, and according to their calendar, it says that such-and-so many years in the future the 13th baktun will end."

"The world ends?"

"The inscription doesn't say anything that will happen on that day. The whole point of it is to project a date into the distant future, basically to anchor the inscription that they're talking about. It would be the equivalent of me saying that in seven years it will be the end of the second millennium. And that's a pretty safe prediction."

"How old will we be?" I thought for a minute.

"It's irrelevant."

James continued to explain that Yax K'uk Mo' conquered Copán at the beginning of the tenth baktun, which gave the new king a critical advantage since the turn of a baktun was deemed a sacred moment and carried cosmic significance for the Maya. Yax K'uk Mo' took the manikan scepter and arrived in Copán from the power center in central Mexico called Teotihuacán, where he had received the emblems of office along with the blessing of this "undisputedly most powerful theater in Mesoamerica." He traveled 153 days 'from the west' until he arrived from Mexico to found the dynasty at Copán in C.E. 435. His arrival carried cosmic importance because it occurred within a few years of the baktun completion. "Yax K'uk Mo' was determined to take Copán from being a backwater village to become a major player among the Maya city-states," he said. The establishment of the new dynasty was a magnificent historical occasion, and Yax K'uk Mo' marked it by building and dedicating new monuments. One such monument was the ball court. Every ritual center in the Maya kingdom had to have a ball court because the ball game was the means through which the king kept the stars and planets in their proper orb. "The implication is"—the man's entire world was built upon implications —"Copán, having become a premier ritual center, had similarly become the dynasty of Yax K'uk Mo'. This is evident in the cosmological imagery he had carved on the ball court, the recording of inscriptions, the stucco decoration, and the architecture styles, which are all very new, very different and very notable. He seems to be the first one at Copán to record inscriptions in stone. This is how he marked the new beginning of his dynasty, the rising city-state of Copán. Interestingly, he died only two years later as an old man."

There we were, standing at that square monument that offered so many clues while James explained how these clues conveyed the story of Copán's founding king and how it thus pointed to his tomb deep within the structure behind us. "Altar Q is set upon four squat stone pillars like a funeral bier—that was the first clue. It was commissioned by Copán's last king, Yax Pasah, and depicts all sixteen kings, four on each side, in conjunction with the four cardinal directions." Furthermore, the image of Yax K'uk Mo' on Altar Q depicts him wearing a pectoral, a single jade bar across his chest. He held a shield with his right arm, which James said suggested he was a left-handed warrior. "He drew his weapon with his left hand and warded off blows with his right, the parrying arm.

When we opened the tomb and examined the mortal remains we noticed a series of combat-style fractures. Most notably the bone of the right forearm had suffered a serious break that hadn't healed properly. A fractured right forearm is consistent with a parrying injury of a left-handed warrior." They also found a single jade bar in the tomb identical to the one Yax K'uk Mo' is shown wearing on here Altar Q. "There is one other thing," he said. "Hieroglyphic inscriptions have referred to Yax K'uk Mo' as the 'lord of the west.' Altar Q also says that, after 153 days of travel, he 'rested his legs' at Copán. So we believe that after his pilgrimage to Teotihuacán he then traveled 153 days from the west until he arrived from Mexico to found the dynasty at Copán. Based upon all these factors, we concluded that this had to be the tomb of the dynasty's founder." He lifted his cap. "The goggles are interesting and important evidence too," he said.

We were now talking about goggles, those saucers about the eyes of the king as depicted in the extant effigies that, in my mind, gave him a look I likened to Bart Simpson. Only he, of all sixteen kings, was depicted as wearing goggles, James said. "Yax K'uk Mo' wasn't buried with goggles. We didn't find goggles in the tomb. But he is portrayed wearing those goggles in the iconography of later rulers. Those, along with his filed teeth, lent further evidence," James said, "that Yax K'uk Mo' arrived from Teotihuacán. We also found pots in the tomb that clearly come from Teotihuacán. But, then again, you can't go by the pots."

"The hallmark of warrior kings," I said dryly. "They

come, they see, they conquer."

James looked at me quizzically. He explained, which I already knew—that before Yax K'uk Mo' asserted leadership around C.E. 400, Copán had been dominated by feuding warlords. He probably married one of their daughters to solidify control and consolidate his power. "The evidence suggests he did so with terror and bloodshed," he said. "We don't know the exact sequence of what happened, but he had established his rule in C.E. 426 near the time of the baktun completion."

At the end of another baktun, some four hundred years and fifteen kings later, the Copán dynasty collapsed, "as if the gods themselves had determined it was time for the dynasty of Yax K'uk Mo' to come to an end."

The discovery of the tomb of Yax K'uk Mo' was "terribly important," he said, for the larger discipline of anthropology in the New World because it proved that the claims made by later kings about the life and times of their founding king were based in history and not in mythology. "When all was said and done, he rested his legs at Copán, according to the inscriptions. So, yes, I guess you could say he came, he saw and he conquered."

21

We entered the passageway to the tomb where we had walked one other time, before the blue body, before the jail, before She of the Rainbow and K'inich Ahau. James repeatedly told me to "stay close." Almost in spite of my otherwise sniveling dependence upon going wherever James led when we were in the tunnels, I found myself instinctively sniffing about as a reporter on other trails. Why would someone bring a dead body through this labyrinth—or, at the very least, an incapacitated body? James walked slowly, switching the flashlight to my feet as we made our descent through the same undulating tunnels and around the same dark corners we had traversed what felt like an eternity before. We lowered our heads. We stepped over holes. We navigated footing. We scraped jagged walls. James was more relaxed then I would have expected, given the circumstances. He assured me security had been doubled and that there was nothing to fear despite the killer remaining at large. James was always relaxed in the tunnels. And I was not afraid. I was, on the other hand, hounded. How had a dead body been navigated through all this? Or maybe the victim had been led here, and then murdered on site? Why here, in the location of the archaeologists' most recent "tantalizing" discovery that had commanded international attention? Why hang the victim, as opposed to leaving him dead on the ground? Why take the trouble to paint him blue? Why the day of the press conference? I did not speak these questions. I simply followed James, my head tilting oddly at various points for second looks at this difficult step or that precarious drop. I lingered a bit longer when we came upon the same wheelbarrow we had passed the last time. Could the ropes we saw bundled in it have been a hammock?

How? How? Unanswered questions assaulted my mind as, at last, we came upon the tomb chamber and I was compelled to refocus. The site had been cordoned off as a "crime scene," but James ignored it. As he did last time, he told me to hold the flashlight while he loosened the padlock. We entered the chamber and he flipped on the light. "Here," he said, extending a hand to secure my footing. We stood on the same spot where we had been when it all began with the sweeping pull of the tarp.

"Wait." He bent over and peeked under it. "No dead bodies." This stole a smile. He pulled back the tarp to expose the sunken chamber. There was the raised stone slab he had mentioned by Altar Q. The remains of Yax K'uk Mo' himself had been removed for tests and preservation. James switched on the flashlight to point out a piece of jade that lay near where the skull had been. "These are his ear flares." He passed the light over something else. "This is his pectoral," the jade bead adornment engraved with a woven mat design that Altar Q depicts. "The image of Yax K'uk Mo' on Altar Q also shows him wearing ear flares like these"—he jiggled the light. I looked, but couldn't tell what I was seeing. "His teeth were filed to points and inlaid with jade. The fanged teeth and goggled eyes are Tlaloc imagery adopted by the Maya from Central Mexico. I told you that, didn't I?" He moved the light. "Here at the base is an early-classic cylinder tripod. It has residue inside, probably the remains of an ritual offering."

Sweat poured from our faces. My shirt was as wet as it had been that first day when we were stranded in the rain. "Where did they find my film cartridge?"

He moved the light. "Back in here." He pointed toward the corner near potsherds. "Mario pulled it out."

I leaned to get a closer look. "Did it damage anything?"

"Nothing of consequence." He switched off the flashlight. "Except you." He wiped the sweat from his face with the tail of his shirt. "Let's get out of here. We can do the interview outside where we can breathe."

The sun's early rays cast long shadows and the dew beneath our feet invigorated our steps. Dirtied and drenched in sweat after our trek to the underbelly of Temple 16, we ambled slowly in the brilliance of the morning's light. We found a cool spot to sit on a ledge north of the ball court. The breeze against our faces, we settled comfortably onto the shaded stone. I looked about me and wondered what stories lay hidden in these temple walls, what dreams had been born and then died here. Everything in this world reaches skyward, the temple pyramids, the stelae, the stairways. Each in its own way seems an attempt to reach the thirteenth level of the Upper World. The mountains swathed in clouds, the mist rising over the valley, the river in its settling movement, and the trees in the wind, each seemed to carry voices of ghosts from behind these fallen houses. They labored and vanished like a turn in the road. I loved these mountains. Yet sadness had come over me.

I pulled from my backpack the photos of Berto and looked at them again with reference to the passage we had just traversed. I looked and looked. The answer to the questions that hounded my mind, I knew, was in those photos. I pondered why James refused to talk about the crime.

James stretched his legs and crossed them, pulling off his baseball cap, and he ran his fingers through his hair the way that had become so familiar to me. "You want your tape recorder? How do you want to do this?" He folded his hands casually on his lap.

How did I want to do this? That was an altogether different story to tell. But that was not this story. This story, it seemed, was writing itself.

I sat cross-legged, facing him, brushed the hair from across my cheeks and began the interview.

"I don't want to record it or write. Just tell me the story of the kings."

We sat beneath the shade of the deciduous forest while James spoke of the great Maya kings—their beginnings and endings—and I listened for the story. He said that Yax K'uk Mo' saw clearly saw the role of the king as the divine sustainer of planetary movements and procurer of sacrifice and therefore, as he put it, was "big on blood rituals." The successors of Yax K'uk Mo' did not lack good ideas about how to continue the tradition. "Especially Yax K'uk Mo's son," who James said "went bananas." He lifted his cap. Under Yax K'uk Mo' Copán prospered as a cohesive political unit in the Middle Classic phase, "though several kings surpassed him in greatness and influence." The key transitional figure that took Copán from the Middle Classic to the Late Classic period was the twelfth king, Smoke Imix God K. Having reigned for sixty-seven years, he was considered Copán's greatest king. Copán reached statehood under him and the population reached between 8,000 and 12,000 by the end of his reign in C.E. 695. "We can infer he had wisdom and staying power," James said. "He was tenacious and well-loved."

Not to be out-done, 18 Rabbit emerged, acceding twenty-one days after Smoke Imix died, and reigned as Copán's thirteenth king for forty-three years. Under 18 Rabbit, James said, "Copán reached new levels of aesthetic and technical sophistication in the arts." In keeping with kingly tradition, he assigned himself supernatural authority and made sure his people understood the cosmos in a way that perpetuated his unique position. 18 Rabbit was particularly active in performing rituals, James said, and built a third version of the ball court—the one over our shoulders, which James repeatedly emphasized was integral to upholding the king's divine status as keeper of the planetary movements. Some think 18 Rabbit was on a journey in search of captives to sacrifice for the dedication of his ball court when he was captured in C.E. 738 and beheaded at Quiriguá, a fiefdom located in present-day Guatemala. "I'll take a sip of that." He pointed to the water bottle. "18 Rabbit's beheading was a seminal event for Copán, but you know that." He paused and pulled the tail of his shirt to wipe the sweat from his face. Then he said, "Why are you going home today?"

"I don't want to talk about that right now."

"Why did you say that to your father? We haven't talked about it."

"Why are you asking me this? I'm interviewing you."

"You're not running your recorder. You're not taking notes. Why did you tell your father you were leaving today?"

"Your job is to answer my questions. What happened after 18 Rabbit lost his head?"

"I want you to stay another day, at least."

"What did the people think when their great god-king didn't come through?"

He sighed and tucked in his shirt. "The death of any king had a destabilizing effect on the society. The loss of 18 Rabbit was all the more traumatic because he lost his head to a subservient fiefdom. It was humiliating, to say the least."

His successor, Smoke Monkey, Ruler 14, thought he could rally the spirits of the people if he shared power with lower lords and decentralized his rule. So he built what the archaeologists call the Mat House, Structure 22A, "in proximity to Structure 22, which was 18 Rabbit's sacred mountain." James emphasized that the two structures served two very different purposes and highlighted the distinction between these two dissimilar kings. "18 Rabbit's Structure 22 rests on the mountain top overlooking the valley of maize, with two large molars flanking the entrance representing the mouth of the god-king himself, who communed with his ancestors there," he said. "The Mat House, in contrast, shifts the focus from the king to the people. Smoke Monkey still reigned at the top of the heap, but the emblematic mat weave design over both sides of the entrance represent unity and people power. Plus, he didn't place his own image on the stela in front of the building, which says something. Despite an otherwise lack-luster career, Smoke Monkey's strategy enabled the city to survive the trauma of losing 18 Rabbit. His reign lasted eleven years."

"Might one say Smoke Imix would be like Ronald Reagan and Smoke Monkey like Harry Truman and 18 Rabbit like Bill Clinton?"

He looked at me blankly. "Political dissent notwithstanding, kind of."

He went on to describe how Smoke Shell, Ruler 15, feeling confident that the good will of the people had been revived thanks to Smoke Monkey's Mat House, went in the opposite direction of his predecessor's "people power" and reasserted the divine role of the god-king.

He ordered the construction of Structure 26 and the Hieroglyphic Stairway, dedicating it to the great king Smoke Imix, hoping to rekindle the spirit of the glory days of that great god-king. "It was like a revivalist movement,"

James said.

"Images of all the kings abound on glyphs through-out the stairway and all are carrying shields. Some hold ropes, which represent the binding of captives for sacrifice. Some are wearing headdresses and holding lances. Smoke Shell intentionally portrayed Copán's kings as great warriors."

The stairway itself represents an elaborate inverted jaguar head, and all the kings on the various inscriptions are being belched forth from the open mouth of this beast, his lower jaw at the top. The stairway is flanked on its four corners and on the front and back doorways with large goggle-eyed masks of the Tlaloc jaguar deity, the patron god of the warrior and his sacrifices. The whole complicated picture is meant to symbolize that the rulers of Copán were consummate warriors, and the procurers of victims for sacrifice.

Just south of the stairway, he said, Smoke Shell added Structure 230, "a nasty structure" decorated with human skulls and fleshless human bones carrying the glyph sign *na*, for 'house'—the 'house of human bones and skulls.' "It was the locus for sacrificial rituals, for storage, dismemberment, embalming and other manipulations of human remains."

"Manipulations?"

"In a manner of speaking." He looked at his watch. "You getting tired?"

"No."

He rubbed his eyes. Wearily, he spoke of the irony of the Hieroglyphic Stairway being the only major structure the Maya at Copán hoped would be an everlasting monument to the glory of the warrior kings, and it was the first to collapse. "The fill they used to construct it was the weakest we've found in Copán. The stones were set in loose dry earth and were never completely consolidated." Smoke Smell's reign lasted about fourteen years. James looked at me. He said, "He would be George Steinbrenner," and we laughed.

"Carlos told me that toward the end of the eighth century the warfare changed and the Maya became more concerned with taking captives for sacrifice than with political expansion."

"By the time we get to the last king, Yax Pasah, in 763, things were unraveling at Copán," he said. The population was increasing and the urban nucleus expanding, swallowing up arable land that should have been used for farming. Added to this, Copán had become a regional center for the production of Copador polychrome pottery, which, he said, meant more and more people were coming and going to the Valley, including non-Maya peoples. "This disseminated Copán's hold on the hinterland sites. It was losing its own power hold of centralized rule from within," and, he said, Yax Pasah reacted "with extreme measures." He undertook massive renovations of Temple 11 and Temple 16. The facade of Structure 11 was the largest anthropomorphic figure ever carved in the Maya area, with an enormous cosmogram on the north face that sent the message that the king was the one who controlled supernatural forces of the world. The renovation of Temple 16, where Yax K'uk Mo' was buried, was intended to mimic Smoke Shell's Hieroglyphic Stairway, only Yax Pasah's version was a gruesome affair. "It became the most gory temple in Copán," James said. "There is a final-phase stairway that's got the big skull rack displaying the skulls that came from sacrificial victims mounted on poles. Really nasty." He said Yax Pasah took desperate measures in the effort to try and keep things together.

His greatest gift to us however, James said, was Altar Q. He called it "a compact version of the Hieroglyphic Stairway" since it carries the portraits of Copán's sixteen kings, fifteen of whom are seated on their name glyphs. Yax Pasah's glyph meant 'lord.' "Only Yax K'uk Mo' was not seated atop his name glyph," James said. "It took us the longest time to figure out who this guy was." Finally, the epigraphers discovered that his name was in his headdress, the combination of the quetzal and the macaw. "So Yax K'uk Mo', with his name in his hat, passes the scepter of office to Yax Pasah. The first king anoints the last.

"It had become evident that things were getting pretty messy under Yax Pasah. At the central axis of Temple 16 he constructed the world's largest jaguar Tlaloc visage surrounded by ropes and a large skull, reminiscent of Structure 230, that gory building used for 'manipulations', " James said. "By the end of Yax Pasah's reign, Temple 16 was the single most gruesome temple ever built in Copán."

I reminded him he still hadn't answered my question about Carlos's comment.

He paused and rubbed his face. "It is clear the entire Maya area was deeply involved in warfare toward the end, as Carlos said. Tikál was trying to hold its own against

Calakmul, and the conflict spilled over all the Maya lowlands. It seems to have gotten worse rather than better
toward the end, and I now think warfare was a major factor in the collapse of the Maya civilization at the end of
the Classic period. Everyone was involved in it. Like it or
not, they got swept up in war. I have come to believe that
the intense warfare of the late Classic period did have a
cataclysmic effect on the fall of Copán's dynasty. Other
things did too, such as the loss of usable farming land
and deforestation. But expanded warfare had more of an
impact than I had previously thought."

He took off his cap and wiped his brow and took a swig
of water. "Their cosmology of the king-as-god in the end,
couldn't provide the internal stability needed to sustain
unity in the face of warfare and local rivalries. That, plus
environmental deterioration, brought about the internal
collapse of Copán. The last inscription we have is on an
unfinished monument called Altar L, commissioned by
a pretender to the throne. The fact that his accession
monument was never finished shows the chaotic political
environment of the moment."

"So Yax K'uk Mo's dynasty lasted a baktun?"

"It came within thirty years of a baktun completion."

"Did the Maya cannibalize themselves?"

He looked at me.

"Can we talk about something else?"

"One more question." James sighed. "Why did Yax K'uk
Mo' choose the Copán Valley in the first place to establish
his regal ritual center?"

James Fee perked up, answering happily despite his

fatigue. He liked talking about the geological composition of the Copán Valley and its "distinct environmental zones." He spoke in a gentle monotone, with lavish descriptions the flowed like a peaceful river from his ocean of knowledge. Steep hills. Gently rolling foothills. Ancient high river terraces. Fertile low river terraces. The floodplain. The way he said "ancient high river terraces" and "fertile low river terraces"—particularly the word "terraces"—made me wish I had my pen. He described the sacred importance of the hills and caves, which were considered the passageway to the Underworld. "The bat is the denizen of sacred caves," he said. "That is why the hieroglyph that names the ancient kingdom of Copán is the leaf-nosed bat." He frequently attached the words "that is why" to what he was explaining and this reassured me. It made me feel safe in this otherwise bewildering world. He mentioned the granite outcrop in the eastern valley and the kaolin used for pottery in the north. He made a passing reference to small limestone outcrops and the geographically stable green volcanic tuff. I liked the way he said those words. "The Maya used it for their dressed stone," he said. "That is why so many sculptures have remained in such good condition." He spoke of jade and obsidian and the hydration layer on obsidian tools that helped archaeologists date things.

He made a clear distinction between the Copán Valley and the Copán pocket, a 'pocket' being a tributary formed by a river in sharp descent, "cutting through deep escarpments before leveling out." When he said the word "escarpments" I wanted to write it down. He said people wrongly refer to the 'valley' when they really mean the 'pocket.' I thought it must annoy him when people did that. "The Principal Group and adjacent settlements are in the 'pocket.' " I wanted to write down "adjacent settlements." The various pockets in the valley contained some of the richest soil in Central America, high in nitrogen content, which is optimal for growing tobacco. "The Maya were big smokers," he said. "The flooding of the bottomlands renewed the soil, which was fertile to begin with." But it was when he said, "the rolling hillsides and the alluvial bottomlands made the pocket an attractive location to settle" that I started to weep.

It was the words "alluvial bottomlands." I wanted to write them down. I wanted to hear him say them again. I looked into the face of James Fee, bronzed by the sun with his brooding eyes and sculpted brow. I measured the cadence of his voice and felt mesmerized by its gentility. When he said "alluvial bottomlands" I realized I loved his National Geographic voice. I thought, What if I never hear the words "alluvial bottomlands" again from that voice? What if I never again hear him talk about limestone outcrops or green volcanic tuff? Dressed stone or the obsidian hydration layer? Or about alluvial plains and the river's descent through deep escarpments, the difference between a pocket and a valley? What if this is the last interview I conduct with James Fee? What if I never again see that chiseled brow, that hair, those Jesus eyes? What if I walk away with two-hundred lines and never come back to this place that feels to me so much like home?

I looked at him and he looked at me. Everything I

wanted to become rose up into my face. Everything he had been and wanted to become, rose up in his. He was saying something about the pocket being distinguished by the bottomlands and expanses of foothills with steep slopes higher up, and tears rolled down my face. I wiped my cheek. His eyes never left mine. I knew, as he knew, that everything between us hung in this moment. "The foothills contain ancient alluvial terraces," he said. "The bottomlands are like alluvial fans formed by tributary streams"—he lifted his hand and held it to me. "The diverse land-forms, soil types, and distinct precipitation regimes of the Copán drainage basin made for a great deal of variation in the pre-Maya vegetation cover." Without a conscious act of will I found myself there, under his arm, my wet face against his, my tears in his beard. "The sheer beauty of the lush and tropical bottomlands, defined by crests of mountains and rolling hills" —he lifted my chin—"made it a desirable location for an agriculture-based population."

Then he stopped talking about environmental zones. I remember little about what we did and said in the next moments. I touched a finger to his lips and closed my eyes. I listened to his breathing and felt the beating of his heart. His face smelled like sweat and Lifebuoy soap. I knew the smell of Lifebuoy soap from the barrels of supplies we received in the jungle. Lifebuoy soap came wrapped with birthday candles and peanut butter. His shirt smelled like pressed cotton. The string holding his sunglasses was tied in a square knot, the same knot Gabe had taught me to tie. Right over left, left over right, the strongest knot you'll ever tie, Bu. Only my fingers on his beard and his touch of my hair, the smell of Lifebuoy soap hung over this moment. That, and my longing to hear the words 'alluvial bottomlands.'

22

"I think it was a woman."

He brushed his beard against my cheek. "You think who was a woman?"

"Whoever did it."

"Why do you think it was a woman?"

"I've been thinking."

"I don't want to talk about this, Lucy."

"Something happened to me while I was in the jail. I saw something I hadn't seen before, I mean, about God." I looked at James.

"Lucy, I don't want to talk about this." He slid a finger up the sleeve of my T-shirt.

"I called to him but he didn't answer."

"Who didn't answer?"

"God. It's like archaeology." He laughed out loud. I sat up straight. "He speaks when he is silent. You start with silence, don't you, in your work? You start with nothing and you dig. You build a story from what you find, backward to forward. That is where you begin, right?"

"Well, we start with dirt and mounds and an idea about what is likely to be buried there, but I see your point."

"You get clues. You piece them together. You see a picture. You see the Maya."

"Yes. We see the Maya. You're right," he said.

"When I was in the jail I was surrounded by voices. But the one voice I called to, didn't answer. Like when Jesus was dying. He was surrounded by voices, but the one he called to—God—didn't answer him. It's like an archaeological project."

"How is Jesus dying like an archaeological project?"

"What were the Maya trying to achieve through their sacrifices?"

"The gift of the blood nourished the gods. It satisfied their demands. You know all this."

"Is it fair to say the sacrifices were an attempt to be heard by the gods and move them to action?"

"It is fair to say that, yes."

"Is it fair to say the sacrifices were a gesture of longing?"

"Longing?" He rubbed his eyes. "I wouldn't say longing had a whole lot to do with it."

"But why else would they go to all the trouble? There was something inside them that wanted to touch the gods. The best way to do it, they thought, was to offer human blood. Isn't that an expression of longing?"

He waved a hand. "Okay. Longing. Fine."

"Was the sacrifice a means of resolution?"

"Only in so far as their deeming human blood the worthiest conduit to repay the debt owed to the gods to

perpetuate the cycles of life. Otherwise, I'd say no. Resolution was not the point."

"Okay, maybe not resolution."

He folded my fingers into his. "I thought journalists
were gifted with the ability to get to the point."

"Was it guilt that compelled the Maya to pull the hearts
out of their captives?"

"They offered the blood of the captives as a sacrifice to
the gods to maintain the dominance of the king, to keep
the planets in motion. I've already said that."

"So without the blood they—meaning the rulers—
sensed there was an impediment to winning the favor of
the gods. The Maya sacrificed who they could seize in
war and felt the need to appease the gods with more and
more blood, yeah?"

"Close enough."

"I sat in the jail and God didn't speak, which made me
think that maybe God's silence is telling a story another
way, backward to forward. It's like archaeology. Archaeology is about finding the story out of the dirt that the
Maya left behind, backward to forward. It's not just dirt.
It's evidence of a narrative.

"That's why I think it was a woman. I think this murder-
slash-sacrifice is telling the story about the one who did
it, backward to forward. Don't you think?"

"Does it matter what I think?"

"What do you think?"

"I think I don't want to spend what little time we have
dealing with a blue sacrificed body. We are working on it.
The police are working on it. It's not your problem, Lu.

How long are you staying? What are we going to do? Can we talk about that? That's what I want. That's what I think." He rubbed his beard. "But something tells me you have other thoughts in mind."

"Well, in a way, it is my problem. Because our talking about what we are going to do relates to coming to terms with who did this."

"Why?"

"Because in the story I am hearing you are the antagonist." He looked at me equally alarmed and bewildered. "You start with what you know, then move backwards.

"When we were making our way to the tomb I couldn't shake the question about how a dead body could have been navigated through these tunnels. So I wondered if Berto been led there first and then murdered on site? But then I wondered why *there*—why in the location of the archaeologists' most treasured discovery, and one that commanded international attention? And when we were in the tomb I couldn't help wondering why the killer suspended the victim over the tomb, rather than simply leaving him dead on the ground? And why paint him blue? Why the day of the press conference?

"That's what we know. The body was either led through the tunnels then killed, or killed before the tunnels and carried through them. The target location had been the tomb of Yax K'uk Mo' and rather than risk damaging the site that the killer had to know you cherished, she went to great lengths to suspend the victim over the site, that is, after she painted him blue."

"You still haven't told me why you think it is a woman."

"Because she left her story behind her. The sacrifice suggests she is wanting to move cosmic forces to action. She is expressing a gesture of longing. She is asking for the favor of the gods. It's a well-known fact that women are more religious than men."

James sighed.

"Whoever sacrificed the victim wanted appeasement. Women regularly feel such things, especially Honduran women."

"How could a woman get the body through the tunnels?"

"Regardless of how the body made it through the tunnels, whoever got it there knew the way. And only a few people know how to access the tomb of Yax K'uk Mo', Berto being one of them. Therefore, the implication is (as you yourself so often say), that whoever did it is someone who is closely connected to your work.

"There's something else." I pulled the pictures of the body from my backpack. "I was looking at these this morning." I flipped through the photos and stopped at the image of the bound arms. "Look at the hands." James took the photo and examined it. "When you and I were locked inside the grounds that day and Berto unlocked the gate, as he was flipping through the keys I noticed his fingers were bent and crippled from arthritis. Those aren't the same hands. Those fingers aren't bent the same way." I looked at him. "Didn't Berto say something about being eight minutes older than a brother? I think the person hanging here is Berto's twin brother, and that whoever did this wanted us to think it was Berto." I paused.

"This is the story I am hearing. Someone closely related to Berto, who knew about Maya rituals and had access to the tunnels used this moment to invoke the only power she had. She understood the value of the tomb, so did not damage it. She got into the tunnels with someone who had a key and she was outraged enough to paint a dead man blue. And she wanted us to think it was Berto.

"The most telling part of this, to me anyway, is that she waited until the day of the press conference to make her statement. The timing would hurt you more than anyone. That is the story she is telling.—Oh, and she had dandruff, which explains the soapy smell and the blue."

He stared incredulously. "Dandruff?"

"I faintly recognized that soapy smell inside the tomb, that morning we found him, along with all those other smells. Then, in the jail, I remembered what it was. When Gabe and I were in high school, he contracted an infection on his skin and the doctor told him to rub on Selsun Blue, dandruff shampoo. Gabe used to rub it all over his arms and chest and back and let it soak in before showering. That was the soapy smell I recognized in the tomb. Selsun Blue. That's what she used to paint him. But it hadn't soaked in, the way Gabe's did, which means he must have been dead before she covered him with it."

James groaned. He looked at me wearily.

"Every mystery writer knows that the only way to solve a murder is to reconcile motive, means and opportunity. The motive was to hurt you. The means would have been access to the tunnel, which Berto had. And opportunity points to the evening before the press conference when the grounds would have been empty. Except that you and I made an unexpected visit to the tomb. Did Berto ever say where he was when we found he was not at the gate and so we were locked inside? Where was he?

"I remember when I bought yuca from the vegetable lady the other day, she told me she worked on the grounds as a maid and she asked if I was going to 'the party.' She brushed dandruff from her shoulder."

23

Workers began to overtake the site and our solitude was overthrown. James heaved my pack over his shoulder and said, "Let's get out of here." We mounted the hillside to depart when Virgilio Fuentes, the park overseer, intercepted us. He wanted to speak with James, as everyone always wanted to speak with James whenever they would happen to catch him walking the grounds. He chatted with Virgilio while I tried to pull my hand from his, but he would not release me. James held my hand as I turned in one direction, while he faced the other direction to speak with Virgilio.

I didn't know what Virgilio wanted. I know only that he went on and on. I felt unsettled and grieved. Why would a woman commit murder to humiliate James?

Freed from Virgilio at last, tension mounted in James's face. He led me into the wood and down the dirt road just west of the Principal Group. The canopy cooled us and the breeze lifted our faces, but James walked in a slow gate, with no leaning strides. Pebbles popped under foot. The moist air and singing birds elicited for me a calming effect and I settled. I said, "It's peaceful here. I feel human here."

"Humanness also involves chaos, Lucy," he said. Then he was silent.

The path opened to a small hidden plaza that I had not seen before. It was clearly a playing court with two alleyways, but not nearly of the size and extravagance of the Ball Court in the Principal Group. "Is this a ball court?"

"A Late Classic court. We think it was used only locally, not for state games. It had a dirt floor instead of stone or plaster." James didn't point, or turn, or lift his cap, or put hands on his hips the way he had done so naturally on other occasions. He walked on toward a winding path that picked up on the other end of the ball court.

"Were they rituals?"

"Were what rituals?"

"The games played here. Or was it pick-up ball?"

"We found evidence for a number of stone incense burners, but it was probably a local lineage court used for contests that were not of state-level importance." He spoke blandly. "It's strictly Late Classic, between C.E. 700 and 800."

"Where are you taking me?"

"We're almost there." On through the thick wood, batting away bugs and bowing beneath looping branches, the trail led to a hidden Ceiba tree, its root buttresses twelve feet high, twice the size of James when he stood between them.

"I come here when I want to be alone," he said. We sat at the base of the roots.

He pulled me between his legs and folded his arms about me from behind, the way the root buttresses enfolded him.

"What's the matter?" I said.

"I've made a mess of my life, Lucy, and other peoples' lives. You were right when you said I ruin lives." His eyes grew dark, his brow was in knots. "Several years ago I made a woman pregnant and she bore a son." He pressed his cheek against mine. "I have a son, Lu."

I turned to face him. "Paco."

He nodded.

"Paco's your son."

"Yes."

"He told me he didn't have a mother."

"He doesn't live with his mother. I took him away from his mother."

"Who is his mother?"

"Berto's niece. Her name is Yamileta. You bought vegetables from her at the air strip."

"The vegetable lady is Paco's mother?" He nodded. "Does he know you're his father?" He nodded again. "He calls you Mr. Fee." I turned away. Then, just as quickly, I turned my eyes back upon him. "He told me his father didn't want him to live with him. He said that's why you let him sleep in your bodega." James didn't speak.

"How old is he?"

"He's eight. I was twenty-five, just out of grad school." He explained, with less than polished diction and without his signature spell-binding effect, that he took the child from his mother after he was born, but at the time didn't feel capable of caring for him. So he asked his maid, Brigida, to keep him while he paid the boy's expenses. James had named him Tomás. Brigida nicknamed him Paco and that's what stuck. Over the years, as the boy got older, she would bring him to work at James's home. Paco began to perceive the unique connection between them, which James himself could not resist, and when Paco was about six he wanted to be around his father more. That's when he started sleeping in the bodega. The boy had been with Brigida when I visited Copán a year ago, which is why I didn't see him then. When James returned with me to Tegucigalpa and, later joined me in Wisconsin, Paco was with the maid.

"Why did you take him from his mother if you weren't going to raise him yourself?"

"I wanted him to have a better life than he would have had there, with Yamileta. But I also had to protect my work and my standing in the community. It seemed like a good solution at the time." He lowered his head. I felt myself stiffen. "Lucy," he said.

I stood. "The great founder of the Copán dynasty Yax K'uk Mo' is dead. His flesh and his bones rotted in the grave. Your son is alive." He didn't answer. I felt heat rise to my face. "Have you ever tucked him in at night? My God, James, he begged for money to bring me food in the jail. He *begged*." I backed away and turned around. Then I faced him again. "Do you love the Maya more than life?"

He stood and faced me and looked at me coldly. "Go back to Larry, Lucy. I won't stop you." He took three steps in the direction of the path and waved a hand. He turned to look at me again, then walked away. And the land of Maya tilted off course. A second time the warrior king attempted to control the forces of the world of his own making. He procured his sacrifice and there I sat alone on the ground. The moon, once bright and full of light, fell from her rising, faded and disappeared behind the sun. That is death. I closed my eyes.

Then, in the time it took for me to close my eyes and turn my head away from the direction of his leaving, he had returned. He held me. Lillian would have pronounced, "Rebirth!" The truth is, I can't say which of us was holding the other one up. It didn't matter. In that singular moment, cradled amid the roots of the giant Ceiba, we both knew who we were. We knew I would be his wife and the mother of the child born from seed he spilled with a woman he did not love. He had left her the way he once left me. He left his son too, the son who slept in his storage closet.

But the king did not fall. The stars stayed in their courses. He took my hand.

We trod the long path back through the wood to his truck. He said, "We need to go see Yamileta." After that we did not speak. Weariness settled over us, and James's brow was still in knots as he drove, knuckles white upon the wheel. The thought occurred to me: I shall be a mother now. This kind little boy who begged tortillas for me, is to be my son. Is this why I came back to this place? Because a shoeless boy needed a mother?

We would go to the woman I had spoken with on the airstrip, whose hair fell loose upon her crooked neck.

Who asked me about the party she knew she intended to hijack with a dead man painted blue. She would ruin the man who stole her child, the man in the truck sitting next to me. But he was not ruined. He found his way around her plan.

24

It took four-wheel drive to scale the rutted roads leading to the ridge called Brisas de Olancho. We pitched and bounced in silence on that unfinished road ascending the hill to the village of her home. James parked as close as he could to the village edge. We would have to walk the final distance. He paused before leaving the truck and looked at me. I said, "We have to give her the chance to keep him." He didn't answer. We met at the front of the truck and he led the way up the dusty road, beyond the pulperia with its carnival of accoutrements—soap, tooth-paste, Chiclets and lottery tickets. We passed a withered old woman sitting listlessly behind piles of pineapples and limes. We passed roosters and chickens and pigs and goats, dogs nursing puppies and flies on the dogs. Most of the homes had been built from hand-cut branches with grass and palm leaves for roofing. The "doors" were little more than cloth pulled back to reveal residents inside sitting on three-legged stools stoking fires built on dirt floors in the center of the home.

The typical Maya three stone arrangement served as their stovetop on which they boiled their beans and corn despite the oppressive heat.

Finally we came upon Yamileta's adobe hovel set off the road amid tall grass and wild palms. Rocks held its rusted tin roof in place and the only window showed a piece of cloth tied back with a string. A metal drum, fully exposed, held the household water supply. They kept it under a make-shift shelter near a basket on the ground. I recognized it as the basket I had helped ease off her head when she sold me the yuca at the airstrip. James pulled open the bamboo fence and let himself in. "Yamileta?" He looked at me and I followed. "Yami?" He called her in a familiar way and I wondered if this is what he had called her in the moment of passion that brought them this child.

Yamileta appeared at the door. She wore polyester that made her bosom bulge and her eyes seemed to drop to her cheeks, as if the sadness she carried was too great for a single pair of eyes. "Did you bring the pensión?" she said.

"That's not why I came." James paused. There was no love there, from her nor from him. He held my hand. Yami looked at me. "Páse." She nodded stiffly.

A hot plate on a wood table in the corner, a lawn chair, and a small refrigerator accounted for the sum total of her home furnishing—luxuries for a village such as this, the home that might have been Paco's. We stood in the dark, the air smelling of sweat and kerosene.

James said, "Yami, where's your father? I haven't seen

him since Berto died." He paused. "Your father is Berto's twin brother, right?" She nodded. Her eyes were as stone. "Yamileta, it wasn't Berto who died, was it? It was your father." She didn't speak. Berto appeared from behind a doorway. James turned away. "Oh God, Berto." He pulled off his baseball cap.

"I'm sorry, Señor Fee. Miss Lucy." He nodded to me.

"Do not speak, Tío." Yamileta threw him a glaring look. James shifted, rubbing the back of his neck. He sighed.

"Why, Yami?"

Yami. Is that the name she hears in her dreams? Does she dream of the one who took from her the only thing in this life rightfully belonging to a woman, her child? I saw two small girls outside hiding behind barrels. But her first born son she did not have.

Berto waved a stiff bony hand, shaking his head. "He was drunk. He drank all the time. He fell down."

James looked at Yami, who responded blankly, "That is when I ended him and decided to tie him up. He felt no pain."

James stood paralyzed. I stepped forward from behind him. "Why did you dress him to look like Berto?"

"My father only drank. He never worked. He used our wage on drink. We need Tio's pensión. We are moving to the north. Tio can work. If he is thought to be dead, we receive his pensión. Otherwise we have no money to move to the north." She looked at me coldly. "Now you know everything about your lover."

"What about the timing? You put him there the day of the press conference," I said.

"It was my surprise for the party."

"How did you get him through the tunnels? Why go to the trouble of hanging him? Why not simply dump him?"

"Tio carry him in the wheelbarrow." I threw James a knowing look, remembering the wheelbarrow we saw the morning as we groped out of the tomb. "I don't throw him in the tomb with the sacred bones because Tio won't do it. He said we hang him. He said he won't damage the work of El Doctor. Only for that, my dead father did not lay with the bones of Copán's great king."

She looked at James. "What do you want me to say, Mister Fee? My son calls you that, verdad? *Mister Fee*? Why did I paint blue my father and put him in your tomb?"

James looked at her sadly. "Yes."

"Blue is the color of the priests in Maya stories, yes? I hear many things while cleaning the rooms of the great archaeologists. The Maya painted human sacrifices blue."

"Yes, some."

"My dead father is my prayer. I am asking the gods to pity me." James didn't speak. "There is a stench before the great Mister Fee, the man who is the father of my only son." I looked at James. His eyes were wetting. "The sacrifice was for me and for you, Mister Fee, for your crimes against me and against your son."

James choked on his words. "Will you take the boy with you when you go to the north?"

She did not answer.

He heaved a weary sigh. "He could grow to know you, and to love you." He curled his cap in both hands. "I will bring him to you if that is what you want."

That broken sad woman in that moment held our world in her hands, dirty hands she had wiped on an apron when she handed me the yuca. I knew in that moment that I loved that boy. I knew James loved him too. We were bargaining his destiny as if his life was for barter like cacao beans or the feathers of the quetzal. James knew then he did not want to lose the son he had not yet claimed. Yamileta's hands tied her dead father's and then painted him blue and carried him, with Berto, in a wheelbarrow through the tunnels. She would not be Nobody. If no one else knew it, she would know. The blue body would ensure that the boy's father knew it too. Dear woman, take your son. We'll pray for him and for you too, that the wounds of our loss would heal your wounds from these failings. We will cry for him. Our hearts will be broken because of the love for a son we discovered too late. But we will find comfort knowing a mother has her son, that you are somebody.

"To him I am not his mother." Wetness covered James's face, sweat or tears I did not know. His life poured out of him as it did from my own face too.

"I won't fail him," he said.

"You have already failed him," she said.

I loved James then more than I had ever loved him. I saw the little boy climbing stacking shelves, his little head bobbing to read his father's name. Then his world collapsed. I saw that he needed me as much as this boy needed his father. I had looked at my veins with a knife in my hand. I had made calculations. I understood what would drive a woman to paint a dead man blue.

25

Goody said it's the in between times when a soul is won or lost. I reckon that the trip back from Yamileta's was one of those times. James and I did not speak. He drove in silence, jaw tight and eyes narrow, until he pulled up to his little house on the corner near the Quebrada. He turned off the engine, then sat. "James." He looked at me. "We have to find Paco." He stepped out of the truck without a word and unlocked the front gate. Then he walked to the house and unlocked the door. He returned to the truck, where I waited, and took his place behind the steering wheel, shutting the door behind him.

"What are you going to do?" I said.

"Dig."

"Don't you want to talk to Paco?"

He looked at me. "Don't tell me what to do, Lucy. He's *my* son." I sat momentarily, then pulled my backpack to my shoulder and opened the passenger door to leave. I thought to peek my head in the window to say something, but before I could speak James threw his baseball cap onto the passenger seat, turned the ignition and pulled away. The truck disappeared up the cobbled street and around a corner as I watched, alone, in stunned silence. I collected myself enough to enter the gate. That is when I found Paco waiting outside James's house.

"Where is Mr. Fee?" He looked at me with sullen eyes.

"Do you want some food? Juice?"

I prodded him in and closed the gate behind me.

"Where is Mr. Fee?"

"He said he went to dig."

Paco shook his head. "He is not digging."

I walked inside. He followed. "He told me he was going to dig. That is what he said. Do you want something to drink?" I pulled open the refrigerator.

"Are you going to leave, Miss Lucy?" He tugged at my elbow. "Are you going to leave, Miss Lucy?"

I stopped.

He shook his head as if the words were stuck to his tongue. "Go find Mr. Fee. He is not digging. Go find him, Miss Lucy."

I sat at the kitchen table. "Paco," I said, "whenever I find myself looking for Mr. Fee I end up losing myself."

Paco stood close so that we were eye to eye. He shook his head. "Tell him you are sorry, Miss Lucy. He'll forgive you."

"Sorry?" I laughed out loud.

His eyes narrowed. "You shamed him. You shamed him. He told you he's my papi and you shamed him."

"He hasn't treated you the way a papi should treat a son."

"Say you're sorry." He stiffened. "Say you're sorry, Miss Lucy."

I reached to him. He batted me away, tears falling down his cheeks. He turned away from me. "I wish you never came on the plane. I wish you were still in the jail." He looked at me coldly. "I hate you." He ran away. The door slammed behind him.

I stood, shocked, and then looked out the window. I sat down. Then I stood. What do I do? What am I doing here? What is happening? I grabbed my backpack. I dug out the water bottle, the same bottle James and I shared during the interview. I pulled out the tape recorder I had not used. I pulled out the camera, my notebooks. Before I reckoned with what I was doing, I had picked up the phone and found myself dialing Larry. I heard it ring on the other end and a chill came over me. I hung up. I dropped into a chair at the kitchen table, my head in my arms.

Then I lifted my eyes and dialed my brother Gabe, who picked up the phone on the third ring, as if he knew it would be me.

"Why did you ruin everything and get married?"

"What's going on, Bu. You still at Fee's?"

"You and I were supposed to live out our days together. Now you're married and I'm alone."

"Pack your things leave. Go home. Take a bus."

I didn't respond.

"Can you do that, Bu? Can you do it right now?"

I didn't respond.

He paused.

"There's your answer."

"You still ruined everything."

"Bu, why does it take heaven and earth to move either one of you two when it comes to each other? Can you answer me that?"

Leonardo says I don't always understand what I want. He says that sometimes I need someone to tell me what I want, but that I am stubborn and won't listen to anybody. I do not deny it. The single exception to this is Gabe. Only he could have shown me that I could not pack my bag and walk away from James Fee. I sat at his kitchen table and stared into the silence of his home and saw him everywhere, his imprint on the couch where he had dropped next to me and smirked when I labeled my notes as our final interview. I saw him in the empty space where he kept his baseball cap on the table by the door. I saw him snatching it and adjusting it to his head on his way out. I saw him in the dish rack that held the frying pan he had used to scramble the eggs he served me without salt.

Where was Paco? I thought surely he would have reappeared by now. I looked out the kitchen window. I went outside and peered beyond the gate. "Paco?" He did not answer.

I returned to the bedroom to wash my arms and legs. I powdered myself and tied a bow at the waist of my summer dress. I colored my lips and pulled up my hair. I wanted to surprise James, he so rarely saw me in a dress. I wanted to be for him the spinner.

I went to the courtyard to pick a handful of flowers

and was placing them in a vase atop the kitchen table when the doorbell rang. Paco at last had returned. And just in time. I knew he would be able to tell me where I could find Mr. Fee. I opened the gate and stood stunned to see staring back at me, not Paco, but the brooding eyes of Mario Lopez. He seemed equally surprised.

"Lucy."

He wore white chino pants and a blue denim shirt, minus the utility belt. His face was tanned and the sunlight glinted off the shocks of gray hair. His eyes warmed to me. "Mario."

"I'm looking for James."

I peeled back hair that the breeze brushed over my face. "He's not here."

"When will he be back?"

"I don't know. He said he was going to dig." I hesitated, then thought of my needed two hundred lines for magazine copy. "Have you got a minute?"

It may have been the dress. It may have been the breeze in my hair. It may have been the lipstick. Anyway, whatever the reason, Mario Lopez was not thinking in that moment that all journalists were wolves. He said he would be glad to talk to me.

We went to the kitchen and I pulled out a chair. "Do you want something to drink? Juice? Coffee?" In my self-appointed role as hostess in James's house, I pulled a glass from the cupboard and poured him a drink from James's refrigerator.

Mario was the picture of helpfulness. He waited patiently, sipping and smiling awkwardly as I set up the recorder and tested the tape. I grabbed a pen and opened my notebook.

I wrote at the top of a fresh page: Saturday, March 6/The royal tomb/Yax K'uk Mo'/Mario Lopez.

"Are you ready to begin the interview?"

He smiled. "A su orden."

"Where did you grow up?"

He looked surprised. "You're not going to ask me about the tomb?"

I leaned on an elbow. "We'll get to that."

"Outside Tegucigalpa. A town called Yuscarán."

"Do you have brothers? Sisters?"

"An older sister." He sipped his juice.

"Did you play games?"

He looked at me. "No." He shook his head, turning his glass.

"What did your father do?"

"He was in the rum business. Yuscarán is known for rum."

"Your mother?"

"*Ama de casa*. She took care of her children. I was close to my mother. She suffered a lot." He stared at his glass. "My father was gone days at a time. My father had another wife and child in Tegucigalpa. Another family. I didn't know it growing up." He looked at me and sipped. "He paid for their dwelling and stayed with them when he traveled to the capital on business." He paused and then lifted his eyes. "What about your family? Who are your parents? Do you have brothers and sisters?"

I recounted for him moments from my childhood, how Gabe and I swam in the lake by our house and how we often had to paddle from the piranhas. "They went after scabs and moles," I said, and Mario gaped.

I told him of drinking coconut milk and eating fried yuca at the tribe. He seemed genuinely affected when I told him of the chigger bites after sitting in the grass at the top of the ridge.

"Your childhood was mysterious and happy," he said, smiling faintly.

"It was a good childhood."

"You and your brother shared many happy moments. That's nice. It sounds like you are close with your father." He paused. "That is why you are bold and ask so many questions. You do not have to fight battles inside yourself." He paused and sipped. "You are a good journalist. I cannot deny it. And your magazine upset me. I cannot deny that either." I leaned toward him and put a hand on his arm.

"They gave me two hundred lines this time, Mario."

He straightened. "Then we had best fill the space." He pulled in his chair, folding his hands and resting his elbows flat on the table. "Copán." He paused. "I came to the ruins the first time when I was thirteen. It left an impact on me. I saw the Maya as part of my heritage. I am Honduran." He paused again. "These are my people. I wanted to understand what happened to them. It was a question I was always thinking about. Who were they? Why did they disappear?

"I was a grad student in the late seventies with my friend, James Fee. We came here together. We were going to solve all the mysteries of the Maya." He laughed. "We did not. We created more mysteries." I put down my pen. "James and I focused our work in the Acropolis. He had his part. I had mine. I focused on Temple 16. That is where we found the tomb of K'inich Yax K'uk Mo'. " He lifted the recorder. "Is the tape running?"

"It's going."

"Structure 16 is a typical royal structure. Therein lies the challenge." He shifted his angle, crossing his legs and folding his hands around a knee. "For the Maya certain spaces were sacred. They would collapse the upper levels of an existing structure and encase what was left with fill. Then they built the new structure around it. In our work we live inside a labyrinth of tunnels. So many levels require us to work in three dimensions, up, down, sideways, and in between, all at once. It is easy to get lost. Sometimes you can't see what you're looking at." He shook his head. "By the time we got to the third level inside Structure 16 we discovered it was very different than the first two levels. We found a beautiful temple, perfectly preserved. We removed the loose dirt. Exposed on the face of the temple we found a set of giant masks tinged with traces of the original paint, red paint. It was all over the place. It is the best preserved Maya temple we've ever found. We called it Rosalila because of the red.

"Two giant birds frame the central doorway. They are facing the setting sun. Above them, undulating serpents extend their bodies to the sky. Rosalila once crowned the highest point in Copán. From miles around you could look in the direction of Copán and see the shocking red temple mounted over the city. We found a hieroglyphic step on the stairs of Rosalila that tells us it was built by Moon Jaguar, Copán's tenth king, in C.E. 571. It is dedicated to K'inich Yax K'uk Mo'. "

He emptied his glass and lifted it. "Is there more?"

I paused the recorder to refill the glass.

"Usually the kings smashed to bits other kings' structures so they could build something bigger and better over it. But one of the kings decided to bury Rosalila intact. It is completely entirely preserved, as if it had been embalmed. This got us wondering—why was this building so revered that it was essentially mummified? What was inside of it? It was obviously sacredly related to Yax K'uk Mo'."

"How did you know that?"

"The temple, which measures about eighteen meters by twelve, represents an allegory in Maya cosmology. It contains no tombs, which suggests it was used only for ceremonial purposes. Rosalila mentions Yax K'uk Mo' in the imagery in many different ways. The birds on the bottom on either side of the doorway are placards of the name of Yax K'uk Mo'. Then, over the doorway, is the face of the sun god, his long wings emerging from both sides of his face. It is an avian form of the sun. He is Yax K'uk Mo' but he has become apotheosized, or deified, as the sun. One of his titles is 'K'inich,' which means 'great sun' or 'sun face.' So he is the sun over the doorway of Rosalila. All of the temple is focused on Yax K'uk Mo'." He leaned with his elbows flat against the table.

"James and I found a small cache of flint eccentrics hidden inside Rosalila. You would not believe how sharp the edges of those things were. These were powerful works of art. A bundle of blades chipped from the sacred fire stone—flint." He paused, his eyes shining. "They were emblems of power, probably used on ceremonial occasions. Some were meant to be hafted onto shafts of spears. Others were hafted to sacred objects used in rituals. There were nine of them. Some people interpret this as representing the nine lords of the night, in accordance with the nine levels of the Maya Underworld. Others think at least one of them was a portrait of Yax K'uk Mo'. They're amazing."

I interrupted. "How does Rosalila fit into the significance of the discovery of Yax K'uk Mo's tomb?"

He crossed his legs, leaning back. "One of the holiest sites in Copán's sacred geography is the place where Yax K'uk Mo' is buried, in the heart of the Acropolis, Structure 16. We found Rosalila also buried within Structure 16, and in it, incense burners, stingray spines, and jade flowers. Incense burners and sting ray spines were the implements used in the ritual of auto-sacrifice, or blood-letting, when the king would pierce himself to communicate with his ancestors. He would use a stingray spine on his tongue or genitals and drip the blood onto bark paper, which was then burned in an incense burner. The king's blood was sacred. His vision of the ancestors would come in the smoke. Finding the implements of auto-sacrifice inside Rosalila meant the kings used the sacred temple as the doorway to the ancestors. Finding the tomb of Yax K'uk Mo' also in Structure 16 meant the kings used Rosalila to communicate with him. This strengthened their authority. All the kings of Copán legitimized their power by linking themselves to Yax K'uk Mo'.

"Finding his tomb put all the pieces of the puzzle into focus. I already said Structure 16 is at the heart of Copán's sacred geography. Rosalila is buried inside Structure 16.

The temple was used by kings for auto-sacrifice to communicate with the ancestors. The bones of Yax K'uk Mo' are buried at the lowest level of Structure 16. He is at the center, he is the cornerstone that holds the other pieces in place." He paused. "Now that we know he was a real man, we are able to understand the significance of Rosalila, Altar Q, the Hieroglyphic Stairway, Structure 11—everything. His bones brought the whole picture into clarity." He touched my arm. "I will never forget the day James and I found those flint eccentrics. The two of us were alone in the tunnel, squeezed between the narrow walls. We had only a single light bulb and it cast many strange shadows. The walls looked blue because of the angle of the light. James's face looked bronze, like the face of a god. We were dripping in sweat, he more than I because of that beard. I pulled the flints out and placed the first one in the box he held. I carefully laid it in. I said, 'You cannot believe how sharp those edges are.'

"One by one I pulled them out. We examined each closely with the flashlight. We found all nine." He shook his head and smiled faintly. "Sometimes you forget that human beings made these things, and that it was very important to them when they did." He stared at his glass. "It is amazing to think that yours are the first eyes to see something this powerful, that no other eyes have seen them for over a thousand years." He looked at me. "It is a special feeling. It doesn't happen everyday. It touches me." Mario shook his head. "Sometimes we forget why we are doing this."

I inclined myself to him. "I don't know what you mean."

"In our grad school days we felt we were going to solve all the mysteries of the Maya. We would crown the efforts of our beloved forebears. When we found those flint eccentrics buried inside Rosalila, just he and I, we understood that we weren't there to solve mysteries or crown the work of our forebears. We were there for our love of the tunnels. Ours were the first eyes to see the flints in 1,300 years, the first hands to touch them since the hands that so carefully put them there. No one knows how long it would take to make an implement like that today because no one today has the skill to do it." He lifted his chin. "We make our measurements. We take our photos. We hold our press conferences. Sometimes we forget to think about the human hands that made these specimens. It is a special trust we have been given. It doesn't happen to everyone. It is a privilege." He paused. "Those are the moments that explain why we do this. Those are *our* moments, James's and mine. The Maya are giving up their secrets. How do you explain that at a press conference? How do you tell a reporter that the world shakes beneath your feet when you find things like those flints? How do you explain that you hear the ancestors whisper?" He looked at me. "They don't want to hear it. They want to know what treasures we found and how it will enhance our international reputation and if it will help tourism. We give them stories. Then they reduce our discoveries to ten lines." He smiled and drained the remainder of his juice. Then he stood.

"You are too dressed up to be on assignment at Copán. You are going to find my friend, I presume." He smiled.

"I understand." Rising, his hands on his belt, he said, "I will be going. Thank you for the juice." I followed him to the gate. Before leaving he turned to me. "By the way, I came to tell James the coroner determined Berto was was already dead by the time he was painted and placed in the tomb."

"How do they know?"

"They could tell by the absorption of the paint in the skin. Or, I should say, by the lack of absorption. Anyway it was not paint. It was dandruff shampoo. We have a very sick act on our hands."

"Do they know how he died?"

"They found high levels of alcohol in his blood and a crack in his skull and swelling in his brain. They concluded he fell down drunk and was hit in his head. That caused the swelling. They believe they have a suspect. But I will leave it to James to give you an explanation." He looked at his watch. "Half past two. Can I give you a ride to the park?"

"I'm going to straighten up here a little. I'll catch a cab."

He hesitated. "I apologize for what happened about the jail. I regret it."

"I survived. And that day doesn't exist in my memory anymore, Mario." We shook hands.

"Tell James I will catch up with him later. Good-bye, Lucy." He waved.

26

I thought by now Paco would have made an appearance, given his propensity to show up at the needed moment. But I determined not to allow someone else's bad timing to derail my resolve. I would go to the tunnels and look for James myself. I checked my backpack for a flashlight and water and started out the door. As an afterthought, I darted back and plucked a flower from the vase to put in my hair. I dropped the pack to fuss in the mirror, then left in haste, closing the gate behind me. It was a matter of only a minute before I hailed an oncoming taxi.

"Las ruinas. Cuanto?"

"Seis lempiras."

I went to pull the lempiras from my wallet when I realized I had dropped my backpack when fussing with my hair, and there it still sat, inside the house behind the locked gate, the keys in it. I turned helplessly to the taxista. "I forgot my wallet. I'm locked out of the house." I intended to plead with him that El Doctor would pay the fare when I found him at the ruins. But the driver peeled away before I uttered another word. I determined not to allow someone else's bad manners to deter my intention. I would walk. It was only a half mile to the park, though, admittedly, the sun was hot and I was wearing sandals, which didn't do well on cobbled streets. But I knew the cobble ended just beyond the Quebrada. Anyway I decided to take off my shoes and walk freely. Just beyond Comedor el Casteo on the edge of the village, I started to sweat. A bus that read "We Are The Champions" over its windshield belched smoked and exhaust as it passed, which turned my stomach and caused me to slow my pace. I decided there was no point in hurrying to find James, only to look like a wilted flower and smell like an old shoe. I ambled, dangling my sandals between fingers and greeting a woman sweeping her step. The cobblestone gave way to asphalt about where the cows were munching weeds in a grassy lot piled with truck carcasses. At that point I abandoned strolling and decided to pick up the pace to make up for lost time. I was pleased with the ground I covered in vigorous strides, avoiding Jugo cartons and mounds of horse dung, sweating, but undeterred. I passed Stelae 5 and 6 on the left, two forlorn outcasts beyond the perimeter of the grounds, and then the Pupuseria Comedor. Approaching the entrance to the archaeological park, as I neared vendors sitting along on the roadside selling miniature stelae, I felt a stab on the bottom of my foot. I yelped. Blood trickled steadily where I pulled out a shard of broken glass. I pressed my finger to it, but doing so made it difficult to walk. So I hopped a few steps, then walked—more like a half-skip—then hopped some more and sometimes stopped to continue to apply pressure to the bleeding. I eventually landed myself on the verandah at the Visitor's Center and decided to give it some solid pressure to stop the bleeding. It slowed, and I was relieved. I determined not to allow a little physical pain to get in the way of a mission.

I welcomed the coolness of the dirt on the pathways against the stinging heat of the asphalt and allowed my feet to luxuriate in it with only fleeting thoughts of rabid infection.

I reached the watchman's shelter where Berto had worked, where James and I had met him in the rain that day when we were locked in. I felt sadness that Berto was gone. But this was tempered with relief that he hadn't been painted blue and hung up. His replacement was a vigilant watchman and he wouldn't let me pass without a ticket. He didn't believe me when I made the plea about my admittedly incongruous relationship with Dr. Fee. "I cannot let you pass without a ticket," he said, waving a finger.

"El Doctor would want you to let me in," I said, hopping and pressing. "Call him on the radio. He'll tell you." He waved me off.

Bands of sweat had formed around my waist and under my breasts. For all the wetness overtaking me, I might as well have been caught in the rain again. I found a rock to sit upon and loosened the bow around my waist and tied it around my bleeding throbbing foot. Sweat drenched the hair around the nape of my neck.

In the distance I heard guides telling stories on the

Great Plaza. "Yax Pasah established the cosmic symmetry of the dynasty at Copán on Altar Q." And, "18 Rabbit was a very proud king." I immediately recognized that voice as Raúl's. Evidently he was leading a group of English speaking tourists. They had gathered near Structure 4, within sight of the entrance.

I stood and waved. "Raúl!" He looked up, but didn't see me. "Raúl! Over here!" He looked again and this time I saw him nod to the visitors and jog to the gate. He smiled and bobbed.

"Have you rested? Are you feeling better?"

I wasted no time presenting my case. With the wave of a hand Raúl promptly got me admission. I walked with him back to the tourists who were waiting dutifully at Structure 4.

"Why do you limp?"

"Have you seen Mr. Fee? I'm looking for him."

He shook his head. "No. I have not seen him. I will tell him you are looking for him if I see him." He bobbed. "Why you are not wearing your shoes? You should be wearing them. We have the chichicaste. We have scorpions."

"Do you think he's in the Acropolis?"

"That might be a guess. Possibly," he said.

I left him with thanks and he watched as I scaled the stairs up the western side of Structure 11. Despite the limp I mounted them in leaping strides with intermittent hops. I waved from the top. He watched as I jumped a root and navigated blocks and stones, my sandals flailing in my hands.

Near the top, I missed a step and landed hard. He called to me and I raised the sandals to signal I was fine. I incurred a sizable scrape on the side of my arm, and took a deep, clean, bluish gash on the knee. But otherwise, fine. Blood from the knee drained in rivulets, not unlike the blood that had come from my foot. Anyway, I determined that I would not allow minor calamity to overrule my goal.

I stood and brushed off my dress. By this point, it was drenched from sweat and soiled with dirt from the fall. It had not been easy scaling the steps of Temple 11 and I had worked up a thirst, but soldiered on, beyond the Ceiba tree where James and I had stood so many times. I descended the steps on the southeast face of Temple 11, over a patch of grass and rocks. Beyond the court of the dancing jaguars to my left, down a little and over a rocky path, I skirted the northern edge of Temple 16. I felt sure James would be waiting for me there. It took some finessing to navigate the descent of that rocky ridge, what with the scrape on my arm, the gash in my knee and partial use of one foot. It leveled out as I neared the cusp of the corte, the steep face that had yet to be descended to get to the tunnel entrances. I made my way to the portion that had not yet been consolidated since it still held plenty of grass and roots to cling to. The consolidated sheer surface of well-ordered stone would have been impossible to descend without disaster. Yet (I was to learn) even upon the unconsolidated surface, I should have known not to attempt reckless strides at such an angle of descent. The grassy surface was a straight drop, which I didn't realize until I began to lose my footing. I would have made it to the bottom without injury were it not for that one brief but disastrous misstep. I leaned badly into what I felt was becoming an inevitable tumble. I raised my arms to break the fall and managed to curl my legs at odd angles, which lowered my center of gravity and accelerated what ended up to be a rolling finishing flourish. I came to rest at the bottom, leveling out after two, maybe three, complete rotations. I tore my dress on a jutting root. I lost a sandal. Achingly, I stood. I couldn't get away from the throbbing in my foot. Nor the burning of my arm. Nor the bleeding knee. Nor my aching legs and, now, a spasming back. My head hurt. My eyes twitched. My face, in any case, was resolute. I determined not to allow loss of body control and disorientation to get in the way of one's plan.

I located the tunnel system where James had taken me many times and found the entrance open and unguarded. This signaled hopefulness that James would indeed be there. I went onward with confidence, feeling sure I knew the way in and sensing only a slight disadvantage at not having a flashlight, remembering the team's rustic lighting system. I mounted the stairs leading to the entrance and stepped inside. Overtaken with darkness, I thought it best to stay close to the inner wall. I remembered James turning right at some point, so I took several steps and turned right. I remembered James turning left at some point and proceeded to make the first left I came upon. I found myself making turns that felt unfamiliar. I stopped, staying close to the inner wall, in keeping with my plan.

A flashlight would have been helpful.

I retreated a few steps and cursed myself for not paying better attention all those times I had walked with James through these tunnels. A second tunnel intersected with the one where I stood. Optimistically I concluded this must be the right tunnel. I stepped forward tentatively, but made a hasty retreat. James's words about Temple 16 came to my mind—" . . . the goriest temple in Copán. Really nasty." This was where Yax Pasah's final-phase stairway displayed human skulls from sacrificial victims mounted on poles.

I inched forward. With each step I became more disoriented. I felt sure I remembered James bearing left. So I followed a tunnel that went left. Then I was forced to make a second immediate left, which I hadn't remembered James doing. He had never made two successive immediate lefts. I proceeded, clutching my one sandal. It grew darker and more silent and the air more stifling the farther I went.

I stopped, hopelessly lost, though still hugging the inside wall. I broke out in a sweat and let out a whimpering plea for James who, evidently, was not there. Surely by now he would be looking for me the way I had come looking for him. Surely, not finding me, he would know I was lost inside Temple 16.

I turned a corner, bumping and scraping against cold rugged walls that led me to nowhere. I abandoned all thoughts of pleasing James with my dress and him thinking of me as the spinner. Hope left me. The darkness had overtaken me and, in a way I can't explain, had entered me. I collapsed to the ground unable to move. Every step I had taken only led me deeper into the shadows. Bats darted over me, "denizens of the Underworld," James called them. I recalled my long hours in the jail with longing. There, I had had visitors and apparitions of old friends who spoke comfort to me. I tasted warm soup from Lillian and heard Carlos whisper to me. There, I had lost myself in other worlds, such as Nobody's grave where I stood with my father and brother. Here, in this tunnel, I felt nothing but the weight of darkness. Ghosts and friends were beyond my reach. I groped along haltingly, crouched on my knees. I kept my hands awkwardly about my head to stave off the bats. I lost all spatial orientation and did not know the time of day, or even if it was still day. It felt it was the end. It seemed good to me to die and to leave my pitiful story buried in these tunnels. I languished for water, but took comfort knowing that soon I would be dead. I thought of others before me who had died languishing for water and that they got through it, which consoled me. I longed for daylight. I tried to picture it. I thought water and daylight must be what heaven is like. I would be there soon. How would they find my rotting bones?

I pitched forward in my crawl and scraped my head. I fell flat and came to rest in a niche carved into a wall. I don't know how long I had lain there fading in and out of fitful imaginings, vipers and fire. I groaned and tried to turn. I dropped a hand. I thought I was touching a snake. It was sliding between my fingers, narrow and smooth. I felt it again and again. Then, I recognized it differently. It was not a snake. It was the taut rubbery coil of an electrical cord. I followed it, dazed, yet awakening. With groping desperate hands it led me to a light bulb and—I found a light switch. It felt like the beginning of a new day. I wept.

Light filled my tomb with an orange-bronze glow. My eyes came into focus and I saw a creature carved into the facade of the niche. Feathers splayed outward from both sides of its face, its faraway eyes like the snake I thought I was touching. Its haunting half-smile had the look of a bad joke.

You have come with me this far, dear reader, and here I ask you to forbear a little longer. For when you are lost, as I was, fatigued by a sense of doom, fired by imaginings and bereft of hope, you see things that, after the fact, you can't explain. Nor can you recall if they were real or imagined. In these dark places it becomes evident that there exists a world behind a veil, a world we cannot see. And in moments such as that which I faced, the veil between that world and this one becomes very thin. I heard things. In fact, I heard very specific things to the extent that, insofar as one can converse with a being beyond the veil, I did so. The haunting image before me that had been carved into the niche seemed indifferent as I lurched around in opposing directions trying to get my bearing and pulling a pincher bug from my hair. Then I heard it say, What do you know about dark places? I stopped. My blood ran cold. What do you know about the tunnels? About dwelling underground?

"Who is speaking?"

You take three steps in and you are hopelessly lost.

"Who are you?"

Who are *you?*

"Stop talking to me." I buried my head in my arms. "I'm losing my mind. I'm insane."

Because you are insane do you think I will stop talking? Where is your archaeologist? Have you driven him to the ground?

I put my hands over my ears. "Blah blah blah blah blah blah."

Do you mock me?

I didn't answer.

A believer in God, and she mocks.

"Are you of God or of the devil?"

Is the one who mocks of God or of the devil?

"Are you real? Are you of God?"

The one who puts his hope in many gods is attempting to know the God of gods.

"I've stopped listening to voices."

What does Lucy Shaw know about dark places? She takes three steps in and is hopelessly lost.

"I'm going to die here." I turned my face to the wall and chafed my wet cheek against its jagged edges.

The God of all gods excels in dignity. He delights in mercy.

"I'm insane. I won't listen to voices. And today is the day I am going to die."

27

Lost in misery I did not notice the approach of a lone worker who stumbled upon me. He saw me in the dim light where I sat in a heap, my head in my arms, sobbing with shallow gulping breaths. It was Raúl, that happy bobbing, dipping guide who (he later said), sensed I was not finding El Doctor Fee. I looked up. He was removing his hat. "Why you are not wearing your shoes? You should be wearing them."

"How did you find me?"

"It was not difficult. I follow the trail of broken things. And here you are," he said. "They are looking for you. Dr. Fee and the pilot. They are very nervous."

"The pilot?"

"They found me on the Great Plaza by Structure 4, where you found me. I was with a group of Germans. They give me the Germans because I am good with the gutturals. They are easy for me.

"Dr. Fee asks if I have seen you. I said I watched you climb the steps of Temple 11. I tell him it is not easy to climb the steps of Temple 11 in single strides but you climbed them in double strides. Then I tell them I saw you fall and wave your shoes."

At that moment James rounded the corner and came upon us. Raúl turned to him, dipping and smiling and shaking his head pointing at me, then departed. James halted, then came and kneeled and picked grass from my matted hair while I choked and heaved. "I was looking for you. I got lost." I pressed my wet eyes to his shirt. He held me tentatively, not wanting to aggravate my wounds.

"Where don't you hurt?"

"My face," I said. "My face doesn't hurt." He kissed my face and the wetness from my cheeks. He pushed back my hair and smiled. "You look pretty in your dress." He pulled his canteen from his shoulder and lifted it to my lips. He saw in degrees the dried blood on my legs and arms and dress, all of it mingled with dirt and sticks and grass and sweat. He curled my hand into his. "Larry is here. He came to take you home. He's waiting outside." I rose achingly and brushed off my dress.

"Can you walk?"

James led me by the hand out of the tunnel, out of the darkness. If someone in that moment had asked which I would have preferred, twenty-fours hours in a Honduran jail with cockroaches and a caffeine headache or three hours in the belly of Temple 16 with oozing bodily fluids and apparitions of Yax K'uk Mo', I would have said it was irrelevant. The result was the same: during both nightmares James Fee was on the other side of the darkness and led me into light.

We stepped out of the tunnels into the open air and the brilliance of the sun caused me to recoil. When my sight returned I saw plainly that Larry was not there and knew why. James glanced around. "I told him to wait here."

"Larry doesn't take orders. He came in to the tunnels. He saw us." I looked at James. "What time is it?"

He checked his watch. "Five-thirty."

"He's going to try and fly back to the capital. He won't be able to land. There are no lights at the airport. We have to stop him. I have to talk to him."

James began darting about looking for the boy who always seemed to know where to be. "Paco! Paco, come here!" The boy appeared from behind the wall of the corte. He ran to James's side without so much as a fleeting glance my way. "I need you to run after Mr. Larry. He is walking to his plane. Run and catch him. Tell him Miss Lucy wants to talk to him."

Paco said, "You want me to tell Mr. Larry to wait for Miss Lucy to get into the plane?"

James kneeled and put his hands on the boy's shoulders. "That is not what I said. Listen to me, now. Run and tell Mr. Larry not to get into the plane. Tell him Miss Lucy is coming to talk to him. Now run! You don't have a lot of time."

He is a fleet-footed runner. Whenever there is running to be done Mr. Fee always calls on Paco and he runs. He ran the length of the park that day. He caught up with Larry McCully who was standing at the plane, the pilot who had brought me to Copán only a few days before. Paco did not speak to me when I approached the plane, limping badly. He ran to the Visitor's Center where James waited. Larry's back was turned to me. He leaned against the Cessna, palms pressed against its side, his arms out straight. His head was bowed between his shoulders. He looked at me with wet eyes. "Please don't fly until tomorrow," I said.

I do not remember what else passed between us during those hard sad moments. I stood erect, my head tilted slightly, holding the one sandal left to me after my fall. I looked him in the eyes and didn't turn away. Larry shifted his weight. He folded his arms, then unfolded them. He placed them on his hips, lowered his head, then raised it. He sometimes shook his head. He put his arms on my shoulders, then pulled them away. We had spoken for several minutes when Leonardo appeared. He looked at me and the three of us talked briefly. Leo kissed my cheek and sent me on my way. I left Larry with Leo at the plane. James and Paco waited at a distance. I came to them and told them I agreed to have dinner with Larry later that night. "He's going to sleep in the plane tonight."

Paco disappeared and James took me home. I showered and washed my cuts and tried to fix my hair. I had no dress to wear, only safari shorts, my Fighting Illini T-shirt, and Renegade hiking shoes. James dressed my wounds. He sat me on a chair so I could soak my cut foot. He dotted my scrapes with ointment. He was wrapping my knee in gauze, circling it with white tape, when I touched his hair. "K'inich Ahua, full of light and fire." He looked up. "He marries the new moon, the mother of rain and rivers, keeper of the three stones." He smiled. "This is my real life," I said. He kissed my knee.

Later that evening I left for the hotel in town where I would be meeting Larry for dinner. I was half-way up the steep cobbled incline to the corner when I realized I had forgotten my backpack and returned to the house to fetch it. I approached and promptly recognized Paco's voice arising from inside. I waited before opening the door. He was sitting at the kitchen table where James had served him tortillas and beans. Paco was saying, "You are not sad Miss Lucy is having dinner with Mr. Larry?" His little mouth curled painfully.

"What's wrong?" James said, "You haven't been yourself today." He poured Paco some juice.

The boy didn't answer. He lifted the beans with a fork and let them drop onto the plate. I watched from behind the screen door as James spread his elbows flat on the table, folding his big hands, and inclined himself to his son. "Tell me what's wrong."

"Why is Miss Lucy with Mr. Larry?"

"She needs to talk to Mr. Larry."

"Is she going to go with Mr. Larry on the plane?"

"Yes. She has to go back with Mr. Larry on the plane."

"Is she going to kiss Mr. Larry by the plane?" He pressed a fist to his wet eyes.

"Is that what's bothering you?" I inclined myself nearer to hear better. "No," James said. "Miss Lucy is not going to kiss Mr. Larry by the plane. Miss Lucy is not going to kiss Mr. Larry anymore. There will be no more kissing."

"I told Miss Lucy I wished she never came on the plane."

A tear spilled down his cheek. "I don't want Miss Lucy to go home on the plane." James pushed his plate away, then pulled away Paco's. He put both his big hands around Paco's little hands.

"Miss Lucy has to go home tomorrow on Mr. Larry's plane. Then, in a few weeks, you and I are going to drive my truck to Miss Lucy's house and bring her back here to live with us." Paco coughed and breathed heavily, then lowered his head in his arms. "Don't you want Miss Lucy to come back and stay with us?" He touched Paco's head.

"She will go on the plane with Mr. Larry and she won't come back. I told Miss Lucy I hated her and wished she never came on the plane." He coughed and choked. "I love Miss Lucy. But she'll never come back. I love Miss Lucy." James stroked that little head. He put his other hand on Paco's arm, so small an arm inside so big a hand. Paco did not speak.

James said, "You're telling me that the words of Tomás Fee are mightier than God?" Paco raised his head. "Is that what you're telling me?"

James placed his arms around his son and lifted him. He carried him to the couch and sat, Paco curled in his lap. James saw me then as I looked through the window. I saw the lines on the edges of James's eyes as he held his son and I knew he would never walk away again. I saw then that all the sadness and loss and ruined hearts were but passing moments on a landscape filled with assertions of goodness more fierce and persistent than all sorrows. Paco lifted his face. I saw, standing there behind the screen door, strong bones carrying fragile ones and that beauty lived and would not be held back. Paco lifted his face to his father. "That is my name. My name is Tomás Fee."

James was waiting asleep on the couch when I returned later that night. I lumbered in, stiff, swollen-eyed, covered with bandages. I sat near him and touched his face. He opened his eyes and played his fingers in my sleeve. "I brought in his bed," he said. "I told him to shower." He took my hand. "He asked when you were coming back."

We slept where we were, on the couch, utterly exhausted, my head on James's lap. Neither of us detected Paco slip out the door the next morning with the rising sun. The time had come for James to take me to the plane. He looked for his son, but Paco would not be found. James hoisted my bag into the bed of the truck and I called to Paco. James told me he did not want to say good-bye.

Leonardo met us in the parking lot of the Visitor's Center. He took my bag to the plane. I watched from afar as Larry heaved it into storage, where four days and a lifetime earlier he had pulled it out and carried it on his shoulder to this spot, duty-bound, as missionaries tend to be.

James carried my pack, given the pain in my arm and my back and the stiffness in my legs from all the falls I took. Larry sat in the pilot's seat adjusting headphones and pushing buttons, looking this way and that, ready to go. Leonardo smiled and shook James's hand. "I will take care of her until you come."

James and I did not touch before I looked at him and

said good-bye. I turned to step into the plane.

"Miss Lucy!"

I stopped and looked up. "Miss Lucy!" I saw him running, that fleet-footed boy with the fire-blazed eyes and hair like a pixie. I caught him in my arms. "I love you. I love you, Miss Lucy." He promised he would come for me in the truck. "In two weeks," he said. He kissed my wet face. I looked at James, who winked at me, and I kissed my son's wet face in return. "That is for you," I whispered. I kissed the other cheek. "And that is for Papi."

James took Paco's hand and pulled him from me. He handed me my pack and said, "Good-bye." They walked to the Center, James's hand on the shoulder of his little boy. Leo sat with Larry up front. And Larry did not turn to me to ask if I was ready, but I was. The plane roared. It lurched forward and coursed the dry airstrip and tears formed at the edges of my eyes, the way they always did when small planes went aloft. We turned in the sky, banked and settled. The wings of the Cessna carried me into the clouds and over the mountains.

PART TWO
(James)

28

In Lucy's mind this story reached its resolution when I, for once, kept with the plan. I drove out two weeks later to claim her as my bride. For my part, my vocation requires that I make peace with speculation that never quite reaches resolution. Yet a kind of resolution did come to me through all this. So for me, the story had not yet reached its conclusion. Lucy left it to me to finish the story as I would see it resolved. Therefore, if you, the reader, are satisfied with Lucy's ending—the murder solved and our marriage assured—then read no more. But if you are of a mind to linger a bit longer, you will hear from me about an account of a fuller completion to this narrative, which—as Lucy noted—seemed to transcend its own script. I told Lucy I would love to finish her story.

But first I must tie up loose ends related to the events surrounding her tantalizing visit to the ruins of Copán. The investigation into the crime at the tomb unfolded. Inevitably it led to Yamileta and, of necessity, to Berto. The investigators had no help from me on that count.

They came to it on their own. In fact, I testified that I believed Berto and Yamileta had acted out of extreme duress and felt that neither posed a threat to the community. I have heard nothing about the outcome. Yet I know from experience that duress, such as it is in these poor countries, is irrelevant in the eyes of the court. It does not portend a hopeful ending, as is too often the case in the criminality of the poor.

Lucy and I were married in a civil court in Tegucigalpa, as is mandated by the law in Honduras, two weeks after her departure from Copán. Tomás had promised her then we would return, and we did. We arose that day with the roosters and made the five-hour drive to the capital where Lucy and I were married that very day. She looked like a flower, as Leo so often describes her. Leonardo and his sister Marisela stood as our witnesses. Lucy cried. She said she missed her family.

Lucy would want me to highlight Doña Nora's utter delight with her article about the tree campaign. Its completion was not without a degree of spectacle, as tends to be the case with Lucy Shaw's assignments. The day after we were married, before returning to Copán, my new wife, our son and I met Leo at the familiar office of La Primera Dama. Leo said he had a promise to fulfill and Lucy needed a photo for the tree campaign article. Doña Nora floated out of her office, took my wife in her arms and kissed both her cheeks. Then she turned to me and kissed my cheeks. "So this is man who stole Lucy Shaw's heart. What *are* you made of?" Doña Nora listened sympathetically as Lucy retold the already well-known story about the blue sacrifice, the night in the jail, and getting lost in the tunnels. Leo, in the meantime, fulfilled his promise when he pulled me by the elbow toward the reception desk. "Have you met Eva Rosales, Dr. Fee? She was very helpful getting Lucy out of the jail." Leo threw my wife a knowing look who reciprocated with her rolling eyes.

I took the hand of Eva Rosales and squeezed it warmly, thanking her. She turned red in the face—an effect Lucy says I have on people. Then Eva said, "It was my honor to help. I have always admired very much the work of Lucy Shaw." When Eva spoke these words, all chattering went silent and Lucy looked at Leonardo incredulously, and he grinned. Then she looked at me. I humored her with that jaguar jig and whispered in her ear, "Come with me to the floor and dance."

By now Doña Nora had pulled Tom by the hand and led all of us to her inner chamber. She boasted of her children, highlighting their photos displayed in silver frames on her mahogany shelving. Then my friend El Presidente Philip Mondragón stepped in. "James Fee." He shook my hand.

"James and Lucy are newlyweds, Philip. Did you know that?" said La Primera Dama.

"Felicidades, amigo." He squeezed my hand a second time and took Lucy by the shoulders to kiss her cheeks. "You are a blessed and beautiful couple. I wish you a lifetime of happiness and, of course, many children." Then he turned to me abruptly and said, "You got a minute? We can meet me down the hall." He looked at Leo. "You come too."

El Presidente kissed my wife a second time and with a look and a wave I gained her consent to excuse myself from the presence of Doña Nora.

What happened next Lucy may not want me to recount. But she gave me the mandate to finish the story and so I tell it as it happened, as any journalist would. Leo and I followed Philip Mondragón down the hallway and sequestered ourselves behind a closed door while Doña Nora insisted the photo for the article be taken on the berm outside her office. She said she wanted Tom in the photo with her. El Presidente was explaining to us a Maya summit he wanted to convene at Copán to which he intended to invite presidents of all Central American countries along the Maya route. He was saying he wanted Leo to work with me as liaison from the capital city and then, with a knock, Lucy popped in. "Excuse me, I need Leonardo." We turned our faces to her. She lifted the camera and tossed Leo a nod. Leo said, "You take the pictures, Lucy. I am busy." She'll discover upon reading this the amusement we could not contain upon seeing the look on Lucy Shaw's face when Leonardo told her to take her own pictures.

She did indeed take charge of the photo session. She led the way to the berm, Doña Nora in her flowing black pants and shiny black shoes clutching Tom's hand as they reached the right location for the shoot. By that point the shoes of La Primera Dama were layered with dust, but her sculpted hair had not budged in the breeze. Eva Rosales held my wife's backpack. Lucy established the location. She's quite resolute about establishing locations. A man in a suit carried a small tree and placed it on the berm as Lucy directed him. She told Tom to stand with Doña Nora. She instructed the man in the suit to turn the tree this way, then that way. She checked the angle of the sun. She nudged Tom closer to La Primera Dama. Doña Nora said to Tom, "You won't let me embarrass myself, will you?" Tom promised he wouldn't. "Put your little hands on mine, mi amor. We're planting together," she said. Tom dropped to his knees and placed his dark little hands on her delicate white fingers. I was glad I had checked to see that his fingernails were clean.

"Look at me." Lucy embraced the photographer's mandate wildly, brandishing a waving arm to evoke surprise and hilarity. Leo and I soon joined them outside in time to see the display. Tom said it hurt to keep smiling. Eva Rosales glanced at me warmly. I laughed at Lucy, which made Tom smile without it hurting so much.

Leo said, "Try it from over here, Lucy," waving a hand downward. Then the picture taking stopped. Lucy stood up, faced Leo, inclined on a hip, and offered him the camera.

"Lucy, it's better from over here." Leo waved a second time.

She said, "Am I stupid?"

He said, "No, Lucy, but that face could convince anyone." I turned away to hide my amusement, placing a sympathetic hand on Leo's shoulder. He said, "You are Lucy Shaw, yes. You are the *Los Tiempo* bureau chief, yes. Anyway, do it the way I am telling you. It is better."

"Two more." She raised two fingers as the shooting

resumed from the angle of Leo's commendation.

Down to her last shot, Lucy said, "make it good." That's when Tom turned to La Primera Dama and looked into her smiling eyes. The moment Lucy released the shutter, to everyone's utter surprise, he planted his brown little lips squarely on Nora's shiny red ones. Lucy gaped, lifting her face from behind the camera. We all gaped, that is, except Doña Nora who promptly seized Tom's cheeks and kissed him right back on the lips a second time. My beloved photographer ambled red-faced to me and buried her embarrassment in my shoulder. "Where did he learn that?" she said. I kissed her cheek and whispered, "We both know the answer to that question."

Tiempo appropriately titled Lucy's story, "A Tree Is Like a Kiss." The national papers requested permission to reprint the photo. It won press awards and made the 1993 edition of *Los Tiempo*'s "The Year in Pictures." Lucy Shaw once again captured national headlines.

In deference to my wife's journalistic heroics, I am also compelled to note, in tying up these loose ends, that Mario Lopez no longer regards journalists as wolves. He loved her article on the tomb of Yax K'uk Mo'. She quoted him extensively. Thereafter he referred to her as a "premier reporter."

29

Lucy spent much time in my world trying to understand baktuns, bakabs, Maya cosmology and the significance of discovering *al fresco* pottery (and she paid dearly for it; she'd want me to note that). Therefore, I draw this story to its conclusion with a final adventure wherein I traveled into her world, a world long unfamiliar to me and one that I did not understand nor cared to. When I told a colleague from Columbia I would be traveling into the Amazonian jungle basin in Peru to visit a missionary family, he promptly responded, "You're going where? With missionaries? What do you think of all that?" I will do my best to answer my colleague's question. It is a question for which at the time I possessed no answer and one that remained always on my mind, just beneath the surface, throughout our trip. The question carried dread for me. But by this point, I had confronted and overcome so much dread in my life with Lucy that I went forth to Peru with a sure step and in prudent happiness. I wanted to try and understand her world as she had tried to understand mine.

It is, after all, what made her what she is.

We traveled to Peru a month after our civil marriage in order to attend the dedication ceremony of her parents' life work, the translation of the Ninganahua New Testament. Except for the few days we stayed in the jungle out with the tribe for that event, we remained at Lucy's childhood home on the mission compound near Pucallpa. Being back where she grew up Lucy became as a little girl again, highlighting Jack Thatcher's house where the Ningabors made their ground-breaking jungle music; telling stories at the lakeside about how she and Gabe swam with piranhas; lying flat on her back on the same grassy airstrip mimicking the way tailwinds once rolled over her and carried her to tears.

The morning when we were to fly into the heart of the jungle to spend two days and one night with the tribe, I arose from the bed of my wife's youth, she lying near, and joined her father on the porch for coffee. Rain poured in rivulets from the tin corrugation of the roof over our heads. Despite my living in Honduras, the minor inconveniences of the quaint village of Copán Ruinas paled in comparison to what I experienced in Peru—and we had not yet made the flight into the jungle. So much of their life here was measured by water. Whether it was the hammer of rain upon the tin roofs, or the rustic faucets spitting muddy tap water in random explosions after a day or two of solid rain; or in the sound of rushing rivers that, during the wet, could pull down mountainsides and homes, dogs and chickens and maybe a bus or a village; or in the imprint of a jungle boot pulled from a mud-soaked path; the movement of water defined their lives. Edie Shaw spent a disproportionate amount of time managing it—storing it for when there would be no water in the pipes; filtering the brackish water when there was; boiling the filtered water for drinking. The kitchen had no hot water so washing dishes and even something as innocuous as making coffee, took forethought and precision. These little decisions had been woven into the slightest nuances of their everyday habits.

We sipped our coffee, the rain slowing. Gene was telling me about a friend of his in Pucallpa who was also a professor. "Of what?" I asked.

"Electricity."

I sat in that porch, sipping coffee made from water that had been spit from a half-clogged faucet, filtered, boiled, then heated again to be poured through the linen sieve filter over the grounds and felt a little ashamed at never having considered becoming a professor of electricity. I was a professor of anthropology and, in this world, that couldn't get the coffee made. Most people in the jungle don't read "the news" and if they could it wouldn't mean a thing. Trends. Elections. Tantalizing archaeological discoveries, none of it mattered. It was all about the water.

Rain levels and river levels, the impact on the banana crop and the beans and corn and yuca. It is about knowing how to run a generator when the electricity goes out and knowing how to fix the electricity without being electrocuted. Knowing electricity is indispensable. Without it, it is impossible to boil water without otherwise building a fire, which is not easy done in a downpour. The professor of electricity was someone I felt I would like to meet.

Lucy soon appeared robed and looking like a rag doll. I lifted my arm to her and she tucked easily to my chest. Then Tom appeared. He huddled under the arm of his abuelito, Gene. I forgot what Gene and I had been chattering about seeing Tom under his arm and feeling Lucy under mine. Tom and Lucy were each being warmed by the others' fathers' arms and it seemed to me, in that fleeting ordinary moment, that all the pieces fit. I couldn't get a finger on what pieces exactly. I knew only that they were pieces of something I had not pulled out of the earth.

Gene said, "Sebastian would like to give your marriage a blessing as part of the dedication ceremony, and so would I." Lucy hesitated. She said she did not want to take away from celebration of her parents' moment by stealing the spotlight. Gene nudged Tom off his lap. Standing, arms wide in a stretch, he said, "I can't think of anything I'd rather have happen at the Ninganahua New Testament dedication then to use that book to consecrate your marriage to James." She looked at me. Then Gene added, "But, it's up to you." He took Tom's hand. "Come on, Tom, let's go find Tío Gabe and kick the ball before breakfast."

The rain stopped that morning long enough for the first plane to depart around 8:30, a Cessna 206 six seater. Lucy was on that flight, along with Gabe and Dottie and Edie, who had appealed to Lu to come early and help set up mosquito nets and prepare the food. Three remaining plane-loads of guests and colleagues were scheduled to arrive behind them. Lucy said she wanted to fly with Tom and me. But at Gabe's behest she deferred to her mother's wishes. "We'll be right behind you," I said, kissing her forehead as she stepped into the plane. Fully loaded and ready to depart, the Cessna's wheels promptly sank into the mud. Gabe disembarked and began motions to lift the rear of the Cessna to turn it. Gene and I mounted motorbikes from the hangar and sloshed through the mud to lend help. Finally the little plane coursed down the airstrip, the wheels spitting water like fire hoses.

Two more planes got off during that brief window of fleeting blue skies. Only Gene, Tom and I were left behind when a wet ceiling of clouds again rolled in. We spent most of that day at the hangar passing time with Pete, our pilot. The office at the hangar smelled of fuel oil and old newspapers and was plastered with maps and littered with dog-eared flight manuals. We drank coffee from mugs that looked like they hadn't been washed since the jungle basin was penetrated. "Okay Tom, here's a question for you," Pete said, sipping his coffee. Tom listened attentively perched on a stool, chin up, his black hair sprouting. "A plane is flying. There is a bird inside the plane also flying. Does the bird add weight?"

Tom thought a minute.

Pete said, "What's holding the bird? The plane or the bird itself?"

Tom said, "Its wings."

Pete said, "What's holding its wings?"

Tom shrugged. "Air."

"What's holding up the air?"

Together Tom and I learned that the answer is, yes, a flying bird adds weight to a flying plane. Pete called it down draft, one of many tidbits of aviation trivia we picked up during our seven-hour delay.

Those long hours also served as an opportunity for me to hear from Gene Shaw himself how it came to pass that he and his wife came to choose this kind of life. He said that after his years at college he began to feel a strong urge to serve some place faraway. He wasn't sure where at the time, and his mother strongly resisted. To win validation for her conviction, she took her son to wise woman of faith (he said) whom his mother felt sure would side with her. The woman said to Gene's mother, "Well, Gene is young. Why don't you give him your blessing and let him go. If it's not the place for him, then he'll find out."

After spending a year and two summers of intensive linguistic training, his mission agency intended to send him to Bolivia where many tribes still needed their language deciphered. But Gene said he "didn't feel called to Bolivia." The long and short of it is, after many discussions, appeals and "fleeces"—a concept I did not understand but didn't ask—he and Edie ended up in Peru. Even then, however, they had not been assigned to work with the Ninganahua. They had been sent to work with the another tribe in the jungle called the Daranahua. To get to their village they had to travel by canoe for many days. After seven days on the river they took a short rest with the tribe known as the Ninganahua.

During that time they got to know them somewhat. Gene said he and Edie were thankful they had not been sent to the Ninganahua because they seemed more proud than the Daranahua. "We thought they would be much more difficult to work with." He said, "Never say where you don't want to go. Sure as you do, that's where the Lord will ask you to go."

With no warning, plans changed and the Shaws were assigned—not to the Daranahua, as had been intended— now to the Ninganahua. He said that later, when people at various missionary gatherings asked their fellow missionaries how they "got the call" to go to their respective tribes, many answered by describing epiphanies and overwhelming conviction and so on. But when the question was put to Gene, he would answer, "The director told me to go. That's how I got my call."

Edie was in shock the first time she walked into the hut that was to be their home. She thought, well, this is it; this is where I am intended to live and I might as well get used to it. They enclosed the entire hut in muslin cloth, walls and ceiling, to make it bug proof. But it also made it darker and hotter. They removed the muslin from the roof when they would put fresh palm leaves up. "As long as you have a new roof you're okay. When it gets old, every time the wind blows pieces of it fall on to your table and into your food."

The Ninganahua welcomed them somewhat warmly because they arrived for the first time with medicines that helped the people. This became the focal point of their early interactions with them.

Most people from the tribe suffered from parasites or the flu or both. Some had Whooping Cough. One year, he said, fifteen babies died from it. So they received the medicines gratefully. "They didn't boil their water, you see. They drank it straight out of the river," Gene said. "But we boiled ours. Slowly, people caught on that it was a good idea to boil water and wash dishes with soap and hot water and let them dry in the sun. They built tables where they dried their dishes so the dogs couldn't get at them."

Once they had established enough trust within the tribe they began the slow tedious work of deciphering the language. Needless to say, they did not have computers in the jungle so they wrote everything on 3 x 5 cards. They often asked a member of the tribe to come and speak with them. They would ask things such as "How do you say 'our house' and 'my house'?" Sometimes the tribe member would give them the correct answer, sometimes they didn't. Gene explained how, on one occasion, when they visited a second Ninganahua village nearby, the tribes people made fun of them because they spoke the language so badly. "We were butchering the language, but the Ninganahua at the primary village hadn't corrected us. We didn't realize we were saying anything wrong until we went to that second village."

At their linguistic school they learned how to write a symbol for each sound they heard in the language. They would listen and write sounds, then they would try to decipher where word breaks existed until, slowly, they would begin to cobble together a structure for the grammar.

He said, "We're still learning things."

The alphabet would be created on what was called a phonemic paper that included their own notations highlighting differing sounds used to pronounce the same word. These are called allatones, he said, or tonal increments of the two basic tones that served as the foundation of the language of the Ninganahua. Allatones are differing aspects within these two primary tones. Some are high. Some are low. Some may be mid-high or mid-low. So, he said, "you have to set things up in frames." For example, the word in Ninganahua for mosquito is *feen*. The word for rubber is also *feen*. So, in the alphabet as the Shaws decipher it, both words contain the same symbols that spell the word *feen*. But speaking them in a way that can be understood requires finding the correct tone and allatone. "In the word *feen* the 'f' is really closer to sounding like a 'p'. You don't bring the lips clear together the way we pronounce 'f' in English. In English we don't have the sound. It's more nasalized. Nasalization is very significant in the Ninganahua," Gene said.

As they progressed to the place where they acquired enough vocabulary to put together words and sentences, they started to tell stories from the bible. The first story they told the Ninganahua was the story about Noah and the great flood. It was a story about how God told a man named Noah to build a boat in preparation for the great flood, though at the time the sun was shining and he couldn't see the sense of it. But Noah obeyed and built the boat incurring the derision of his neighbors. Then the rain came and Noah was told to corral animals and rescue them from the flood. Even that didn't make sense to Noah, though again, he obeyed. According to the story, as Gene told it to me, the waters covered the land and all the friends and neighbors who had derided Noah perished. After a period of forty days, Gene said, the waters began to subside and eventually Noah's boat spotted land. He and his family, along with the animals, disembarked and, according to the legend, began rebuilding life from scratch. The first thing Noah did was plant a vineyard.

Gene told me that when he had finished telling this story to the Ninganahua, the chief, Sebastian, began to laugh out loud. Gene asked why he was laughing. Sebastian said, "I'm laughing because my grandmother told me this story." Evidently all the tribes have a flood story, which is why Gene introduced his work with it. Sebastian said that the story his grandmother told him did not involve a man called Noah. But, since Gene had read it to him, as he had written down in the Ninganahua language, Sebastian deduced that his grandmother had gotten parts of the story wrong. He concluded that, since Gene's story is written, it must be the true story.

Over time, Gene said, the Ninganahua took him and Edie into their tribal kinship system, giving them the tribal names Fasanahua and Yambacora. He said the tribe used the kinship name for a brother or sister or uncle, or any person whom they deemed an intimate part of their lives or family. Until the Shaws arrived, they had been accustomed to rubber traders coming and pillaging their land and taking their wood and women. They came to the

Ninganahua only to take from them. But Fasanahua and Yambacora, they said, came to weep with them when someone died and give them help when someone was sick. "One of the most meaningful moments for Edie and me was the day Sebastian stood up and said to the tribe that we hadn't come to them to take anything away from them. We hadn't come to take their women, as the traders had done. They have come to give us our language."

The year of the great flood, that is, as Lucy describes it—the year they pushed the button you push when you are going to die, the Ninganahua had told the Shaws not to worry about the rising waters because the river never rose above the airstrip, which was atop a very high ridge. But the river kept rising. By late afternoon, Gene said, the river had almost reached the airstrip and continued to rise. It wasn't gentle water either, but was wild, rushing water that washed away huts and animals and people along with them. Some in the tribe took their canoes and searched for higher ground. Other canoes had been swept away. But Gene and Edie did not have a canoe. Cuscobundi and his family came to their hut by canoe and asked for refuge. He said their house was tilting and asked if they could stay with them in their house because the poles holding their hut were deep. Gene told them to come. Then he said that maybe all of them should try to get away. Cuscobundi said, "No. We can't. The water is too fast. We will be swept away."

The water kept rising and the Shaws were able to hear it rushing just beneath the planks of their floor. That is when Gene looked at Edie and asked if she thought they should push the alarm button. She said, "If ever there was a time to press the button, this seems to be it." Wes Thatcher was at the ready on the other end, back at the base, and said promptly, "Do you have a problem, Gene?" Gene explained to Wes that the water was four inches from overtaking the house and that two families were stranded there and would he please pray that the water would stop rising.

The water stopped rising. Their home was not washed away. Even so, the village had been devastated. The water had covered their yuca and there was barely any food left. Many homes were gone. Even the Shaws hut had incurred damage that left them little more than a quarter of their already confined space inside. None of them ate for two days, until the water receded and planes could throw down hundred-pound sacks of rice. They lived for over a month with no walls, only a roof over their heads.

As we waited at the hangar that long gray day, these and other stories, carried the time and took me to a world that seemed to me so forbidding and strange.

30

The last possible hour to make it to the tribe and still arrive before sundown was drawing near. One of the pilots who had already departed radioed to say skies were looking good past the jungle periphery. If we were going to get out that day, this was the moment. We wasted no time. Tom and I squeezed into the rear of the Helio Courier H295 float plane that awaited at the dock near the air strip. We nestled in amid sleeping gear, coolers, cereal boxes, mosquito nets, water bottles, and a generator, all meticulously weighed in deference to the mission's scrupulous safety regime. Gene sat in front with Pete. He held in his hand the single copy of the New Testament that would be presented to the tribe at the dedication service the following day. The other four hundred ninety-nine copies were stalled in customs. He called this single copy "the pearl of great price."

Pete passed out "sick sacks for everyone," as he put it, then he settled into the cockpit and pulled away from the dock, engines humming, as he positioned the plane in the middle of the lake. Soon we were skirting the surface of our shimmering runway. As we took flight the windows cleared of the spray and I looked below to see Pucallpa's salt-box shanties fade into a carpet of green. Only the muddy Ucalayi River cut through the rain forest in its tortured twists and turns.

The guidebook noted that where we were headed was "inaccessible." As I looked out the window, I couldn't fathom how the pilots knew where we were, or where to put down the plane. It felt like we were heading straight into the ends of the earth. We flew more than two hours over solid green with only a snaking river for orientation. Gene Shaw, sitting in front, kept that single copy of the New Testament sealed in a zip-lock bag to fend off the jungle rot. His "pearl of great price" was the fruit of forty years of floods, fires, fevers and chigger bites. Forest coverage alone could dissuade even the most stout-hearted pioneer from penetrating this terrain. I looked out my window and saw nothing but trees, mile after mile, hour upon hour. What would compel a simple man like Gene Shaw, or anyone, to choose this life? There was nothing to appeal to anyone, no roads or electricity. Heat so punishing you never cooled off and the place so bug-infested you wore long pants despite the heat. Only ninety-eight percent deet held off the gnats and we had to rub sulfur on our ankles so the chiggers wouldn't get us. Lucy's parents traveled in canoes for weeks up the river that first time to find the Ninganahua. I, in my life, have never traveled for two weeks, by canoe or other means, looking for anyone.

After two and a half hours I felt the cabin pressure change. My ears popped. We tilted left, then banked right. Pete turned to Gene. "We'll be down in 20 minutes." I saw a village cut into the jungle perimeter along the riverside. Gene turned and said, "They're Yashinahua."

Cabin humidity increased with our descent. Shadows were long by the time Pete pitched and turned to align the plane with the river. Gene smiled at Tom and me. "The river is up. Lots of water to land on." I wondered to myself what we would have done if the river had been "down."

Lucy told me that Ninganahua children could hear a plane approach long before anyone else could, their ears were so attuned to their surroundings. From my window I saw them running to gather at the ridge and watch us descend. We dropped low and skimmed the river with a dip and a bob. Pete idled to the edge and secured the plane to dug-out canoes tied along the riverbank. Gene pointed and laughed as Lucy ran down the ridge in sliding leaps to meet us.

Greeted by the children, the plane unloaded, we heaved supplies on our backs and started the trek up that steep ridge to the village, Lucy behind me holding my belt. I measured with my eye the distance of the vertical cut and understood in a way that shocked me how high the water had risen during that terrible flood.

The dirt landing strip above, hacked out with machetes by Gene and Wes Thatcher, dictated the lay-out of the village, its raised thatch-roofed huts lining both sides. The other planes had positioned themselves at the end, near the government built school house, where we were headed. We walked single file, so ordered by Edie Shaw, as she pointed to the ground saying, "Stay on the path, otherwise you'll get chiggers, remember Lu dear?"

Tom and I would be sleeping the night in the school, Lucy said, because her father felt it was best until the tribe had officially blessed our marriage. "I'm with my parents in their hut." Then she whispered, "I'll miss you." The Ninganahuas greeted us from their open huts as we passed by. Some dangled in hammocks draped from high beams. Some sat on wood floors, legs crossed, nursing babies. Others squatted by little fires under palm shelters. Maw maw owa, they said. "You have come."

31

Goody told Lucy once that he couldn't imagine anyone experiencing a true movement of God in a way that would eliminate all doubt, and survive it. I have pondered this thought, as I have pondered my colleague's incredulity toward my newly formed alliance with missionaries. I myself am staggered by it. I have wondered if it might not be due to the fact that those of us in the academic world have not been schooled in recognizing such things as "God's movements," or even in possessing a category for them. We have managed quite capably without noting them. I write my journal articles that highlight obscurities relating to the Motmot Structure and the Papagayo, themes that tantalize me. It has been my privilege to invoke these names with the self-possession I bring to my vocation. Yet resolution of a different kind came to me here, in this place, when I stepped inside a world that was so strange to me. It had nothing to do with self-importance and my knowledge of the Motmot or the Papagayo. It is not about my place of privilege. Coming here took a kind of resolve that risked all that.

When someone of my ilk conceives of the missionary enterprise the Spanish conquest immediately comes to mind. We understand that it is numbered among the most dramatic events in human history that devastated the legacy of New World peoples, which we have spent our lifetimes trying to recover. Most estimates indicate between eighty and ninety percent of the indigenous population perished within a hundred years of the coming of the Spanish because of diseases brought from the Old World. It was an unwitting use of biological warfare against New World peoples who had no immune responses. The Old World exploited mineral resources in the New World, such as gold and silver, and benefited from the quick diffusion of highly prized commodities such as chocolate, corn, beans, squash, potatoes, and peanuts. Tobacco made it around the world within sixteen years of European contact.

Still, even we see that the arrival of the Spanish wasn't all bad for the New World. They gained technologies and an infusion of new blood lines from the Old World. Genetic resistance to all those diseases eventually came about through intermarriage. Agriculture, mining and other industries came with the Spaniards and Portuguese and gave New World peoples tremendous advantages in their economic aspirations.

Religious ideals were a nominal driving force behind the conquest. In fact, the indigenous peoples had already embraced many ideas Catholics thought they were introducing to the New World. The notion of gods dying for the people and being resurrected existed in virtually all New World Amer-Indian religions. These concepts are present all over Mesoamerican cosmology and are represented in their art in a myriad of ways. Even the symbol of the cross, four arms extended toward the four cardinal directions crossing in the center, pervades pre-Colombian Mesoamerican art and worldview. These were not difficult concepts for them to latch onto. The Spaniards believed they were converting the Indians. But the truth is, it was more a matter of the Indians taking on a new name for old beliefs. Many scholars now tend to view the imposition of Catholicism as a religious system Mesoamerican peoples selectively borrowed from. Perhaps it is not unlike the way the Ninganahua appropriated the translator's version of the story about Noah.

The Spanish conquest aside, anthropologists such as I have a harder time justifying the social inequality colonial rule imposed upon these indigenous peoples, championed and perpetuated for over three and a half centuries, in no small way by the missiological impulse of the Christian religion. I am compelled, however, to qualify this by conceding that tremendous social inequality already existed in the pre-Colombian world and among these indigenous peoples. At most, about five percent of the ancient Maya could actually read those marvelous hieroglyphs carved on to stone monuments that we have slowly, tortuously deciphered. Ninety-five percent of the population couldn't. Alas, it seems to be the nature of human civilizations that those in power, the haves, are quite careful to design effective strategies that defend their rights and privileges vis-à-vis the powerless, the have-nots. They managed it through information control. And information control was as important in pre-Colombian Amer-Indian civilizations as it was in the Old World civilizations. The notion of the few ruling the many has been around for a long time.

I carried these thoughts with me in my mind as I disembarked the plane on the river and walked the narrow pathway up the ridge and through the village, ever hounded by my colleague's question.

The contingent of scholars, missionaries, family members and other guests who had come to the jungle for the dedication ceremony gathered later that first evening on the schoolhouse porch.

We looked at the stars in the southern sky and tried to identify these new constellations. Gene lit a lantern and we sat on the floor of the porch leaning against poles, some sitting on camp stools. Wes Thatcher was saying, "Translation is nothing compared to putting together the dictionary, I'll tell you what." The way the light shadowed his tanned weathered face betrayed the many hard years he had spent in the jungle. He said, "When you translate a sentence, you know the meaning you want to give a word. But when it comes to putting together the dictionary, well,—" he folded his arms—"that requires every meaning every word can have, which means consulting tribal experts and sure as I'm standing here that ends up in a fight. 'This word means this—no, it means that.'"

Wes, who with his wife Billie worked with the Bora tribe, went on to say, "Fifty percent of the world's languages are tonal and these usually have only two or at most three tones. The Bora have five. The good Lord knew what he was doing when he sent Billie to the Bora." He went on to tell the story about the day Billie and a Bora woman were paddling in a canoe and ran into some brush. "Jack used to tell his mother never to paddle on the same side as the other person or the canoe would tip. He knew that river, didn't he, Gabe?" Gabe, chewing on a stem of grass, nodded knowingly. "Well, she and the other woman were paddling happily along when they came upon rapids and debris in the river. Before she knew what she was doing, Billie moved her paddle to the wrong side to avoid the brush and the canoe tipped. Now to say 'Help, I'm drowning' in Bora involves six tones in descending sequence that have the same wording as the phrase, 'I am weighing myself' except for the last tone on the last word."

Gene elbowed me. "This is a great story."

"All other intonations were the same except that last word," Wes continued. "So here Billie has tipped the canoe and was thrashing around in the swirling water"—he lifted his cap and scratched his head—"trying to come up with the right vocabulary, the right pitch, and, most important, the right final intonation. She needed to call for help, but didn't want to send the message that a gringa was in the river weighing herself!" He smiled at Gene. "Glory to God, she did it right. They were saved. She's got perfect pitch. A tribe member came along in another canoe and said, 'Sister, get into my canoe.'" Wes shook his head. "We never could have cracked this language without Billie's ear for music."

A linguist named Iva Lundin happened to be standing near me during this discussion. She and I digressed into a lengthy conversation about theories relating to the Ninganahua and how they ended up so deep in the jungle. "It is widely accepted they are not related to the Inca," she said. "The Inca never penetrated the Amazon basin. The Ninganahua and several other tribes—Shipibo, Yaminahua, and others—belong to a language family that is entirely different from Quechua, the Inca language. They are in their own linguistic pocket in other words, unrelated to any other language group in Peru." A bat darted about us in the darkened sky. "For the Yora—a dialect of the Yaminahua—the Chitonahua, and the Ninganahua the verbs 'go' and 'come' are the same as in Korean." Linguists compared key grammatical features in tribal dialects using "mutual intelligibility tests," she said. "The Yora are very Asian."

She continued, "In our translations, we aim to preserve the meaning of the original text in a way that would be understandable to that tribe. For example, in Papua New Guinea, they do not possess an emotive concept of 'the heart.' They understand things with their stomach. So when translating a verse that says, say, 'set your heart on things above,' we appropriate the tribal word for stomach. If we use 'heart,' then we've lost them. Our translations are not literal. They are idiomatic, but relevant. That is why our missionaries go to live with the tribes. They need to find a way not only to learn the verbal language but also the cultural language. The culture of a society is defined by the way they look at life. Rather than condescend to impose upon them the way we look at life, instead our people move in with them—only after they have been invited to do so—and take the time they need to understand the tribe's way of life and their way of understanding the world. Gene and Edie slept in hammocks and bathed in the river, as the Ninganahua do."

I wondered why they felt the need to go at all. Even showing up in a canoe, by implication, suggests they are bringing something of a foreign element not yet introduced to the tribe. "This is the common dissent we hear from many anthropologists," Iva said. " 'If we truly cared about preserving their culture we would leave them alone.' What this reasoning fails to recognize is that these tribes will not be left alone. They are not being left alone. Change is overtaking them one form or another . . ."

Gabe interrupted. "When the rubber boom hit years ago, rubber barons beat them and made them slaves."

"Before our coming," Iva continued, "every imposition had always and consistently been detrimental to the tribes. Rubber barons and traders came only to get what they could from these people. Our work not only gives them their language and the skills to maintain it in written form, but it also introduced what they themselves have called a good story to people who otherwise lived in fear of the dark, fear of the dead, who beat their women and saw betraying one another as a sign of power. We answer the anthropologists, 'Why would anyone think leaving someone in a place of despair like that is a good thing?' We've chosen not to. If this imposition has introduced a foreign element to their thinking, then it is the same foreign element that confronts every person's thinking, tribal or otherwise. In the case of the Ninganahua, as in the case of the people who serve them, the imposition has delivered them from self-destructive behaviors, from hurting one another, from killing one another and destroying their women. They no longer pride themselves in lying to one another and stealing from one another. They don't fear walking the path at night. If, from the vantage point of anthropology, this has ruined them, then we stand guilty as charged."

"How did the tribes receive the linguists, given the bad experience they had had with the rubber barons?" I asked.

Iva said, "The linguists arrived first with medicines, which helped the tribal people. Then, after they had developed trust, they told us that the mestizos who had come before them had disparaged the linguists, telling the tribes people they were rich gringos who wanted to steal their language and sell it. They told us as well that they had been waiting for a message from Our Father the Sun. So when the linguists arrived with good things—such as the medicine—the tribal chief spent many nights chewing the coco leaf waiting for a message about why they had come. When, in time, the translators read to them in their own language about he who says 'I am the One who is habitually true'—the translation of John fourteen six—the chief concluded, 'This is the message from Our Father the Sun. These are the words we've been waiting for.' "

I stood before her helpless. And yet I was able to see

the part of Lucy that had been forged in the crucible of this jungle. I was shocked by the tenacity and lucidity these people brought to their vocation. I was encountering a missionary enterprise that in every way contradicted my limited understanding of it. In contrast to the methods of the Conquistadors, I was witnessing, through these unassuming people, a strategy of information control in reverse. Rather than divest the tribe of their power—their identity—these ordinary people gave up the better part of their lives to assess things such as mutual intelligibility and tonal distinctions, even when drowning in a river, to decipher an unknown language in order to render it back to the people who owned it. Rather than coming to steal from the tribe as so many had done, the coming of people like Wes Thatcher and Gene Shaw gave their lives and their families' lives so that they could do what I dare say few others—myself among them—would have been willing to. There is no place to go to judge the wisdom of such choices.

32

The following morning, the day of the dedication ceremony, the sun rose to sweltering levels before my first cup
of coffee. It was also the day the Ninganahuas would bless
Lucy's and my marriage in the church the Catholics had
built. Tom and I powdered our feet with sulfur and went
looking for Gene and Gabe with whom we had scheduled
a fishing outing for the morning. We found them at a small
fire where the men of the tribe had gathered, as they did
each morning, to drink banana juice and talk about the
business of the day ahead. One lucky man had just butch-
ered a tortoise and felt as if he had won the lottery for the
bundle of golf ball-sized eggs he found inside.

Gene said, "Be glad you didn't see it. It suffered."

The near misses and jousting flourishes of our fishing
adventure pale in comparison to what awaited us upon
our return. Evidently, as Edie Shaw recounted afterward,
Lucy had arisen that morning and hurried down the
path to find me at the schoolhouse in irrepressible ex-
citement about the upcoming marriage blessing, only to

discover that I had gone fishing—"You know how she gets," Edie said. —*"Fishing!"* Lucy found her mother sitting with a neighbor eating fried yuca before a small fire. The neighbor's name was Mosa, which in Ninganahua meant "beautiful." Mosa was frying the yuca in a curved metal lid. "He's always with Gabe," Lucy groused to her mother. Edie said, "He's discovering life with a brother, dear. Can you give him that?"

This response irked Lucy and she wandered off in search of something to do. That is when she stumbled upon Luisa, a ten year old Ninganahua child, whose little angular face was tilted skyward as tears streamed down her cheeks. She explained to Lucy that her bird, a blue macaw with a striking gold hood, had flown up a tree. Evidently it had lighted to the lowest branch of a very tall tree.

Lucy, remembering Larry's bird Bart, whom she had taught to say Don't have a cow man, said to Luisa, "I'll help you. Birds like me." Luisa led Lucy to the edge of the jungle canopy and pointed. Lucy saw the bird on a low branch, but it was a tall tree. The lowest branch was twenty feet up. She told Luisa she would talk to the bird and that the bird would come to her, the way Bart came when she would talk to him. Lucy had been saying things like, "Hi pretty bird. Lucy likes you. You're a pretty bird" when she was seized with the idea to rally the Ninganahua children, who by now had joined the scene. She instructed them to form a pyramid on which she would climb in order to reach the branch. The children stacked themselves four, then three, then two, and Lucy mounted up. Even so, their strong backs and willing spirits could not surmount the six-inch deficit short of the lowest branch.

Lucy had been raised in the jungle with her brother, Gabe Shaw. In keeping with Gabe's never-say-die spirit, she came up with a plan. Jumping the pyramid, she pulled off her leather belt, wrapped it around her wrist, and remounted. The children bore it optimistically. Once steadied she lobbed the buckle over the branch, caught it with the free hand and, now grasping both ends of the belt, swung a leg over the branch and hoisted herself up.

By that point the bird had moved up a branch and Lucy followed it. The pyramid collapsed. Nine sets of eyes, plus Luisa's, followed Lucy up the tree. She was saying things to the bird such as, "Can you say, 'I love you Lucy?'"

Within a breath of grabbing it, the bird hopped yet still higher. But Lucy, ever mindful that she was "good with birds," climbed higher. Besides, everyone else had gone fishing. As she continued to climb the Ninganahua children grew alarmed. They called to her, but she ignored them, hell bent as she was on being good with birds. At about this point we had debarked the canoe after the fishing adventure when a Ninganahua boy named Pedro approached us at the riverside. Pedro spoke to Gabe in rapid staccato Ninganahuan that I did not understand but that clearly signaled alarm. He was pointing to a tree. Gabe reiterated that he said Lucy was stuck in a tree and was sick and that the little boy feared she might fall. By the time we scaled the ridge using both hands and feet, the village had gathered at the tree, all faces skyward. The wind was blowing and the branches leaned. Ninganahua children resurrected the pyramid to mount a rescue, Tom climbing the top. Gabe dispersed them with a wave of his hand. He squatted to load me onto his shoulders so I could take the lowest branch. The wind carried Lucy's muted voice: "I'm sick, James." Gene, who with Edie had joined the commotion, called to her: "Honey, James is coming up. Hang on!"

I wrapped my knees over Gabe's shoulders and he grabbed my ankles. He bounced low to steady himself. Then he grunted "Up" and heaved, keening a little, but standing red-faced with veins bulging, I on his shoulders. He bobbled forward then backward. Still, I could not reach the branch.

In labored movements Gabe inched nearer the tree. By this point he was purple. Edie Shaw held out a hand feeling helpful. Gabe's pregnant wife Dottie repeated, "Gabe, darlin' oh darlin'." Then Gabe buckled.

Getting Lucy out of the tree became a community event. Their mothers smacked all children implicated in the pyramid. The village chief, Sebastian, stood with Gene and Cuscobundi, who motioned a child whom I then saw run off. Moments later, the same child reappeared with Jaime del Aguilar, Cuscobundi's son, Lucy and Gabe's childhood friend. Without hesitation Jaime curled around the tree and squirreled to the lowest branch without breaking a sweat. Gabe and I abandoned our efforts. Jaime was half-way to the top by the time I brushed myself off. Cuscobundi said to me, "I should have named him Tree Climber."

If any member of the tribe had not gathered by this

point it was because he was away on a hunt. Jaime disappeared into the upper branches. We all stood faces fixed on leafy undergrowth, caps lifted, sweat down our necks and backs. Edie joined hands with Ninganahua women who stood in a circle praying. Gene stood with Gabe and me and the other helpless men.

The tree jostled signaling Jaime had reached her. What happened next was recounted to me later by Jaime. Lucy was clutching the trunk with both arms, sweating and heaving. Jaime asked her if she remembered the flood they experience together as children when the river washed most of the huts away. Lucy said she remembered it. Jaime said, "We did not die. That day you saved my life. This day I am going to save your life." He asked if she was ready to be saved. She didn't answer.

He said, "lift a foot because I am going to take off your shoe." Lucy didn't answer. "I am going to save your life today," he said. He tapped her ankle and got her to lift her foot enough to pull off a shoe. Then he yelled something in Ninganahua, which I took to mean "Look out!" since the shoe tumbled to earth through the leaves. He yelled a second time and the other shoe landed.

Foot by foot, branch by branch, Jaime led her down. About half way he started to sing. 'Min imi foni. Cruzhuun afa. Min imi foni. Cruzhuun pacuni.' By the time they were resting on a lower branch, he and Lucy were both singing, 'Aicho Ifo Jesus non mia fanaishoin.' When they came within our view, the villagers too started to sing. 'Min imi foni. Cruzhuun afa. Min imi foni. Cruzhuun pacuni. Aicho Ifo Jesus non mia fanaishoin.' The lowest branch was twenty feet up. Lucy and Jaime sat there singing, along with the entire Ninganahua village who had greeted them with eyes raised and lips curled in song.

Jaime threw himself from the branch, landing in a perfect squat, then rose. "Lucy, you are going to jump now."

She said, "I'm going to hang first."

Before further advice or encouragement could be rendered she dropped, legs flailing, and I did my best to catch her. But we dropped and rolled. "Did you catch me? Or did I drop?" she said. I held her close to me, both of us on the ground. "I caught you. Then we both dropped."

Her father brought her shoes. Her mother pushed back her hair. Dottie leaned to her, cheek on cheek. Cuscobundi, Sebastian, Luisa—now inexplicably holding her bird—looked on curiously. My wife reached for Tom and kissed him. "Mami is a fool. Don't be like me when you grow up," she said. Only Gabe, himself recovering, tended to me. We sat alone on a fallen log hidden in tall grasses. He shook his head. "That girl's a gringa loca, I swear."

"Who taught me how to talk to birds and climb trees, you sanctimonious little snot?" Gabe Shaw smiled at his sister's approach. He stood and placed both hands on her face and kissed her lips. "I love you, Bu," he said. She came to me where I sat alone on the log and slipped her arm through mine. I looked at her.

"You just took ten years off my life, you know that, don't you?" She dropped her head to my shoulder. "No more climbing trees, can we agree on that?"

33

Lucy recovered from the tree climbing fiasco relaxing on her parents' hammock in the few hours remaining before the dedication ceremony. I was with her there when Wes and Billie Thatcher approached. "Lucy, we found something we thought you might like to have," Billie said. I looked at Billie Thatcher standing there in the sun shaded by her straw hat, and Wes in his baseball cap, their faces etched by years of jungle heat, and their eyes shining in a way I could not describe and nor understand. I wondered if they once thought Lucy's wedding day would be the day she would take her place with their son. "We found this, Lucy. It was Jack's." Billie handed her a faded score sheet with scribblings in ink. "It was buried in papers that got filed away, I can't say for how long. I dug them out the other day," said Wes. "It's a song he wrote for your little jungle band. We thought you and Gabe might put it to music and sing it at the dedication service, for Jack, you know," he said. Billie said, "He would have wanted to be here for this." Lucy rose and went to her, that simple woman with shining eyes and perfect pitch that saved her from drowning in the river. They wet each other's faces with their tears. Lucy said, "Billie, I believe Jack is here with us."

There weren't enough benches in the little church to accommodate the many who had arrived by Cessna or Helio or by canoe along the river from other tribal villages. Gabe, Tom, Pete and I carried chairs two at a time from the schoolhouse to the church at the opposite end of that long narrow path. Passing the Shaw's hut on one of these trips, my eye caught a glimpse of a glint of white catching the afternoon sun. I approached for a closer look and Lucy's mother turned me away abruptly and told me to keep carrying chairs. I moved on, under orders.

The dedication service commenced. Gene and Edie Shaw occupied the front pew. I say pew, but it was little more than a hard wood bench and prone to cause splinters. Sebastian and the second of his many wives sat with them, along with Cuscobundi and his wife. Jaime and Juna and their spouses sat in the second row, where Lucy, Tom and I sat with Gabe and a pregnant Dottie, who found no respite from the heat, try as she might by fanning herself. Wes and Billie Thatcher, the pilots and linguists, and the program director from the United States filled what was left of the limited seating space in that dusty little church. The Ninganahuas wore their best clothes, an old woman in a child's dress, tight in the puffy sleeves and pressed firmly against her breasts; young men in Red Sox T-shirts; older men in stiffly pressed cotton, whiter and crisper than any shirt I've worn. Many sat by choice on the dirt floor.

Wes Thatcher spoke first. He stood and lifted his cap. "We've looked forward many years for this moment. Let's pray." All heads lowered except mine. I stood as an onlooker into a mysterious and unfamiliar world. The mystery of it brought to my mind an experienced I encountered in Rome a few years back. I had gone to a symposium on the conquering of the Americas and presented a paper on Maya social organization as reflected in settlement patterns. When I had finished I snatched half a day to sightsee. I found my way to the Church of Santa Maria del Popolo where, in one of the little chapels, hung Caravaggio's painting of St. Peter being crucified upside down. An elderly woman approached and stood next to me, a scarf over her thinning hair, clutching a kerchief in a bony fist. She said, "It is his reward. In death he saw the world as it really is." She looked at me. "The clouds are mountains and the flowers as stars, all hanging on God's mercy."

Wes prayed, "You have given Gene and Edie the strength they've needed to finish this work. At so many points there was no strength. You've been by their side giving them health and breath. Thank you for the privilege of working with them these many years. Prepare this ground that the seed of this book will fall on fertile soil and bear fruit."

Archeologists understand the implications of fertile ground. We know the upper slopes surrounding the Copán Valley were not used agriculturally because of high acidic soil. We know settlement data is very scarce in that area but that the alluvial beds at the base of the foothills fortified the land with nutrient deposits from the river's flooding. We know those terraces were exhaustively cultivated and from the physical evidence we understand landscapes as they are. Archaeologists understand that the alluvial bottomlands in the Copán Valley constitute some of the richest soil in Central America. We classify our findings. We divide evidence into periods and sub-periods, phases and sub-phases. That is what we know about soil and growing fruit.

My father-in-law stepped to the front of the church to join Wes Thatcher. "Gene, I'll never forget all those years ago the six weeks it took us to clear that air strip," Wes said. "Seeing you pull those rocks and hack down that brush in all that heat, I knew then you'd see this work through to its end, whatever it took. And Edie"—he looked at her—"Edie nursed Gene back to health when, many times, he struggled with his fatigue and fevers. She encouraged him."

Watching these people pray, seeing the glint in my father-in-law's eyes, Wes standing next to him strong and plain, I began to feel something give way inside me. Lucy's friend, Jaime had told me earlier that day after saving Lucy from the tree, that when Fasanahua and Yambacora came with their stories, at first, the stories did not sound like anything new. He said that when his father Cuscobundi first heard the story about this man Jesus it sounded like one of the old stories, only this was a nice story. He said Cuscobundi enjoyed hearing it. Jaime said Fasanahua and Yambacora did not stop talking about that story, how the story was always on their lips. He told me that many stories often came from the mouths of the Ninganahua, but this story, the story that was always on the lips of the Fasanahua and Yambacora, was also in their innermost. This is why he said the Ninganahuas began to think that the words about Jesus were not just another old story. They began to think that this was a real story. He said Fasanahua was always saying that Jesus wants us to tell good to each other and that they understood it was a real story because Fasanahua was always telling good to them. He said the Ninganahua used to think it was a sign of power to lie to a person to gain favor for themselves. But Fasanahua had told them to think about what the Owner desires and to truly do exactly what the Owner desires. "So now we don't have to lie to one another to gain favor for ourselves because Fasanahua says 'The bad things that people on earth want to do, don't do them. The Owner made you to be like himself.' " Fasanahua, Jaime told me, "walks the trail with the Owner in his innermost. He does not fear the spirits. He is not afraid of the dark." Jaime told me the Ninganahua have never been afraid of the jaguars in the jungle because they know how to kill them. But it was Fasanahua who showed them not to fear the dark or fear the spirit world that lives in the dark. He said, "Now we know we do not have to fear the spirits. They are nothing." (He did tell me, however, that they still fear snakes.)

"I tried to quit twice," Gene was saying, standing in front of the assembly. Silence fell over the church. "I told the mission supervisor that someone with a Ph.D. ought to step in and take over. He told me, 'Gene, you may not set the linguistic world on fire with your

technical expertise, but I do believe you can do a good translation. For you to step out now would be a disaster.' "
Gene said, "So I prayed, 'Lord'—"

I looked to my wife and saw Lucy's face wet with tears.

—" 'Lord,' I said, 'twice I've tried to step away. I'm not going to do it again.' " Gene paused. " 'Lord,' I said, 'I can't do it without you. Encourage my heart.' " He looked up. "All of you have been that encouragement."

I listened to and watched all that was unfolding before me in that cramped little church. Gene was so comfortable in his own skin, all smiles, even in tears, his cotton shirt wet with sweat, his baseball cap just off his brow. He said he sometimes wondered if the Ninganahua would want to keep them. Lucy's mother was dabbing her eyes, sitting like the rest of us in that stifling heat amid human smells and stoic faces of withered old women in little girls' dresses and toothless warriors who didn't fear jaguars and a tribal chief who used to beat his wives. My father-in-law was describing when he and Wes had made the seven-day canoe trip to the Ninganahua to build the airstrip. When they arrived they discovered Sebastian was not there and they couldn't begin the work without the chief. He learned that Sebastian had gone to Esperanza and he knew, a few days later, that Sebastian had returned because he heard gun shots. The sound of gun shots, Gene said, generally means someone is drunk, as indeed Sebastian was when he pulled up to the riverbank in a canoe and lurched over the side. Gene was saying, "The Lord put it my heart to love him as he was, the way the Lord loves me as I am."

This, I did not understand.

Gene went on, one story after the next, describing episodes and mishaps that defined his life in the jungle with the Ninganahua. When he and Sebastian had a disagreement, the chief often refused to continue to work with him on the translation. Lucy whispered to me, "One time he called my father a dumb linguist." Gene was describing how once, during a disagreement with Sebastian, he did something he had never done before any member of the tribe. "I burst into tears." Even as he said it, tears filled the edges of his eyes and I saw Gabe pressing his fingers to his eyes as Lucy dabbed hers with a crumpled tissue. "Then Sebastian began to weep," Gene said. "There we were, both of us weeping. If anyone had walked into the translation center at that moment they would have thought we were working on the saddest verse in the bible."

Sebastian joined Gene at the front of the church having no idea what Gene had been saying, since he told the story in English. Sebastian began speaking in Ninganahua with Gene translating, and said, "Many years I've worked together with Father Fasanahua to make this book. I'm anxious to teach it to my people. It will be interesting to see when we get to heaven what language we will speak."

Cuscobundi joined them at the front. "For a long time we have seen only Spanish mestizo books," he said. "We understand some of the words. But now we see the bible in the language of the Ninganahua. We possess it in a way that speaks to us and we understand. We understand it from the book of Matthew to the book of the Apocalypse. It makes good sense to us. We are understanding we can love those we see. We are understanding it is not respectable to lie. We are not afraid of death."

By the time Gabe and Lucy went forward to sing Jack's song, I had begun to feel something likened to a mountain falling around me. Gabe had the voice of an angel "in keeping with his name," as Lucy often said. He played guitar facing Lucy, in rhythm with her vocal harmony and the rattle of the seedpods she played, as Jack would have wanted her to. During one sustained note she and her brother, in his clear sonorous voice, reached perfect harmony and I surprised myself when wetness come to my eyes. Tom stood up and began to clap with the rhythms of the seed-pods. This got the whole church clapping. Jaime, who was sitting on the floor near a window at the front, turned a plastic bucket upside down and beat out the rhythms with sticks. Gabe sang with his eyes closed.

The song concluded and the room had settled when Gene and Edie joined Gabe and Lucy at the front of the assembled group. There they stood, the four Shaws, who lived this strange life amid floods and chiggers and jaguars and latrines, Fasanahua holding high the single copy of the New Testament they had been able to get through customs. His pearl of great price, still in a zip-loc bag. Unlike the Spanish Conquest, these simple people gave up all worldly consolations to spend thankless lifetimes in the jungle heat learning codes of mutual intelligibility, not to keep it, but to give it back. Some of us are crowned with the bequeathal of information control, the way I was, having been born of academician parents. Others, like the Shaws, had to scratch it out one allatone at a time.

Who could blame him for wanting to walk away twice? He did not. And when they had finished their work, they gave all they had come to do and put it back into the hands of the people for whom they had sold their lives so dearly. And the mountain fell. I felt waves rolling over me as if I had fallen into a rushing river. I was a drowning man. I was Peter hanging upside down.

34

We don't always see the gifts we're given. Sometimes they creep in shadows. Sometimes they come as bursts of light, the way it happened when Lucy stepped into the church on her father's arm for our marriage consecration. At the end of the dedication ceremony, Gene had taken the book from its wrapping and handed it to Sebastian, who lifted it and looked at me. "It is a privilege to take this book. Its first use will be to consecrate the marriage of this man, our brother James, to our little girl Lucy."

She entered with the rays of the sun wearing that same white dress, the one with the strings I did not pull so long ago. Seeing her in the sunlight, entering on her father's arm, I reckoned I hadn't pulled those strings for the same reason I left her in the airport that sad day. I took more comfort in controlling and understanding my world of isotopes and carbon dating, even if it meant desolation, than risking the desire for something I did not understand. The dress was her mother's surprise to us both. She had found it the year before when Lucy left it crumpled in a ball on the floor in the lake house in Wisconsin. Edie Shaw stuffed it into a mildew-proof sack to present to Lucy when the time was right. That was the glimpse of whiteness my eye caught in the afternoon sun earlier that day and why I was promptly waved off.

It was a very bold dress. Though in the moment Lucy entered the doorway on the arm of her beaming father, it did not seem so, even, I believe, to the missionaries. When I saw her I broke into a smile and then into tears. The mighty waters drowning me proved strong and wide enough to lift me beyond the rubble of my fallen mountain.

She stepped into that cramped church, bare feet on the dirt floor, and fixed her eyes on me. Her father walked her to the front where I waited with Tom and Sebastian behind us. Wes and Billie Thatcher played a violin duet in a way that, by its end, had everyone pressing tissues to their eyes.

Gene stood with Sebastian who, in Ninganahua, asked Lucy and me to come forward. He smiled. Gene translated, but there were moments he had trouble getting the words out. Sebastian spoke quietly. Lucy's father said, "He's asking you to kneel."

I looked at Lucy and helped her to her knees, lifting her dress so it wouldn't soil. I kneeled next to her. Sebastian opened the single copy of the New Testament and said, "I am reading from First Corinthians chapter eleven. 'God made man. Then he made woman. God made man and woman to companion together and so they might cause one another to be happy.'"

I held Lucy's hand and we kneeled under the blessing of the chief, a man who had once beat his wives and shot his gun when drunk in the night, the man who worked forty years with Gene Shaw and who once had called him a dumb linguist. Sebastian spoke words from the little book that had claimed the lifetimes of good people. We knelt on the dirt floor of the church built by the Catholics and Gene translated as Sebastian read in his own language, "For this reason a man shall have his own mosquito net and share it with his wife." He turned and received a mosquito net from his second wife and placed it into my hands. "Tell good to each other. Give yourself to the Owner in order that He will be your Owner. Whatever the Owner desires, think about that. Truly do exactly what he desires. Bad things people here on earth want to do, don't do them. The Owner made us to be like himself. Therefore," he paused, "be hearted like God." He placed his hands on our heads. "I am going to pray for you now. As Father God caused his Son to be raised in order that you become new, be good, as he is good."

At the service's end, as Lucy and I were departing the church, I surprised her when I scooped her into my arms, the mosquito net draped about us, her white dress blowing in the breeze. "What are you doing?"

"Taking my bride to climb under the net," I said.

Gabe snapped our picture. Her arm around my neck and her face inclined to mine, both of us swallowed in white from the dress and the net, we were the only two people on earth in that moment, a moment that seemed to me to capture all moments of every human heart, no more no less than all that is and is meant to be among men and women, tribes and scholars, people with information and those without. The photo became our wedding announcement in all the Honduran papers. The caption read: "The reporter with her head in the clouds marries the archaeologist with his nose in the dirt." They stole the line from Lucy.

Lucy asked me to finish this story. As I write these final words from my cramped little office tucked in the corner of the Visitor's Center at Copán, my mind carries me back to our last night in Peru. The men, myself among them, were returning from playing basketball on a concrete slab near the lake. Tom was riding on Gabe's back and I was drenched in sweat. I approached Lucy, who was standing on the porch of her parents' house in a cotton summer dress. She pointed for me to look at the beauty of the evening sky. I looked up. Seeing Lucy on the porch in her dress waiting for me, the sky behind her crowning her in fire and indigo, the evening breeze upon my face and catching the shards of light off the glimmering lake, I caught a glimpse of what she meant when she said that God sometimes speaks through his silence. I was seeing a little boy, a fleet-footed runner, skirting over rocks and roots. I saw a cold floor of a darkened jail, and a drunken groom, and a buck-toothed guard, and the canal in the corner that was a toilet. I saw orange bobbled earrings and the billowing red dress of my father's old lover, Lillian. (She thinks I never knew.) I saw

Larry McCully's wet eyes when he understood he had lost his love to me. I saw Brigida pat my son's head and Doña Nora's luscious lips planted on his own. I saw Yamileta's crooked neck and sad eyes, and a ruined heart that painted a dead man blue.

I saw village people looking up a tree, their curled lips singing as Jaime brought a rescue. I saw myself standing there among them, my face to the sun, the tree filled with lights, magic stars holding Lucy up while I stood helpless underneath. I saw Gabe turn purple trying to save his sister while the Ninganahuas gathered from their huts. I saw her mother pray and Lucy did not die that day. She dropped to me and I dropped too, and the world came into harmony. I held my wife's head and understood the meaning of so much I had not known before. It came to me wrapped in a moonbeam dress. And after the tribe's blessing on our marriage I carried my wife to her parents' hut, took her under the mosquito net and finally pulled those strings.

That is what I saw as she stood on the porch that evening at the house in Peru. The dedication was behind us, the mosquito net packed in my bag. My wife and son and I would return home the next day.

Leonardo said the gods must have heard a little boy crying. He said they roused themselves to bring Lucy back to Copán. So she came. She spent a day and a night in a Honduran jail and got lost in the tunnels. She said, "Sometimes the story is bigger than the script." Goody said a person dies many times before he comes alive at last. I have seen and known the truth of all of this.

I have learned the importance of a kinship name. The Ninganahua know theirs and will always know them because the family I have come to hold so dear has given them back their words. The Ninganahua put their stories on paper now. As a tribe they will always remain, because the Shaws took other names in order to give them back their own.

Yamileta laid no claim to information control. She could not write her name in letters. So she wrote it in blue, a hue that forever shadows my own. My son said once he could feel God's power and that it hurt. My consolation is this: I understand what it takes for a father to own a son. That is what I answered my colleague at Columbia and what I myself have come to think about "all this." You see, my son is the one they used to call Paco. But his name is Tomás Fee. He is the son of the renowned archaeologist and of the reporter who points to the clouds.

Addenda

Wendy Murray

A Tree Is Like a Kiss
by Lucy Shaw
Los Tiempo

TEGUCIGALPA—More than a thousand fires have been reported since the beginning of the dry season, according to the Forest Protection Campaign chief, Jose Lupe Correa of the Honduran Forestry Development Corps (COHDEFOR). The blazes consumed over 40,000 hectares of pine and mahogany forest in the Departments of Olancho, Gracias a Dios (La Mosquitia), Comayagua and El Paraiso.

The crisis of deforestation has captured the enthusiastic interest of La Primera Dama, Nora Reyes Morales de Mondragón, who has aggressively tried to spread the word for Hondurans everywhere to bring "ecological strength" back to the country's green areas. Last week she launched her "Plant A Tree For Nora" campaign. With the help of a Honduran boy who grew up on the streets, she planted the first tree, a sapling, on the berm outside her office. She patted the soil then watered its roots. In a surprise twist, she kissed the boy to show her solidarity with all Hondurans. "A tree is like a kiss," she said. "It gives life."

A thousand trees have already been planted as a result of the Nora campaign. This has been due in no small way to the collaboration of the Honduran military, which has joined La Primera Dama and COHDEFOR in the tree-planting effort. Says military spokesman, Osvaldo Soto ("El Gordito"), "It is an opportunity for Honduran citizens to get involved and be vigilant in preserving our country's forests. We are a people who respect and honor the outdoors. It is for the welfare of our country and the future of our children."

The young helper who won the kiss described it as tasting like a gumdrop.

The Secret Buried with Yax K'uk Mo'
by Lucy Shaw
LOS TIEMPO

COPÁN RUINAS—"How do you describe to reporters what it feels like when the world shakes beneath your feet? How do you tell them when you hear the ancestors whisper?" So says archaeologist Mario Lopez, with the Honduran Anthropological Institute, of the recent discovery of what they believe to be the tomb of Copán's founding king, K'inich Yax K'uk Mo. "It is the most incredible find of my career," he says.

At first, when you look inside the tomb, you're not sure what you are looking at—broken shards, flecks of paint, some green, some red, brown, lots of black. It's a mess. It's a miracle.

"But you can't go by the pots," adds Lopez's partner, archaeologist James Fee, of Columbia, who oversees the projects in the Acropolis. He was referring to clues that enabled them to identify the remains as belonging to the dynasty founder, most notably, Altar Q. Altar Q was commissioned by Copán's 16th and last king, Yax Pasah. A square carving about the size of the bed of a pickup truck, it is set upon four squat stone pillars and depicts all sixteen of Copán's kings, four on each side in conjunction with the four cardinal directions. Hieroglyphs on the altar describe Yax K'uk Mo' as coming 'from the west,' probably Teotihuacán, Mexico, archaeologists believe, and then traveling 153 days, till he 'rested his legs' in Copán. Another monument elsewhere in the ruins established the date C.E. 426 as the time of his consolidation of power at Copán. The dynasty ended in C.E. 822.

Carved onto the west face of Altar Q, K'inich Yax K'uk Mo' hands the last king—Yax Pasah, the kingly scepter. In the mind of the king who commissioned it, this gesture legitimized his reign, and those of all kings in between, symbolically linking them to the founder.

"The hieroglyphic inscription on top says that this the stone of K'inich Yax K'uk Mo' and those four stones underneath suggest it is imitating the burial place of the guy buried in the Acropolis," says Fee. "His burial slab has four cylinders supporting it the same way. Since Altar Q is placed in front of Temple 16; since it mimics a burial slab; and since it indicates it is the stone of Yax K'uk Mo' we took a good guess that Temple 16 was the funerary temple of the founder."

Says Lopez: "Finding his tomb puts all the pieces of the puzzle into focus. The bones of Yax K'uk Mo' are buried at the lowest level of Structure 16, which is at the heart of Copán's sacred geography. He is the cornerstone that holds the pieces of the puzzle in place. Now that we know he was real, we are able to understand the significance of Rosalila, Altar Q, the Hieroglyphic Stairway, Structure 11, everything. His bones bring the whole picture into clarity."

According to Fee, the discovery of the founder's tomb is signifcant not only for the study Honduran history, but also for the larger discipline of anthropology in the New World. "To be able to demonstrate that there is archaeological evidence to support claims made by later rulers about the founder's role in setting up this distinguished Maya kingdom is terribly important," says Fee. He adds that the distinct environmental zones of the Copán Valley—not to be confused with the Copán pocket—set the stage for their ascent. "The sheer beauty made it desirable, but what made it ideal for an agricultural-based population were its lush alluvial bottomlands."

Dynastic History of the Kings of Copán

Founding Ruler:	K'inich Yax K'uk Mo	C.E. 426 - 435
Ruler 2:	K'inich . . .	C.E. 437 - ???
Ruler 3:	Unknown	
Ruler 4:	K'al Tuun Hix (approximate)	C.E. 485 - 495
Rulers 5 and 6:	(approximate)	C.E. 495 - 500
Ruler 7:	Jaguar Mirror Accession unknown	? 544 ?
Ruler 8:	Unknown	
Ruler 9:	White . . .	C.E. 551 - ???
Ruler 10:	. . . Jaguar	C.E. 553 - 578
Ruler 11:		C.E. 578 - 628
Ruler 12:	Smoke Imix God K	C.E. 628 - 695
Ruler 13	18 Rabbit	C.E. 695 - 738
Ruler 14:	Smoke Monkey	C.E. 738 - 749
Ruler 15:	Smoke Shell	C.E. 749 - 763
Ruler 16:	Yax Pasah	C.E. 763 - 820

Acknowledgments

In the narrative of the novel, the male and female protagonists at one point discuss the conundrum the archaeologists faced trying to identify mortal remains found under the Hieroglyphic Stairway in 1989. The lead archaeologist felt sure they belonged to Copán's Twelfth Ruler, Smoke Imix God K, who reigned for sixty-seven years and was Copán's longest-living king. During the time in which the novel is set, the physical anthropologist determined that the preliminary bone fragments did not show elements that would suggest an aged individual and concluded the remains therefore belonged to a person between thirty-five and forty years old, which eliminated Smoke Imix who died an old man. More recent dating techniques have since been brought to bear on this investigation and the scholars and archaeologists have revised their preliminary assessment concluding definitively, as they originally speculated, that the remains found buried under the Hieroglyphic Stairway do indeed belong to Copán's longest-living and probably greatest king, Smoke Imix God K.

On another note, the landing strip near the Visitor's Center, as it is depicted in the novel, existed during the year in which the novel is set. However that was the last year it functioned as such. The land was designated the site of the Copán Sculpture Museum, which opened in 1996.

For the ongoing gracious and meticulous input regarding details related to the Maya, discoveries noted in the novel, and information rendered subsequent to the time in which the novel is set, the author wishes to the thank the following individuals: William L. Fash, Harvard's Bowditch Professor of Central American and Mexican Archaeology and Ethnology and the William and Muriel Seabury Howells Director of the Peabody Museum, with whom I met on multiple occasions both in Copán and at Harvard; and Ricardo Agurica Fasquelle, Executive Director of the Copán Association and affiliated with the Honduran Institute of Anthropology and History; E. Wyllys Andrews of Tulane University; and Robert Sharer, University of Pennsylvania. The author assumes responsibility for any errors I may have brought to their insights.

For the invaluable opportunity to travel to the Amazonian jungle basin to attend the dedication ceremony of the New Testament translation of the heretofore unwritten language of the tribe they served, the author thanks "Scotty" and Marie Scott, missionaries for the SIL (Summer Institute of Linguistics); David Scott; Steve and Leila Odeh Scott. For helping to understand the intricacies of lingual decipherment, the author thanks the numerous linguists, scholars and translators (too numerous to mention) whom I interviewed at the tribal village.

I thank my journalism students Amanda, Kate, Laura, Jess, Gary, Maggie, Christy, Colleen, Kaelyn, Sarah P., Sarah Pr., Craig, Angela, Tom and Houston, for their invaluable feedback and proofreading skills. I add sincere thanks, as well, to Tim Geisse and Keith Wilson for reading early drafts.

My happiest and most heart-felt gratitude goes to my beloved son Ben, and he knows why.

Maps, etc.

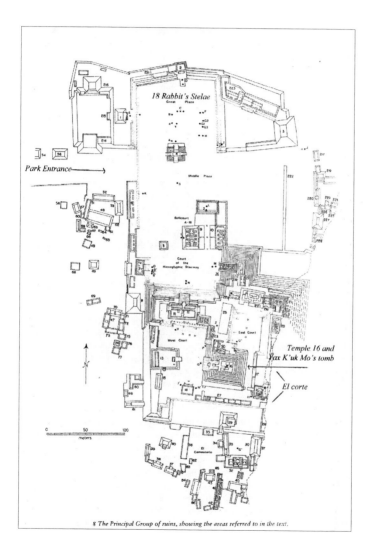

18 Rabbit's Stelae

Great Plaza

Park Entrance ——→

Middle Plaza

Ballcourt

Court of the Hieroglyphic Stairway

West Court

East Court

Temple 16 and Yax K'uk Mo's tomb

El corte

N

0   50   100
meters

El Cementerio

8 *The Principal Group of ruins, showing the areas referred to in the text.*

Censor lid effigy of K'inich Yax K'uk Mo'

Breinigsville, PA USA
08 February 2011
255139BV00001B/10/P